ENSIGN FLANDRY

Ensign Dominic Flandry, Imperial Naval Flight Corps, was in trouble. He had been "rescued"—but with a foul wind, they'd be days at sea in this damned wallowing bathtub. And would the Seatrolls and Merseians let the alien craft alone?

His gravity impeller wouldn't lug him much further until the capacitors were recharged. What power remained in the pack on his shoulders must be saved to operate the pump and reduction valve in the vitryl globe which sealed off his head.

Nobody was to blame for the loss of his blaster. It was torn from the holster in those wild moments of scrambling clear of the shot-down flier. He had kept the regulation knife, boots, and gray coverall, and that was just about the lot.

His chances, you might say, were slim. . . .

ENSIGN FLANDRY

by
POUL ANDERSON

ACE SCIENCE FICTION BOOKS
NEW YORK

ENSIGN FLANDRY

An Ace Science Fiction Book / published by arrangement with
the author

PRINTING HISTORY
First printing / February 1979
Eighth printing / January 1985

ISBN: 0-441-20729-4

Ace Science Fiction Books are published by The Berkley Publishing Group,
200 Madison Avenue, New York, New York 10016.
PRINTED IN THE UNITED STATES OF AMERICA

*To Frank Herbert, and to
Bev in memoriam*

Excerpts (with some expansion of symbols) from *Pilot's Manual and Ephemeris, Cis-Betelgeusean Orionis Sector*, 53rd ed., Reel III, frame 28:

IGC S-52,727,061. *Saxo.* F5, mass 1.75 Sol, luminosity 5.4 Sol, photosphere diameter 1.2 Sol. . . . Estimated remaining time on main sequence, 0.9 begayear. . . .

Planetary system: Eleven major bodies. . . . V, *Starkad.* Mean orbital radius, 3.28 a.u., period 4.48 years. . . . Mass, 1.81 Terra. Equatorial diameter, 15,077 Km. Mean surface gravity, 1.30 g. Rotation period, $16^h 31^m 2.75^s$. Axial inclination, 25° 50' 4.9''. . . . Surface atmospheric pressure, ca. 7000 mm. Percentage composition, N_2 77.92, O_2 21.01, A0.87, CO_2 0.03. . . .

Remarks: Though 254 light-years from Sol, the system was discovered early, in the course of the first Grand Survey. Thus the contemporary practice of bestowing literary-mythological names on humanly interesting objects was followed. Only marginally manhabitable, Starkad attracted a few xenological expeditions by its unusual autochthons. . . . These studies were not followed up, since funds went to still more rewarding projects and, later, the Polesotechnic League saw no profit potential. After the Time of Troubles, it lay outside the Imperial sphere and remained virtually unvisited until now, when a mission has been sent for political reasons.

The 54th edition had quite a different entry.

Chapter One

Evening on Terra—

His Imperial Majesty, High Emperor Georgios Manuel Krishna Murasaki, of the Wang dynasty the fourth, Supreme Guardian of the Pax, Grand Director of the Stellar Council, Commander-in-Chief, Final Arbiter, acknowledged supreme on more worlds and honorary head of more organizations than any one man could remember, had a birthday. On planets so remote that the unaided eye could not see their suns among those twinkling to life above Oceania, men turned dark and leathery, or thick and weary, by strange weathers lifted glasses in salute. The light waves carrying their pledge would lap on his tomb.

Terra herself was less solemn. Except for the court, which still felt bound to follow daylight around the globe for one exhausting ceremony after another, Birthday had become simply an occasion to hold carnival. As his aircar hummed over great dusking waters, Lord Markus Hauksberg saw the east blaze with sky luminosity, multi-colored moving curtains where fireworks exploded meteoric. Tonight, while the planet turned, its dark side was so radiant as to

drown the very metro-centers seen from Luna.
Had he tuned his vid to almost any station, he
could have watched crowds filling pleasure
houses and coming near riot among festively
decorated towers.

His lady broke the silence between them with
a murmur that made him start. "I wish it were
a hundred years ago."

"Eh?" Sometimes she could still astonish him.

"Birthday meant something then."

"Well . . . yes. S'pose so." Hauksberg cast his
mind back over history. She was right. Fathers
had taken their sons outdoors when twilight
ended parades and feasts; they had pointed to
the early stars and said,—Look yonder. Those
are ours. We believe that as many as four million
lie within the Imperial domain. Certainly a hundred thousand know us daily, obey us, pay trib-
ute to us, and get peace and the wealth of peace
in return. Our ancestors did that. Keep the faith.

Hauksberg shrugged. You can't prevent later
generations from outgrowing naïveté. In time
they must realize, bone deep, that this one
dustmote of a galaxy holds more than a hundred
billion suns; that we have not even explored the
whole of our one spiral arm, and it does not appear we ever will; that you need no telescope to
see giants like Betelgeuse and Polaris which do
not belong to us. From there, one proceeded easily to: Everybody knows the Empire was won and
is maintained by naked power, the central government is corrupt and the frontier is brutal and
the last organization with high morale, the
Navy, lives for war and oppression and anti-in-

tellectualism. So get yours, have fun, ease your conscience with a bit of discreet scoffing, and never, never make a fool of yourself by taking the Empire seriously.

Could be I'll change that, Hauksberg thought.

Alicia interrupted him. "We might at least have gone to a decent party! But no, you have to drag us to the Crown Prince's. Are you hoping he'll share one of his pretty-boys?"

Hauksberg tried to ease matters with a grin. "Come, come, m'love, you do me an injustice. You know I still hunt women. Preferably beautiful women, such as you."

"Or Persis d'Io." She sagged back. "Never mind," she said tiredly. "I just don't like orgies. Especially vulgar ones."

"Nor I, much." He patted her hand. "But you'll manage. Among the many things I admire about you is your ability to carry off any situation with aplomb."

True enough, he thought. For a moment, regarding those perfect features under the diademed hair, he felt regret. So his marriage had been political; why couldn't they nonetheless have worked out a comradeship? Even love —No, he was confusing his love for ancient literature with flesh-and-blood reality. He was not Pelléas nor she Mélisande. She was clever, gracious, and reasonably honest with him; she had given him an heir; more had never been implied in the contract. For his part, he had given her position and nearly unlimited money. As for more of his time . . . how could he? Somebody had to be the repairman, when the universe was falling to pieces. Most women understood.

To entropy with it. Alicia's looks came from an expensive biosculp job. He had seen too many slight variations on that fashionable face.

"I've explained to you often enough," he said. "Lot rather've gone to Mboto's or Bhatnagar's myself. But my ship leaves in three days. Last chance to conduct a bit of absolutely essential business."

"So you say."

He reached a decision. Tonight had not seemed to him to represent any large sacrifice on her part. During the months of his absence, she'd find ample consolation with her lovers. (How else can a high-born lady who has no special talents pass her time on Terra?) But if she did grow embittered she could destroy him. It is vital to keep closed that faceplate which is pretense. Never mind what lies behind. But in front of the faceplate waits open ridicule, as dangerous to a man in power as emptiness and radiation to a spacefarer.

Odd, reflected the detached part of him, *for all our millennia of recorded history, for all our sociodynamic theory and data, how the basis of power remains essentially magical. If I am laughed at, I may as well retire to my estates. And Terra needs me.*

"Darlin'," he said, "I couldn't tell you anything before. Too many ears, live and electronic, don't y' know. If the opposition got wind of what I'm about, they'd head me off. Not because they necessarily disagree, but because they don't want me to bring home a jumpin' success. That'd put me in line for the Policy Board, and everybody hopes to sit there. By arrangin' a *fait accompli,* though—d' you see?"

She rested a hard gaze on him. He was a tall, slender, blond man. His features were a little too sharp; but in green tunic and decorations, gauze cloak, gold breeches and beefleather halfboots, he was more handsome than was right. "Your career," she jibed.

"Indeed," he nodded. "But also peace. Would you like to see Terra under attack? Could happen."

"Mark!" Abruptly she was changed. Her fingers, closing on his wrist beneath the lace, felt cold. "It can't be that serious?"

"Nuclear," he said. "This thing out on Starkad isn't any common frontier squabble. Been touted as such, and quite a few people honestly believe it is. But they've only seen reports filtered through a hundred offices, each one bound to gloss over facts that don't make its own job look so fiery important. I've collected raw data and had my own computations run. Conservative extrapolation gives a forty per cent chance of war with Merseia inside five years. And I mean war, the kind which could get total. You don't bet those odds, do you, now?"

"No," she whispered.

"I'm s'posed to go there on a fact-findin' mission and report back to the Emperor. Then the bureaucracy may start grindin' through the preliminaries to negotiation. Or it may not; some powerful interests'd like to see the conflict go on. But at best, things'll escalate meanwhile. A settlement'll get harder and harder to reach, maybe impossible.

"What I want to do is bypass the whole

wretched process. I want plenipotentiary authority to go direct from Starkad to Merseia and try
negotiatin' the protocol of an agreement. I think
it can be done. They're rational bein's too, y'
know. S'pose many of 'em're lookin' for some
way out of the quicksand. I can offer one." He
straightened. "At least I can try."

She sat quiet. "I understand," she said at
length. "Of course I'll cooperate."

"Good girl."

She leaned a little toward him. "Mark—"

"What?" His goal stood silhouetted against a
crimson sheet.

"Oh, never mind." She sat back, smoothed
her gown, and stared out at the ocean.

The Coral Palace was built on an atoll, which
it engulfed even as its towers made their crooked
leap skyward. Cars flittered about like fireflies.
Hauksberg's set down on a flange as per GCA,
let him and Alicia out, and took off for a parking
raft. They walked past bowing slaves and salut-
ing guardsmen, into an antechamber of tall wa-
terspout columns where guests made a shifting
rainbow, and so to the ballroom entrance.

"Lord Markus Hauksberg, Viscount of Ny
Kalmar, Second Minister of Extra-Imperial Affairs, and Lady Hauksberg!" cried the stentor.

The ballroom was open to the sky, beneath a
clear dome. Its sole interior lighting was ul-
traviolet. Floor, furnishings, orchestral instruments, tableware, food shone with the deep pure
colors of fluorescence. So did the clothing of the
guests, their protective skin paint and eyelenses.
The spectacle was intense, rippling ruby, topaz,
emerald, sapphire, surmounted by glowing

masks and tresses, against night. Music lilted through the air with the scent of roses.

Crown Prince Josip was receiving. He had chosen to come in dead black. His hands and the sagging face floated green, weirdly disembodied; his lenses smoldered red. Hauksberg bowed and Alicia bent her knee. "Your Highness."

"Ah. Pleased to see you. Don't see you often."

"Press of business, your Highness. The loss is ours."

"Yes. Understand you're going away."

"The Starkad affair, your Highness."

"What? . . . Oh, yes. That. How dreadfully serious and constructive. I do hope you can relax with us here."

"We look forward to doin' so, your Highness, though I'm 'fraid we'll have to leave early."

"Hmph." Josip half turned.

He mustn't be offended. "Goes without sayin' we both regret it the worst," Hauksberg purred. "Might I beg for another invitation on my return?"

"Well, really!"

"I'll be even more bold. My nephew's comin' to Terra. Frontier lad, y' know, but as far as I can tell from stereos and letters, quite a delightful boy. If he could actually meet the heir apparent of the Empire—why, better'n a private audience with God."

"Well. Well, you don't say. Of course. Of course." Josip beamed as he greeted the next arrival.

"Isn't that risky?" Alicia asked when they were out of earshot.

"Not for my nephew," Hauksberg chuckled.

"Haven't got one. And dear Josip's memory is rather notoriously short."

He often wondered what would become of the Empire when that creature mounted the throne. But at least Josip was weak. If, by then, the Policy Board was headed by a man who understood the galactic situation. . . . He bent and kissed his lady's hand. "Got to drift off, m'dear. Enjoy yourself. With luck, things'll still be fairly decorous when we dare scoot off."

A new dance was called and Alicia was swept away by an admiral. He was not so old, and his decorations showed that he had seen outplanet service. Hauksberg wondered if she would return home tonight.

He maneuvered to the wall, where the crowd was thinner, and worked his way along. There was scant time to admire the view above the dome's rim, though it was fantastic. The sea marched ashimmer beneath a low moon. Long waves broke intricately, virginally white on the outer ramparts; he thought he could hear them growl. The darkness enclosed by the Lunar crescent was pinpointed with city lights. The sky illumination had now formed a gigantic banner overhead, the Sunburst alive in a field of royal blue as if stratospheric winds bugled salute. Not many stars shone through so much radiance.

But Hauksberg identified Regulus, beyond which his mission lay, and Rigel, which burned in the heart of the Merseian dominions. He shivered. When he reached the champagne table, a glass was very welcome.

"Good evening," said a voice.

Hauksberg exchanged bows with a portly man

wearing a particolored face. Lord Advisor Petroff was not exactly in his element at a festival like this. He jerked his head slightly. Hauksberg nodded. They gossiped a little and drifted apart. Hauksberg was detained by a couple of bores and so didn't manage to slip out the rear and catch a graveshaft downward for some while.

The others sat in a small, sealed office. They were seven, the critical ones on the Policy Board: gray men who bore the consciousness of power like added flesh. Hauksberg made the humility salute. "My sincere apologies for keepin' my lords waitin'," he said.

"No matter," Petroff said. "I've been explaining the situation."

"We haven't seen any data or computations, though," da Fonseca said. "Did you bring them, Lord Hauksberg?"

"No, sir. How could I? Every microreader in the palace is probably bugged." Hauksberg drew a breath. "My lords, you can examine the summation at leisure, once I'm gone. The question is, will you take my word and Lord Petroff's for the moment? If matters are as potentially serious as I believe, then you must agree a secret negotiator should be dispatched. If, on t'other hand, Starkad has no special significance, what have we lost by settlin' the dispute on reasonable terms?"

"Prestige," Chardon said. "Morale. Credibility, the next time we have to counter a Merseian move. I might even be so archaic as to mention honor."

"I don't propose to compromise any vital interest," Hauksberg pleaded, "and in all events, whatever concord I may reach'll have to be ratified here. My lords, we can't be gone long without someone noticin'. But if you'll listen—"

He launched his speech. It had been carefully prepared. It had better be. These six men, with Petroff, controlled enough votes to swing a decision his way. Were they prevailed on to call a privy meeting tomorrow, with a loaded quorum, Hauksberg would depart with the authority he needed.

Otherwise. . . . No, he mustn't take himself too seriously. Not at the present stage of his career. But men were dying on Starkad.

In the end, he won. Shaking, sweat running down his ribs, he leaned on the table and scarcely heard Petroff say, "Congratulations. Also, good luck. You'll need plenty of that."

Chapter Two

Night on Starkad—

Tallest in the central spine of Kursoviki Island was Mount Narpa, peaking at almost twelve kilometers. So far above sea level, atmospheric pressure was near Terran standard; a man could safely breathe and men had erected Highport. It was a raw sprawl of spacefield and a few score prefabs, housing no more than five thousand; but it was growing. Through the walls of his office, Commander Max Abrams, Imperial Naval Intelligence Corps, heard metal clang and construction machines rumble.

His cigar had gone out again. He mouthed the stub until he finished reading the report on his desk, then leaned back and touched a lighter to it. Smoke puffed up toward a blue cloud which already hung under the ceiling of the bleak little room. The whole place stank. He didn't notice.

"Damn!" he said. And deliberately, for he was a religious man in his fashion, "God damn!"

Seeking calmness, he looked at the picture of his wife and children. But they were home, on Dayan, in the Vega region of the Empire, more parsecs distant than he liked to think. And remote in time as well. He hadn't been with them for over a year. Little Miriam was changing so he'd never recognize her, Marta wrote, and David become a lanky hobbledehoy and Yael seeing such a lot of Abba Perlmutter, though of course he was a nice boy. . . . There was only the picture, separated from him by a clutter of papers and a barricade of desk machines. He didn't dare animate it.

Nor feel sorry for yourself, you clotbrain. The chair creaked beneath his shifted weight. He was a stocky man, hair grizzled, face big and hooknosed. His uniform was rumpled, tunic collar open, twin planets of his rank tarnished on the wide shoulders, blaster at belt. He hauled his mind back to work.

Wasn't just that a flitter was missing, nor even that the pilot was probably dead. Vehicles got shot down and men got killed more and more often. Too bad about this kid, who was he, yes, Ensign Dominic Flandry. *Glad I never met him. Glad I don't have to write his parents.* But the area where he vanished, that was troubling. His assignment had been a routine reconnaissance over the Zletovar Sea, not a thousand kilometers hence. If the Merseians were getting that aggressive. . . .

Were they responsible, though? Nobody knew, which was why the report had been bucked on to the Terran mission's Chief of Intelligence. A burst of static had been picked up at Highport from that general direction. A search flight had revealed nothing except the usual Tigery merchant ships and fishing boats.

Well, engines did conk out occasionally; matériel was in such short supply that the ground crews couldn't detect every sign of mechanical overwork. (When in hell's flaming name was GHQ going to get off its numb butt and realize this was no "assistance operation to a friendly people" but a war?) And given a brilliant sun like Saxo, currently at a peak of its energy cycle, no tricks of modulation could invariably get a message through from high altitudes. On the other hand, a scout flitter was supposed to be fail safe and contain several backup systems.

And the Merseians were expanding their effort. *We don't do a mucking thing but expand ours in response. How about making them respond to us for a change?* The territory they commanded grew steadily bigger. It was still distant from Kursoviki by a quarter of the planet's circumference. But might it be reaching a tentacle this way?

Let's ask. Can't lose much.

Abrams thumbed a button on his vidiphone. An operator looked out of the screen. "Get me the greenskin cinc," Abrams ordered.

"Yes, sir. If possible."

"Better be possible. What're you paid for? Tell his cohorts all gleaming in purple and gold to tell him I'm about to make my next move."

"What, sir?" The operator was new here.

"You heard me, son. Snarch!"

Time must pass while the word seeped through channels. Abrams opened a drawer, got out his magnetic chessboard, and pondered. He hadn't actually been ready to play. However, Runei the Wanderer was too fascinated by their match to refuse an offer if he had a spare moment lying around; and damn if any Merseian son of a mother was going to win at a Terran game.

Hm . . .promising development here, with the white bishop . . . no, wait, then the queen might come under attack . . . tempting to sic a computer onto the problem . . . betcha the opposition did . . . maybe not . . . ah, so.

"Commandant Runei, sir."

An image jumped to view. Abrams could spot individual differences between nonhumans as easily as with his own species. That was part of his business. An untrained eye saw merely the alienness. Not that the Mersians were so odd, compared to some. Runei was a true mammal from a terrestroid planet. He showed reptile ancestry a little more than Homo Sapiens does, in hairless pale-green skin, faintly scaled, and short triangular spines running from the top of his head, down his back to the end of a long heavy tail. That tail counterbalanced a forward-leaning posture, and he sat on the tripod which it made with his legs. But otherwise he rather resembled a tall, broad man. Except for complex bony convolutions in place of external ears, and brow ridges overhanging the jet eyes, his head and face might almost have been Terran. He wore the form-fitting black and silver uniform of his service. Behind him could be seen on the wall a bell-mouthed gun, a ship model, a curious statuette: souvenirs of far stars.

"Greeting, Commander." He spoke fluent Anglic, with a musical accent. "You work late."

"And you've dragged yourself off the rack early," Abrams grunted. "Must be about sunrise where you are."

Runei's glance flickered toward a chrono. "Yes, I believe so. But we pay scant attention here."

"You can ignore the sun easier'n us, all right, squatted down in the ooze. But your native friends still live by this cheap two-thirds day they got. Don't you keep office hours for them?"

Abrams' mind ranged across the planet, to the enemy base. Starkad was a big world, whose gravity and atmosphere gnawed land masses away between tectonic epochs. Thus, a world of shallow ocean, made turbulent by wind and the moons; a world of many islands large and small, but no real continents. The Merseians had established themselves in the region they called the Kimraig Sea. They had spread their domes widely across the surface, their bubblehouses over the bottom. And their aircraft ruled those skies. Not often did a recon flight, robot or piloted, come back to Highport with word of what was going on. Nor did instruments peering from spaceships as they came and went show much.

One of these years, Abrams thought, *somebody will break the tacit agreement and put up a few spy satellites. Why not us?— 'Course, then the other side'll bring space warships, instead of just transports, and go potshooting. And then the first side will bring bigger warships.*

"I am glad you called," Runei said. "I have thanked Admiral Enriques for the conversion unit, but pleasure is to express obligation to a friend."

"Huh?"

"You did not know? One of our main de-salinators broke down. Your commandant was good enough to furnish us with a replacement part we lacked."

"Oh, yeh. That." Abrams rolled his cigar between his teeth.

The matter was ridiculous, he thought. Terrans and Merseians were at war on Starkad. They killed each other's people. But nonetheless, Runei had sent a message of congratulations when Birthday rolled around. (Twice ridiculous! Even if a spaceship in hyperdrive has no theoretical limit to her pseudovelocity, the concept of simultaneity remains meaningless over interstellar distances.) And Enriques had now saved Runei from depleting his beer supplies.

Because this wasn't a war. Not officially. Not even among the two native races. Tigeries and Seatrolls had fought since they evolved to intelligence, probably. But that was like men and wolves in ancient days, nothing systematic, plain natural enemies. Until the Merseians began giving the Seatrolls equipment and advice and the landfolk were driven back. When Terra heard about that, it was sheer reflex to do likewise for the Tigeries, preserve the balance lest Starkad be unified as a Merseian puppet. As a result, the Merseians upped their help a bit, and Terrans replied in kind, and—

And the two empires remained at peace. These were simple missions of assistance,

weren't they? Terra had Mount Narpa by treaty
with the Tigeries of Ujanka, Merseia sat in
Kimraig by treaty with whoever lived there.
(Time out for laughter and applause. No Starkadian culture appeared to have anything like an
idea of compacts between sovereign powers.)
The Roidhunate of Merseia didn't shoot down
Terran scouts. Heavens, no! Only Merseian
militechnicians did, helping the Seatrolls of
Kimraig maintain inviolate their air space. The
Terran Empire hadn't bushwhacked a Merseian
landing party on Cape Thunder: merely Terrans
pledged to guard the frontier of their ally.

The Covenant of Alfzar held. You were bound
to assist civilized outworlders on request.
Abrams toyed with the notion of inventing some
requests from his side. In fact, that wasn't a bad
gambit right now.

"Maybe you can return the favor," he said.
"We've lost a flitter in the Zletovar. I'm not so
rude as to hint that one of your lads was cruising
along and eyeballed ours and got a wee bit over-
excited. But supposing the crash was accidental,
how about a joint investigation?"

Abrams liked seeing startlement on that hard
green face. "You joke, Commander!"

"Oh, naturally my boss'd have to approach
you officially, but I'll suggest it to him. You've
got better facilities than us for finding a sunken
wreck."

"But why?"

Abrams shrugged. "Mutual interest in pre-
venting accidents. Cultivation of friendship between peoples and individual beings. I think

that's what the catchword is back home."

Runei scowled. "Quite impossible. I advise you not to make any such proposal on the record."

"Nu? Wouldn't look so good if you turn us down?"

"Tension would only be increased. Must I repeat my government's position to you? The oceans of Starkad belong to the seafolk. They evolved there, it is their environment, it is not essential to the landfolk. Nevertheless the landfolk have consistently encroached. Their fisheries, their seabeast hunts, their weed harvests, their drag nets, everything disturbs an ecology vital to the other race. I will not speak of those they have killed, the underwater cities they have bombed with stones, the bays and straits they have barred. I will say that when Merseia offered her good offices to negotiate a modus vivendi, no land culture showed the slightest interest. My task is to help the seafolk resist aggression until the various landfolk societies agree to establish a just and stable peace."

"Come off that parrot act," Abrams snorted. "You haven't got the beak for it. Why are you really here?"

"I have told you—"

"No. Think. You've got your orders and you obey 'em like a good little soldier. But don't you sometimes wonder what the profit is for Merseia? I sure do. What the black and red deuce is your government's reason? It's not as if Saxo sun had a decent strategic location. Here we are, spang in the middle of a hundred light-

year strip of no man's land between our realms.
Hardly been explored; hell, I'll bet half the stars
around us aren't so much as noted in a
catalogue. The nearest civilization is Betelgeuse,
and the Betelgeuseans are neutrals who wish
emerods on both our houses. You're too old to
believe in elves, gnomes, little men, or the disin-
terested altruism of great empires. So *why*?"

"I may not question the decisions of the
Roidhum and his Grand Council. Still less may
you." Runei's stiffness dissolved in a grin. "If
Starkad is so useless, why are you here?"

"Lot of people back home wonder about that
too," Abrams admitted. "Policy says we contain
you wherever we can. Sitting on this planet, you
would have a base fifty light-years closer to our
borders, for whatever that's worth." He paused.
"Could give you a bit more influence over
Betelgeuse."

"Let us hope your envoy manages to settle the
dispute," Runei said, relaxing. "I do not precisely enjoy myself on this hellball either."

"What envoy?"

"You have not heard? Our latest courier in-
formed us that a ... *khraich* ... yes, a Lord
Hauksberg is hitherbound."

"I know." Abrams winced. "Another big red
wheel to roll around the base."

"But he is to proceed to Merseia. The Grand
Council has agreed to receive him."

"Huh?" Abrams shook his head. "Damn, I
wish our mails were as good as yours. . . . Well.
How about this downed flitter? Why won't you
help us look for the pieces?"

"In essence, informally," Runei said, "because we hold it had no right, as a foreign naval vessel, to fly over the waters. Any consequences must be on the pilot's own head."

Ho-ho! Abrams tautened. That was something new. Implied, of course, by the Merseian position; but this was the first time he had heard the claim in plain language. So could the greenskins be preparing a major push? Very possible, especially if Terra had offered to negotiate. Military operations exert pressure at bargaining tables, too.

Runei sat like a crocodile, smiling the least amount. Had he guessed what was in Abrams' mind? Maybe not. In spite of what the brotherhood-of-beings sentimentalists kept bleating, Merseians did not really think in human style. Abrams made an elaborate stretch and yawn. " 'Bout time I knocked off," he said. "Nice talking to you, old bastard." He did not entirely lie. Runei was a pretty decent carnivore. Abrams would have loved to hear him reminisce about the planets where he had ranged.

"Your move," the Merseian reminded him.

"Why . . . yes. Clean forgot. Knight to king's bishop four."

Runei got out his own board and shifted the piece. He sat quiet a while, studying. "Curious," he murmured.

"It'll get curiouser. Call me back when you're ready." Abrams switched off.

His cigar was dead again. He dropped the stub down the disposal, lit a fresh one, and rose. Weariness dragged at him. Gravity on Starkad

wasn't high enough that man needed drugs or a
counterfield. But one point three gees meant
twenty-five extra kilos loaded on middle-aged
bones. . . . No, he was thinking in standard
terms. Dayan pulled ten per cent harder than
Terra. . . . Dayan, dear gaunt hills and wind-
scoured plains, homes nestled in warm orange
sunlight, low trees and salt marshes and the
pride of a people who had bent desolation to
their needs. . . . Where had young Flandry been
from, and what memories did he carry to
darkness?

On a sudden impulse Abrams put down his
cigar, bent his head, and inwardly recited the
Kaddish.

*Get to bed, old man. Maybe you've stumbled on a
clue, maybe not, but it'll keep. Go to your rest.*

He put on cap and cloak, thrust the cigar back
between his jaws, and walked out.

Cold smote him. A breeze blew thinly under
strange constellations and auroral glimmer. The
nearer moon, Egrima, was up, almost full, twice
the apparent size of Luna seen from Terra. It
flooded distant snowpeaks with icy bluish light.
Burus was a Luna-sized crescent barely above
the rooftops.

Walls bulked black on either side of the un-
paved street, which scrunched with frost as his
boots struck. Here and there glowed a lighted
window, but they and the scattered lamps did
little to relieve the murk. On his left, unrestful
radiance from smelters picked out the two spaceships now in port, steel cenotaphs rearing
athwart the Milky Way. Thence, too, came the

clangor of night-shift work. The field was being
enlarged, new sheds and barracks were going
up, for Terra's commitment was growing. On
his right the sky was tinted by feverish
glowsigns, and he caught snatches of drumbeat,
trumpets, perhaps laughter. Madame Cepheid
had patriotically dispatched a shipful of girls
and croupiers to Starkad. And why not? They
were so young and lonely, those boys.

Marta, I miss you.

Abrams was almost at his quarters when he
remembered he hadn't stashed the papers on his
desk. He stopped dead. Great Emperor's elegant
epiglottis! He was indeed due for an overhaul.

Briefly he was tempted to say, "Urinate on
regulations." The office was built of ferrocon-
crete, with an armorplate door and an automatic
recognition lock. But no. Lieutenant Novak
might report for duty before his chief, may his
pink cheeks fry in hell. Wouldn't do to set a bad
security example. Not that espionage was any
problem here, but what a man didn't see, he
couldn't tell if the Merseians caught and hypnoprobed him.

Abrams wheeled and strode back, trailing bad
words. At the end, he slammed to a halt. His
cigar hit the deck and he ground down a heel on
it.

The door was properly closed, the windows
dark. But he could see footprints in the churned,
not yet congealed mud before the entrance, and
they weren't his own.

And no alarm had gone off. Somebody was
inside with a truckload of roboticist's gear.

Abrams' blaster snaked into his hand. Call the guard on his wristcom? No, whoever could burgle his office could surely detect a transmission and was surely prepared for escape before help could arrive. By suicide if nothing else.

Abrams adjusted his gun to needle beam. Given luck, he might disable rather than kill. Unless he bought it first. The heart slugged in his breast. Night closed thickly inward.

He catfooted to the door and touched the lock switch. Metal burned his fingers with chill. Identified, he swung the door open and leaned around the edge.

Light trickled over his shoulder and through the windows. A thing whirled from his safe. His eyes were adapted and he made out some details. It must have looked like any workman in radiation armor as it passed through the base. But now one arm had sprouted tools; and the helmet was thrown back to reveal a face with electronic eyes, set in a head of alloy.

A Merseian face.

Blue lightning spat from the tool-hand. Abrams had yanked himself back. The energy bolt sparked and sizzled on the door. He spun his own blaster to medium beam, not stopping to give himself reasons, and snapped a shot.

The other weapon went dead, ruined. The armored shape used its normal hand to snatch for a gun taken forth in advance and laid on top of the safe. Abrams charged through the doorway while he reset for needle fire. So intense a ray, at such close range, slashed legs across. In a rattle and clash, the intruder fell.

Abrams activated his transmitter. "Guard! Intelligence office—on the double!"

His blaster threatened while he waved the lights to go on. The being stirred. No blood flowed from those limb stumps; powerpacks, piezoelectric cascades, room-temperature superconductors lay revealed. Abrams realized what he had caught, and whistled. Less than half a Merseian: no tail, no breast or lower body, not much natural skull, one arm and the fragment of another. The rest was machinery. It was the best prosthetic job he'd ever heard of.

Not that he knew of many. Only among races which didn't know how to make tissues regenerate, or which didn't have that kind of tissues. Surely the Merseians—But what a lovely all-purpose plug-in they had here!

The green face writhed. Wrath and anguish spewed from the lips. The hand fumbled at the chest. To turn off the heart? Abrams kicked that wrist aside and planted a foot on it. "Easy, friend," he said.

Chapter Three

Morning on Merseia—

Brechdan Ironrede, the Hand of the Vach Yn-vory, walked forth on a terrace of Castle Dhangodhan. A sentry slapped boots with tail and laid blaster to breastplate. A gardener, pruning the dwarfed koir trees planted among the flagstones, folded his arms and bent in his brown smock. To both, Brechdan touched his forehead. For they were not slaves; their families had been clients of the Ynvorys from ages before the nations merged into one; how could they take pride in it if the clan chief did not accord them their own dignity?

He walked unspeaking, though, between the rows of yellow blooms, until he reached the parapet. There he stopped and looked across his homeland.

Behind him, the castle lifted gray stone turrets. Banners snapped in a cool wind, against an infinitely blue sky. Before him, the walls tumbled down toward gardens, and beyond them the forested slopes of Bedh-Ivrich went on down, and down, and down, to be lost in mists and shadows which still cloaked the valley. Thus he could not see the farms and villages which

Dhangodhan dominated: nothing but the peaks on the other side. Those climbed until their green flanks gave way to crags and cliffs of granite, to snowfields and the far blink of glaciers. The sun Korych had now cleared the eastern heights and cast dizzling spears over the world. Brechdan saluted it, as was his hereditary right. High overhead wheeled a fangryf, hunting, and the light burned gold off its feathers.

There was a buzz in the air as the castle stirred to wakefulness, a clatter, a bugle call, a hail and a bit of song. The wind smelled of woodsmoke. From this terrace the River Oiss was not visible, but its cataracts rang loud. Hard to imagine how, a bare two hundred kilometers west, that stream began to flow through lands which had become one huge city, from foothills to the Wilwidh Ocean. Or, for that matter, hard to picture those towns, mines, factories, ranches which covered the plains east of the Hun range.

Yet they were his too—no, not his; the Vach Ynvory's, himself no more than the Hand for a few decades before he gave back this flesh to the soil and this mind to the God. Dhangodhan they had preserved little changed, because here was the country from which they sprang, long ago. But their real work today was in Ardaig and Tridaig, the capitals, where Brechdan presided over the Grand Council. And beyond this planet, beyond Korych itself, out to the stars.

Brechdan drew a deep breath. The sense of power coursed in his veins. But that was a familiar wine; today he awaited a joy more gentle.

It did not show upon him. He was too long

schooled in chieftainship. Big, austere in a black robe, brow seamed with an old battle scar which he disdained to have biosculped away, he turned to the world only the face of Brechdan Ironrede, who stood second to none but the Roidhun.

A footfall sounded. Brechdan turned. Chwioch, his bailiff, approached, in red tunic and green trousers and modishly high-collared cape. He wasn't called "the Dandy" for nothing. But he was loyal and able and an Ynvory born. Brechdan exchanged kin-salutes, right hand to left shoulder.

"Word from Shwylt Shipsbane, Protector," Chwioch reported. "His business in the Gwelloch will not detain him after all and he will come here this afternoon as you desired."

"Good." Brechdan was, in fact, elated. Shwylt's counsel would be most helpful, balancing Lifrith's impatience and Priadwyr's over-reliance on computer technology. Though they were fine males, each in his own way, those three Hands of their respective Vachs. Brechdan depended on them for ideas as much as for the support they gave to help him control the Council. He would need them more and more in the next few years, as events on Starkad were maneuvered toward their climax.

A thunderclap cut the sky. Looking up, Brechdan saw a flitter descend with reckless haste. Scalloped fins identified it as Ynvory common-property. "Your son, Protector!" Chwioch cried with jubilation.

"No doubt." Brechdan must not unbend, not even when Elwych returned after three years.

"Ah . . . shall I cancel your morning audience, Protector?"

"Certainly not," Brechdan said. "Our client folk have their right to be heard. I am too much absent from them."

But we can have an hour for our own.

"I shall meet Heir Elwych and tell him where you are, Protector." Chwioch hurried off.

Brechdan waited. The sun began to warm him through his robe. He wished Elwych's mother were still alive. The wives remaining to him were good females, of course, thrifty, trustworthy, cultivated, as females should be. But Nodhia had been—well, yes, he might as well use a Terran concept—she had been fun. Elwych was Brechdan's dearest child, not because he was the oldest now when two others lay dead on remote planets, but because he was Nodhia's. May the earth lie light upon her.

The gardener's shears clattered to the flagstones. "Heir! Welcome home!" It was not ceremonial for the old fellow to kneel and embrace the newcomer's tail, but Brechdan didn't feel that any reproof was called for.

Elwych the Swift strode toward his father in the black and silver of the Navy. A captain's dragon was sewn to his sleeve, the banners of Dhangodhan flamed over his head. He stopped four paces off and gave a service salute. "Greeting, Protector."

"Greeting, swordarm." Brechdan wanted to hug that body to him. Their eyes met. The youngster winked and grinned. And that was nigh as good.

"Are the kindred well?" Elwych asked super-
fluously, as he had called from the inner moon
the moment his ship arrived for furlough.

"Indeed," Brechdan said.

They might then have gone to the gynaeceum
for family reunion. But the guard watched.
Hand and Heir could set him an example by
talking first of things which concerned the race.
They need not be too solemn, however.

"Had you a good trip home?" Brechdan inquired.

"Not exactly," Elwych replied. "Our main
fire-control computer developed some kind of
bellyache. I thought best we put in at Vorida for
repairs. The interimperial situation, you know;
it just might have exploded, and then a Terran
unit just might have chanced near us."

"Vorida? I don't recall—"

"No reason why you should. Too hooting
many planets in the universe. A rogue in the
Betelgeuse sector. We keep a base—What's
wrong?"

Elwych alone noticed the signs of his father
being taken aback. "Nothing," Brechdan said.
"I assume the Terrans don't know about this
orb."

Elwych laughed. "How could they?"

How, in truth? There are so many rogues,
they are so little and dark, space is so vast.

Consider: To an approximation, the size of
bodies which condensed out of the primordial
gas is inversely proportional to the frequency of
their occurrence. At one end of the scale,
hydrogen atoms fill the galaxy, about one per

cubic centimeter. At the other end, you can count the monstrous O-type suns by yourself. (You may extend the scale in both directions, from quanta to quasars; but no matter.) There are about ten times as many M-type red dwarfs as there are G-type stars like Korych or Sol. Your spaceship is a thousand times more likely to be struck by a one-gram pebble than by a one-kilogram rock. And so, sunless planets are more common than suns. They usually travel in clusters; nevertheless they are for most practical purposes unobservable before you are nearly on top of them. They pose no special hazard—whatever their number, the odds against one of them passing through any particular point in space are literally astronomical—and those whose paths are known can make useful harbors.

Brechdan felt he must correct an incomplete answer. "The instantaneous vibrations of a ship under hyperdrive are detectable within a light-year," he said. "A Terran or Betelgeusean could happen that close to your Vorida."

Elwych flushed. "And supposing one of our ships happened to be in the vicinity, what would detection prove except that there was another ship?"

He had been given the wristslap of being told what any cub knew; he had responded with the slap of telling what any cub should be able to reason out for himself. Brechdan could not but smile. Elwych responded. A blow can also be an act of love.

"I capitulate," Brechdan said. "Tell me somewhat of your tour of duty. We got far too few letters, especially in the last months."

"Where I was then, writing was a little difficult," Elwych said. "I can tell you now, though. Saxo V."

"Starkad?" Brechdan exclaimed. "You, a line officer?"

"Was this way. My ship was making a courtesy call on the Betelgeuseans—on showing them the flag, whichever way they chose to take it—when a courier from Fodaich Runei arrived. Somehow the Terrans had learned about a submarine base he was having built off an archipelago. The whole thing was simple, primitive, so the seafolk could operate the units themselves, but it would have served to wreck landfolk commerce in that area. Nobody knows how the Terrans got the information, but Runei says they have a fiendishly good Intelligence chief. At any rate, they gave some landfolk chemical depth bombs and told them where to sail and drop them. And by evil luck, the explosions killed several key technicians of ours who were supervising construction. Which threw everything into chaos. Our mission there is scandalously short-handed. Runei sent to Betelgeuse as well as Merseia, in the hope of finding someone like us who could substitute until proper replacements arrived. So I put my engineers in a civilian boat. And since that immobilized our ship as a fighting unit, I must go too."

Brechdan nodded. An Ynvory did not send personnel into danger and himself stay behind without higher duties.

He knew about the disaster already, of course.

Best not tell Elwych that. Time was unripe for the galaxy to know how serious an interest Merseia had in Starkad. His son was discreet. But what he did not know, he could not tell if the Terrans caught and hypnoprobed him.

"You must have had an adventurous time," Brechdan said.

"Well . . . yes. Occasional sport. And an interesting planet." The anger still in Elwych flared: "I tell you, though, our people are being betrayed."

"How?"

"Not enough of them. Not enough equipment. Not a single armed spaceship. Why don't we support them properly?"

"Then the Terrans will support *their* mission properly," Brechdan said.

Elwych gazed long at his father. The waterfall noise seemed to louden behind Dhangodhan's ramparts. "Are we going to make a real fight for Starkad?" he murmured. "Or do we scuttle away?"

The scar throbbed on Brechdan's forehead. "Who serve the Roidhun do not scuttle. But they may strike bargains, when such appears good for the race."

"So." Elwych stared past him, across the valley mists. Scorn freighted his voice. "I see. The whole operation is a bargaining counter, to win something from Terra. Runei told me they'll send a negotiator here."

"Yes, he is expected soon." Because the matter was great, touching as it did on honor, Brechdan allowed himself to grasp the shoulders of his son. Their eyes met. "Elwych," Brechdan said gently, "you are young and perhaps do not understand. But you must. Service to the race calls for more than courage, more even than intelligence. It calls for wisdom.

"Because we Merseians have such instincts that most of us actively enjoy combat, we tend to look on combat as an end in itself. And such is not true. That way lies destruction. Combat is a means to an end—the hegemony of our race. And that in turn is but a means to the highest end of all—absolute freedom for our race, to make of the galaxy what they will.

"But we cannot merely fight for our goal. We must work. We must have patience. You will not see us masters of the galaxy. It is too big. We may need a million years. On that time scale, individual pride is a small sacrifice to offer, when it happens that compromise or retreat serves us best."

Elwych swallowed. "Retreat from Terra?"

"I trust not. Terra is the immediate obstacle. The duty of your generation is to remove it."

"I don't understand," Elwych protested. "What is the Terran Empire? A clot of stars. An old, sated, corrupt people who want nothing except to keep what their fathers won for them. Why pay them any heed whatsoever? Why not expand away from them—around them—until they're engulfed?"

"Precisely because Terra's objective is the preservation of the status quo," Brechdan said. "You are forgetting the political theory that was supposed to be part of your training. Terra cannot permit us to become more powerful than she. Therefore she is bound to resist our every attempt to grow. And do not underestimate her. That race still bears the chromosomes of conquerors. There are still brave men in the Empire, devoted men, shrewd men. . .with the experience of a history longer than ours to guide them. If they see doom before them, they'll fight like demons. So, until we have sapped their strength, we move carefully. Do you comprehend?"

"Yes, my father," Elwych yielded. "I hope so."

Brechdan eased. They had been serious for as long as their roles demanded. "Come." His face cracked in another smile; he took his son's arm. "Let us go greet our kin."

They walked down corridors hung with the shields of their ancestors and the trophies of hunts on more than one planet. A graveshaft lifted them to the gynaeceum level.

The whole tribe waited, Elwych's stepmothers, sisters and their husbands and cubs, younger brothers. Everything dissolved in shouts, laughter, pounding of backs, twining of tails, music from a record player and a ringdance over the floor.

One cry interrupted. Brechdan bent above the cradle of his newest grandcub. *I should speak about marriage to Elwych,* he thought. *High time he begot an Heir's Heir.* The small being who lay on the furs wrapped a fist around the gnarled finger that stroked him. Brechdan Ironrede melted within himself. "You shall have stars for toys," he crooned. "Wudda, wudda, wudda."

Chapter Four

Ensign Dominic Flandry, Imperial Naval Flight Corps, did not know whether he was alive through luck or management. At the age of nineteen, with the encoding molecules hardly settled down on your commission, it was natural to think the latter. But had a single one of the factors he had used to save himself been absent— He didn't care to dwell on that.

Besides, his troubles were far from over. As a merchant ship belonging to the Sisterhood of Kursoviki, the *Archer* had been given a radio by the helpful Terrans. But it was crapout; some thimblewit had exercised some Iron Age notion of maintenance. Dragoika had agreed to put back for her home. But with a foul wind, they'd be days at sea in this damned wallowing bathtub before they were even likely to speak a boat with a transmitter in working order. That wasn't fatal per se. Flandry could shovel local rations through the chowlock of his helmet; Starkadian biochemistry was sufficiently like Terran that most foods wouldn't poison him, and he carried vitamin supplements. The taste, though, my God, the taste!

Most ominous was the fact that he *had* been shot down, and at no large distance from here.

Perhaps the Seatrolls, and Merseians, would let
this Tigery craft alone. If they weren't yet ready
to show their hand, they probably would. However, his misfortune indicated their preparations
were more or less complete. When he chanced to
pass above their latest kettle of mischief, they'd
felt so confident they opened fire.

"And then the Outside Folk attacked you?"
Ferok prodded. His voice came as a purr
through whistle of wind, rush and smack of
waves, creak of rigging, all intensified and distorted by the thick air.

"Yes," Flandry said. He groped for words.
They'd given him an electronic cram in the language and customs of Kursovikian civilization
while the transport bore him from Terra. But
some things are hard to explain in pre-industrial
terms. "A type of vessel which can both submerge and fly rose from the water. Its radio
shout drowned my call and its firebeams
wrecked my craft before mine could pierce its
thicker armor. I barely escaped my hull as it
sank, and kept submerged until the enemy went
away. Then I flew off in search of help. The
small engine which lifted me was nigh exhausted
when I came upon your ship."

Truly his gravity impeller wouldn't lug him
much further until the capacitors were
recharged. He didn't plan to use it again. What
power remained in the pack on his shoulders
must be saved to operate the pump and reduction valve in the vitryl globe which sealed off his
head. A man couldn't breathe Starkadian sea-
level air and survive. Such an oxygen concentra-

tion would burn out his lungs faster than nitrogen narcosis and carbon dioxide acidosis could kill him.

He remembered how Lieutenant Danielson had gigged him for leaving off the helmet. "Ensign, I don't give a ball of fertilizer how uncomfortable the thing is, when you might be enjoying your nice Terra-conditioned cockpit. Nor do I weep at the invasion of privacy involved in taping your every action in flight. The purpose is to make sure that pups like you, who know so much more than a thousand years of astronautics could possibly teach them, obey regulations. The next offense will earn you thirty seconds of nerve-lash. Dismissed."

So you saved my life, Flandry grumbled. *You're still a snot-nosed bastard.*

Nobody was to blame for his absent blaster. It was torn from the holster in those wild seconds of scrambling clear. He had kept the regulation knife and pouchful of oddments. He had boots and gray coverall, sadly stained and in no case to be compared with the glamorous dress uniform. And that was just about the lot.

Ferok lowered the plumy thermosensor tendrils above his eyes: a frown. "If the vaz-Siravo search what's left of your flier, down below, and don't find your body, they may guess what you did and come looking for you," he said.

"Yes," Flandry agreed, "they may."

He braced himself against pitch and roll and looked outward—tall, the lankiness of adolescence still with him—brown hair, gray eyes, a rather long and regular face which Saxo

had burned dark. Before him danced and shim-
mered a greenish ocean, sun-flecks and
whitecaps on waves that marched faster, in
Starkadian gravity, than on Terra. The sky was
pale blue. Clouds banked gigantic on the
horizon, but in a dense atmosphere they did not
portend storm. A winged thing cruised, a sea
animal broached and dove again. At its distance,
Saxo was only a third as broad as Sol is to Terra
and gave half the illumination. The adaptable
human vision perceived this as normal, but the
sun was merciless white, so brilliant that one
dared not look anywhere near. The short day
stood at late afternoon, and the temperature,
never very high in these middle northern
latitudes, was dropping. Flandry shivered.

Ferok made a contrast to him. The land
Starkadian, Tigery, Toborko, or whatever you
wanted to call him, was built not unlike a short
man with disproportionately long legs. His
hands were four-fingered, his feet large and
clawed, he flaunted a stubby tail. The head was
less anthropoid, round, with flat face tapering to
a narrow chin. The eyes were big, slanted,
scarlet in the iris, beneath his fronded tendrils.
The nose, what there was of it, had a single slit
nostril. The mouth was wide and carnivore-
toothed. The ears were likewise big, outer edges
elaborated till they almost resembled bat wings.
Sleek fur covered his skin, black-striped orange
that shaded into white at the throat.

He wore only a beaded pouch, kept from flap-
ping by thigh straps, and a curved sword scab-
barded across his back. By profession he was the

boatswain, a high rank for a male on a Kursovikian ship; as such, he was no doubt among Dragoika's lovers. By nature he was impetuous, quarrelsome, and dog-loyal to his allegiances. Flandry liked him.

Ferok lifted a telescope and swept it around an arc. That was a native invention. Kursoviki was the center of the planet's most advanced land culture. "No sign of anything yet," he said. "Do you think yon Outsider flyboat may attack us?"

"I doubt that," Flandry said. "Most likely it was simply on hand because of having brought some Merseian advisors, and shot at me because I might be carrying instruments which would give me a clue as to what's going on down below. It's probably returned to Kimraig by now." He hesitated before continuing: "The Merseians, like us, seldom take a direct role in any action, and then nearly always just as individual officers, not representatives of their people. Neither of us wishes to provoke a response in kind."

"Afraid?" Lips curled back from fangs.

"On your account," Flandry said, somewhat honestly. "You have no dream of what our weapons can do to a world."

"World . . . hunh, the thought's hard to seize. Well, let the Sisterhood try. I'm happy to be a plain male."

Flandry turned and looked across the deck. The *Archer* was a big ship by Starkadian measure, perhaps five hundred tons, broad in the beam, high in the stern, a carven post at the prow as emblem of her tutelary spirit. A

deckhouse stood amidships, holding galley,
smithy, carpenter shop, and armory. Everything
was gaudily painted. Three masts carried yellow
square sails aloft, fore-and-aft beneath; at the
moment she was tacking on the latter and a gen-
oa. The crew were about their duties on deck
and in the rigging. They numbered thirty male
hands and half a dozen female officers. The ship
had been carrying timber and spices from
Ujanka port down the Chain archipelago.

"What armament have we?" he asked.

"Our Terran deck gun," Ferok told him.
"Five of your rifles. We were offered more, but
Dragoika said they'd be no use till we had more
people skilled with them. Otherwise, swords,
pikes, crossbows, knives, belaying pins, teeth,
and nails." He gestured at the mesh which
passed from side to side of the hull, under the
keel. "If that twitches much, could mean a
Siravo trying to put a hole in our bottom. Then
we dive after him. You'd be best for that, with
your gear."

Flandry winced. His helmet was adjustable
for underwater; on Starkad, the concentration of
dissolved oxygen was almost as high as in
Terra's air. But he didn't fancy a scrap with a
being evolved for such an environment.

"Why are you here, yourself?" Ferok asked
conversationally. "Pleasure or plunder?"

"Neither. I was sent." Flandry didn't add that
the Navy reckoned it might as well use Starkad
to give certain promising young officers some experience. "Promising" made him sound too im-
mature. At once he realized he'd actually sound-

ed unaggressive and prevaricated in haste: "Of course, with the chance of getting into a fight, I would have asked to go anyway."

"They tell me your females obey males. True?"

"Well, sometimes." The second mate passed by and Flandry's gaze followed her. She had curves, a tawny mane rippling down her back, breasts standing fuller and firmer than any girl could have managed without technological assistance, and a nearly humanoid nose. Her clothing consisted of some gold bracelets. But her differences from the Terran went deeper than looks. She didn't lactate; those nipples fed blood directly to her infants. And hers was the more imaginative, more cerebral sex, not subordinated in any culture, dominant in the islands around Kursoviki. He wondered if that might trace back to something as simple as the female body holding more blood and more capacity to regenerate it.

"But who, then, keeps order in your home country?" Ferok wondered. "Why haven't you killed each other off?"

"Um-m-m, hard to explain," Flandry said. "Let me first see if I understand your ways, to compare mine. For instance, you owe nothing to the place where you live, right? I mean, no town or island or whatever is ruled, as a ship is . . . right? Instead—at any rate in this part of the world—the females are organized into associations like the Sisterhood, whose members may live anywhere, which even have their special languages. They own all important property and

make all important decisions through those associations. Thus disputes among males have little effect on them. Am I right?"

"I suppose so. You might have put it more
politely."

"Apology-of-courage is offered. I am a
stranger. Now among my people—"

A shout fell from the crow's nest. Ferok
whirled and pointed his telescope. The crew
sprang to the starboard rail, clustered in the
shrouds, and yelled.

Dragoika bounded from the captain's cabin
under the poop. She held a four-pronged fish
spear in one hand, a small painted drum beneath her arm. Up the ladder she went, to stand
by the quartermistress at the wheel and look for
herself. Then, coolly, she tapped her drum on
one side, plucked the steel strings across the re-
cessed head on the other. Twang and thump carried across noise like a bugle call. *All hands to
arms and battle stations!*

"The vaz-Siravo!" Ferok shouted above
clamor. "They're on us!" He made for the
deckhouse. Restored to discipline, the crew were
lining up for helmets, shields, byrnies, and
weapons.

Flandry strained his eyes into the glare off the
water. A score or so blue dorsal fins clove it, converging on the ship. And suddenly, a hundred
meters to starboard, a submarine rose.

A little, crude thing, doubtless home-built to a
Merseian design—for if you want to engineer a
planet-wide war among primitives, you should
teach them what they can make and do for them-

selves. The hull was greased leather stretched
across a framework of some undersea equivalent
of wood. Harness trailed downward to the four
fish which pulled it; he could barely discern
them as huge shadows under the surface. The
deck lay awash. But an outsize catapult
projected therefrom. Several dolphin-like bodies
with transparent globes on their heads and powerpacks on their backs crouched alongside. They
rose onto flukes and flippers; their arms reached
to swing the machine around.

"Dommaneek!" Dragoika screeched. "Dommaneek Falandaree! Can you man ours?"

"Aye, aye!" The Terran ran prow-ward.
Planks rolled and thudded beneath his feet.

On the forward deck, the two females whose
duty it was were trying to unlimber the gun.
They worked slowly, getting in each other's way,
spitting curses. There hadn't yet been time to
drill many competent shots, even with a weapon
as simple as this, a rifle throwing 38 mm.
chemical shells. Before they got the range, that
catapult might—

"Gangway!" Flandry shoved the nearest
aside. She snarled and swatted at him with long
red nails. Dragoika's drum rippled an order.
Both females fell back from him.

He opened the breech, grabbed a shell from
the ammo box, and dogged it in. The enemy
catapult thumped. A packet arced high, down
again, made a near miss and burst into flame
which spread crimson and smoky across the
waves. Some version of Greek fire—undersea oil
wells—Flandry put his eye to the range finder.

He was too excited to be scared. But he must lay
the gun manually. A hydraulic system would
have been too liable to breakdown. In spite of
good balance and self-lubricating bearings, the
barrel swung with nightmare slowness. The
Seatrolls were rewinding their catapult . . .
before Andromeda, they were fast! *They* must
use hydraulics.

Dragoika spoke to the quartermistress. She
put the wheel hard over. Booms swung over the
deck. The jib flapped thunderous until
crewmales reset the sheets. The *Archer* came
about. Flandry struggled to compensate. He
barely remembered to keep one foot on the
brake, lest his gun travel too far. *Bet those she-cats
would've forgotten*. The enemy missile didn't make
the vessel's superstructure as intended. But it
struck the hull amidships. Under this oxygen
pressure, fire billowed heavenward.

Flandry pulled the lanyard. His gun roared
and kicked. A geyser fountained, mingled with
splinters. One draught fish leaped, threshed,
and died. The rest already floated bellies up.
"Got him!" Flandry whooped.

Dragoika plucked a command. Most of the
crew put aside their weapons and joined a firefighting party. There was a hand pump at either
rail, buckets with ropes bent to them, sails to
drag from the deckhouse and wet and lower.

Ferok, or someone, yelled through voices,
wind, waves, brawling, and smoke of the flames.
The Seatrolls were coming over the opposite rail.

They must have climbed the nets. (*Better invent
a different warning gadget,* raced through Flandry's

mind.) They wore the Merseian equipment
which had enabled their kind to carry the war
ashore elsewhere on Starkad. Waterfilled
helmets covered the blunt heads, black absor-
bent skinsuits kept everything else moist. Pumps
cycled atmospheric oxygen, running off powerpacks. The same capacitors energized their
legs. Those were clumsy. The bodies must be
harnessed into a supporting framework, the two
flippers and the fluked tail control four mechanical limbs with prehensile feet. But they lurched
across the deck, huge, powerful, their hands
holding spears and axes and a couple of water-
proof machine pistols. Ten of them were now
aboard . . . and how many sailors could be
spared from the fire?

A rifle bullet wailed. A Seatroll sprayed lead
in return. Tigeries crumpled. Their blood was
human color.

Flandry rammed home another shell and
lobbed it into the sea some distance off. "Why?"
screamed a gunner.

"May have been more coming," he said. "I
hope hydrostatic shock got 'em." He didn't notice he used Anglic.

Dragoika cast her fish spear. One pistol
wielder went down, the prongs in him. He scrab-
bled at the shaft. Rifles barked, crossbows
snapped, driving his mate to shelter between the
deckhouse and a lifeboat. Then combat ramped,
leaping Tigeries, lumbering Seatrolls, sword
against ax, pike against spear, clash, clatter,
grunt, shriek, chaos run loose. Several fire-
fighters went for their weapons. Dragoika

drummed them back to work. The Seatrolls made for them, to cut them down and let the ship burn. The armed Tigeries tried to defend them. The enemy pistoleer kept the Kursovikian rifle shooters pinned down behind masts and bollards—neutralized. The battle had no more shape than that.

A bullet splintered the planks a meter from Flandry. For a moment, panic locked him where he stood. What to do, what to do? He couldn't die. He mustn't. He was Dominic, himself, with a lifetime yet to live. Outnumbered though they were, the Seatrolls need but wreak havoc till the fire got beyond control and he was done. *Mother! Help me!*

For no sound reason, he remembered Lieutenant Danielson. Rage blossomed in him. He bounded down the ladder and across the main deck. A Seatroll chopped at him. He swerved and continued.

Dragoika's door stood under the poop. He slid the panel aside and plunged into her cabin. It was appointed in barbaric luxury. Sunlight sickled through an oval port, across the bulkhead as the ship rolled, touching bronze candlesticks, woven tapestry, a primitive sextant, charts and navigation tables inscribed on parchment. He snatched what he had left here to satisfy her curiosity, his impeller, buckled the unit on his back with frantic fingers and hook in his capacitors. Now, that sword, which she hadn't taken time to don. He re-emerged, flicked controls, and rose.

Over the deckhouse! The Seatroll with the

machine pistol lay next it, a hard target for a
rifle, himself commanding stem and stern. Flandry drew blade. The being heard the slight noise
and tried awkwardly to look up. Flandry struck.
He missed the hand but knocked the gun loose.
It flipped over the side.

He whirred aft, smiting from above. "I've got
him!" he shouted. "I've got him! Come out and
do some real shooting!"

The fight was soon finished. He used a little
more energy to help spread the wet sail which
smothered the fire.

After dark, Eŭrima and Buruz again ruled
heaven. They cast shivering glades across the
waters. Few stars shone through, but one didn't
miss them with so much other beauty. The ship
plowed northward in an enormous murmurous
hush.

Dragoika stood with Flandry by the totem at
the prow. She had offered thanks. Kursovikian
religion was a paganism more inchoate than any
recorded from ancient Terra—the Tigery mind
was less interested than the human in finding
ultimate causes—but ritual was important. Now
the crew had returned to watch or to sleep and
they two were alone. Her fur was sparked with
silver, her eyes pools of light.

"Our thanks belong more to you," she said
softly. "I am high in the Sisterhood. They will be
told, and remember."

"Oh, well." Flandry shuffled his feet and
blushed.

"But have you not endangered yourself? You

explained what scant strength is left in those boxes which keep you alive. And then you spent it to fly about."

"Uh, my pump can be operated manually if need be."

"I shall appoint a detail to do so."

"No need. You see, now I can use the Siravo powerpacks. I have tools in my pouch for adapting them."

"Good." She looked awhile into the shadows and luminance which barred the deck. "That one whose pistol you removed—" Her tone was wistful.

"No, ma'am," Flandry said firmly. "You cannot have him. He's the only survivor of the lot. We'll keep him alive and unhurt."

"I simply thought of questioning him about their plans. I know a little of their language. We've gained it from prisoners or parleys through the ages. He wouldn't be too damaged, I think."

"My superiors can do a better job in Highport."

Dragoika sighed. "As you will." She leaned against him. "I've met vaz-Terran before, but you are the first I have really known well." Her tail wagged. "I like you."

Flandry gulped. "I . . . I like you too."

"You fight like a male and think like a female. That's something new. Even in the far southern islands—" She laid an arm around his waist. Her fur was warm and silken where it touched his skin. Somebody had told him once that could you breathe their air undiluted, the Tigeries would smell like new-mown hay. "I'll have joy of your company."

"Um-m-m . . . uh." *What can I say?*

"Pity you must wear that helmet," Dragoika said. "I'd like to taste your lips. But otherwise we're not made so differently, our two kinds. Will you come to my cabin?"

For an instant that whirled, Flandry was tempted. He had everything he could do to answer. It wasn't based on past lectures about taking care not to offend native mores, nor on principle, nor, most certainly, on fastidiousness. If anything, her otherness made her the more piquant. But he couldn't really predict what she might do in a close relationship, and—

"I'm deeply sorry," he said. "I'd love to, but I'm under a—" what was the word?—"a geas."

She was neither offended nor much surprised. She had seen a lot of different cultures. "Pity," she said. "Well, you know where the forecastle is. Goodnight." She padded aft. En route, she stopped to collect Ferok.

—and besides, those fangs were awfully intimidating.

Chapter Five

When Lord Hauksberg arrived in Highport, Admiral Enriques and upper-echelon staff had given a formal welcoming party for their distinguished visitor and his aides as protocol required. Hauksberg was expected to reciprocate on the eve of departure. Those affairs were predictably dull. In between, however, he invited various officers to small gatherings. A host of shrewd graciousness, he thus blunted resentment which he was bound to cause by his interviewing of overworked men and his diversion of already inadequate armed forces to security duty.

"I still don't see how you rate," Jan van Zuyl complained from the bunk where he sprawled. "A lousy ensign like you."

"You're an ensign yourself, me boy," Flandry reminded him from the dresser. He gave his blue tunic a final tug, pulled on his white gloves, and buffed the jetflare insignia on his shoulders.

"Yes, but not a lousy one," said his roommate.

"I'm a hero. Remember?"

"I'm a hero too. We're all heroes." Van Zuyl's gaze prowled their dismal little chamber. The girlie animations hardly brightened it. "Give L'Etoile a kiss for me."

"You mean she'll be there?" Flandry's pulses jumped.

"She was when Carruthers got invited. Her and Sharine and—"

"Carruthers is a lieutenant j.g. Therefore he is ex officio a liar. Madame Cepheid's choicest items are not available to anyone below commander."

"He swears milord had 'em on hand, and in hand, for the occasion. So he lies. Do me a favor and elaborate the fantasy on your return. I'd like to keep that particular illusion."

"You provide the whisky and I'll provide the tales." Flandry adjusted his cap to micrometrically calculated rakishness.

"Mercenary wretch," van Zuyl groaned. "Anyone else would lie for pleasure and prestige."

"Know, O miserable one, that I possess an inward serenity which elevates me far beyond any need for your esteem. Yet not beyond need for your booze. Especially after the last poker game. And a magnificent evening to you. I shall return."

Flandry proceeded down the hall and out the main door of the junior officer's dorm. Wind struck viciously at him. Sea-level air didn't move fast, being too dense, but on this mountaintop Saxo could energize storms of more than terrestroid ferocity. Dry snow hissed through chill and clamor. Flandry wrapped his cloak about him with a sign for lost appearances, hung onto his cap, and ran. At his age he had soon adapted to the gravity.

HQ was the largest building in Highport, which didn't say much, in order to include a level of guest suites. Flandry had remarked on that to Commander Abrams, in one of their conversations following the numerous times he'd been summoned for further questioning about his experience with the Tigeries. The Intelligence chief had a knack for putting people at their ease. "Yes, sir, quite a few of my messmates have wondered if—uh—"

"If the Imperium has sludge on the brain, taking up shipping space with luxuries for pestiferous junketeers that might've been used to send us more equipment. Hey?" Abrams prompted.

"Uh . . . nobody's committing *lèse majesté,* sir."

"The hell they aren't. But I guess you can't tell me so right out. In this case, though, you boys are mistaken." Abrams jabbed his cigar at Flandry. "Think, son. We're here for a political purpose. So we need political support. We won't get it by antagonizing courtiers who take champagne and lullaby beds for granted. Tell your friends that silly-looking hotel is an investment."

Here's where I find out. A scanner checked Flandry and opened the door. The lobby beyond was warm! It was also full of armed guards. They saluted and let him by with envious glances. But as he went up the graveshaft, his self-confidence grew thinner. Rather than making him bouncy, the graduated shift to Terran weight gave a sense of unfirmness.

"Offhand," Abrams had said when he learned about the invitation, "milord seems to want you for a novelty. You've a good yarn and you're a talented spinner. Nu, entertain him. But watch yourself. Hauksberg's no fool. Nor any idler. In fact, I gather that every one of his little soirées has served some business purpose— off-the-record information, impressions of what we really expect will happen and expect to do and how we really feel about the whole schtick."

By that time, Flandry knew him well enough to venture a grin. "How do we really feel, sir? I'd like to know."

"What's your opinion? Your own, down inside? I haven't got any recorder turned on."

Flandry frowned and sought words. "Sir, I only work here, as they say. But . . . indoctrination said our unselfish purpose is to save the land civilizations from ruin; islanders depend on the sea almost as much as the fishfolk. And our Imperial purpose is to contain Merseian expansionism wherever it occurs. But I can't help wondering why anybody wants this planet."

"Confidentially," Abrams said, "my main task is to find the answer to that. I haven't succeeded yet."

—A liveried servant announced Flandry. He stepped into a suite of iridescent walls, comfortable loungers, an animation showing a lowgee production of *Ondine*. Behind a buffet table poised another couple of servants, and three more circulated. A dozen men stood conversing: officers of the mission in dress uniform. Hauksberg's staff in colorful mufti. Only one girl

was present. Flandry was a little too nervous for
disappointment. It was a relief to see Abrams'
square figure.

"Ah. Our gallant ensign, eh?" A yellow-
haired man set down his glass—a waiter with a
tray was there before he had completed the motion—and sauntered forth. His garments were
conservatively purple and gray, but they fitted
like another skin and showed him to be in better
physical shape than most nobles. "Welcome.
Hauksberg."

Flandry saluted. "My lord."

"At ease, at ease." Hauksberg made a neg-
ligent gesture. "No rank or ceremony tonight.
Hate 'em, really." He took Flandry's elbow.
"C'mon and be introduced."

The boy's superiors greeted him with more interest than hitherto. They were men whom
Starkad had darkened and leaned; honors sat
burnished on their tunics; they could be seen to
resent how patronizingly the Terran staffers addressed one of their own. "—and my concubine,
the right honorable Persis d'Io."

"I am priviledged to meet you, Ensign," she
said as if she meant it.

Flandry decided she was an adequate substitute for L'Etoile, at least in ornamental func-
tion. She was equipped almost as sumptuously
as Dragoika, and her shimmerlyn gown em-
phasized the fact. Otherwise she wore a fire ruby
at her throat and a tiara on high-piled crow's-
wing tresses. Her features were either her own or
shaped by an imaginative biosculptor: big green
eyes, delicately arched nose, generous mouth,

uncommon vivacity. "Please get yourself a drink and a smoke," she said. "You'll need a soothed larynx. I intend to make you talk a lot."

"Uh . . . um—" Flandry barely stopped his toes from digging in the carpet. The hand he closed on a proffered wine glass was damp. "Little to talk about, Donna. Lots of men have, uh, had more exciting things happen to them."

"Hardly so romantic, though," Hauksberg said. "Sailin' with a pirate crew, et cet'ra."

"They're not pirates, my lord," Flandry blurted. "Merchants. . . . Pardon me."

Hauksberg studied him. "You like 'em, eh?"

"Yes, sir," Flandry said. "Very much." He weighed his words, but they were honest. "Before I got to know the Tigeries well, my mission here was only a duty. Now I *want* to help them."

"Commendable. Still, the sea dwellers are also sentient bein's, what? And the Merseians, for that matter. Pity everyone's at loggerheads."

Flandry's ears burned. Abrams spoke what he dared not: "My lord, those fellow beings of the ensign's did their level best to kill him."

"And in retaliation, after he reported, an attack was made on a squadron of theirs," Hauksberg said sharply. "Three Merseians were killed, plus a human. I was bein' received by Commandant Runei at the time. Embarrassin'."

"I don't doubt the Fodaich stayed courteous to the Emperor's representative," Abrams said. "He's a charming scoundrel when he cares to be. But my lord, we have an authorized, announced policy of paying back any attacks on our mission." His tone grew sardonic. "It's a peaceful, advisory mission, in a territory claimed by neither empire. So it's entitled to protection. Which means that bush-whacking its personnel has got to be made expensive."

"And if Runei ordered a return raid?" Hauksberg challenged.

"He didn't, my lord."

"Not yet. Bit of evidence for Merseia's conciliatory attitude, what? Or could be my presence influenced Runei. One day soon, though, if these skirmishes continue, a real escalation will set in. Then everybody'll have the devil's personal job controllin' the degree of escalation. Might fail. The time to stop was yesterday."

"Seems to me Merseia's escalated quite a big hunk, starting operations this near our main base."

"The seafolk have done so. They had Merseian help, no doubt, but it's their war and the landfolk's. No one else's."

Abrams savaged a cold cigar. "My lord," he growled, "seafolk and landfolk alike are divided into thousands of communities, scores of civilizations. Many never heard of each other before. The dwellers in the Zletovar were nothing but a nuisance to the Kursovikians, till now. So who gave them the idea of mounting a concerted attack? Who's gradually changing what was a stable situation into a planet-wide war of race against race? Merseia!"

"You overreach yourself, Commander," said Captain Abdes-Salem reluctantly. The viscount's aides looked appalled.

"No, no." Hauksberg smiled into the angry brown face confronting him. "I appreciate frankness. Terra's got quite enough sycophants without exportin' 'em. How can I find facts as I'm s'posed to without listening'? Waiter—refill Commander Abrams' glass."

"Just what are the, ah, opposition doing in local waters?" inquired a civilian.

Abrams shrugged. "We don't know. Kursovikian ships have naturally begun avoiding that area. We could try sending divers, but we're holding off. You see, Ensign Flandry did more than have an adventure. More, yet, than win a degree of respect and good will among the Tigeries that'll prove useful to us. He's gathered information about them we never had before, details that escaped the professional xenologists, and given me the data as tightly organized as a limerick. Above the lot, he delivered a live Seatroll prisoner."

Hauksberg lit a cheroot. "I gather that's unusual?"

"Yes, sir, for obvious environmental reasons as well as because the Tigeries normally barbecue any they take."

Persis d'Io grimaced. "Did you say you like them?" she scolded Flandry.

"Might be hard for a civilized being to understand, Donna" Abrams drawled. "We prefer nuclear weapons that can barbecue entire planets. Point is, though, our lad here thought up gadgets to keep that Seatroll in health, things a smith and carpenter could make aboard ship. I better not get too specific, but I've got hopes about the interrogation."

"Why not tell us?" Hauksberg asked. "Surely you don't think anyone here is a Merseian in disguise."

"Probably not," Abrams said. "However, you people are bound on to the enemy's home planet. Diplomatic mission or no, I can't impose the risk on you of carrying knowledge they'd like to have."

Hauksberg laughed. "I've never been called a blabbermouth more tactfully."

Persis interrupted. "No arguments, please, darling. I'm too anxious to hear Ensign Flandry."

"You're on, son," Abrams said.

They took loungers. Flandry received a goldleaf-tipped cigaret from Persis' own fingers. Wine and excitement bubbled in him. He made the tale somewhat better than true: sufficient to drive Abrams into a coughing fit.

"—and so, one day out of Ujanka, we met a ship that could put in a call for us. A flier took me and the prisoner off."

Persis sighed. "You make it sound such fun. Have you seen your friends again since?"

"Not yet, Donna. I've been too busy working with Commander Abrams." In point of fact he had done the detail chores of data correlation on a considerably lower level. "I've been temporarily assigned to this section. I do have an invitation to visit down in Ujanka, and imagine I'll be ordered to accept."

"Right," Captain Menotti said. "One of our problems has been that, while the Sisterhood accepts our equipment and some of our advice, they've remained wary of us. Understandable, when we're so foreign to them, and when their own Seatroll neighbors were never a real menace. We've achieved better liaison with less developed Starkadian cultures. Kursoviki is too proud, too jealous of its privacies, I might say too sophisticated, to take us as seriously as we'd like. Here we may have an entering wedge."

"And also in your prisoner," Hauksberg said thoughtfully. "Want to see him."

"What?" Abrams barked. "Impossible!"

"Why?"

"Why—that is—"

"Wouldn't fulfill my commission if I didn't," Hauksberg said. "I must insist." He leaned forward. "You see, could be this is a wedge toward something still more important. Peace."

"How so . . . my lord?"

"If you pump him as dry's I imagine you plan, you'll find out a lot about his culture. They won't be the faceless enemy, they'll be real bein's with real needs and desires. He can accompany an envoy of ours to his people. We can—not unthinkable, y' know—we can p'rhaps head off this latest local war. Negotiate a peace between the Kursovikians and their neighbors."

"Or between lions and lambs?" Abrams snapped. "How do you start? They'd never come near any submarine of ours."

"Go out in native ships, then."

"We haven't the men for it. Damn few humans know how to operate a windjammer these days, and sailing on Starkad is a different art anyhow. We should get Kursovikians to take us on a peace mission? Ha!"

"What if their chum here asked 'em? Don't you think that might be worth a try?"

"Oh!" Persis, who sat beside him, laid a hand over Flandry's. "If you could—"

Under those eyes, he glowed happily and said he would be delighted. Abrams gave him a bleak look. "If ordered, of course," he added in a hurry.

"I'll discuss the question with your superiors," Hauksberg said. "But gentlemen, this is a s'posed to be a social evenin'. Forget business and have another drink or ten, eh?"

His gossip from Terra was scandalous and comical. "Darling," Persis said, "you mustn't cynicize our guest of honor. Let's go talk more politely, Ensign."

"W-w-with joy, Donna."

The suite was interior, but a viewscreen gave on the scene outside. Snowfall had stopped; mountaintops lay gaunt and white beneath the moons. Persis shivered. "What a dreadful place. I pray we can bring you home soon."

He was emboldered to say, "I never expected a, uh, highborn and, uh, lovely lady to come this long, dull, dangerous way."

She laughed. "I highborn? But thanks. You're sweet." Her lashes fluttered. "If I can help my lord by traveling with him . . . how could I refuse? He's working for Terra. So are you. So should I. All of us together, wouldn't that be best?" She laughed again. "I'm sorry to be the only girl here. Would your officers mind if we danced a little?"

He went back to quarters with his head afloat. Nonetheless, next day he gave Jan van Zuyl a good bottle's worth.

At the center of a soundproofed room, whose fluoros glared with Saxo light, the Siravo floated in a vitryl tank surrounded by machines.

He was big, 210 centimeters in length and thick of body. His skin was glabrous, deep blue on the back, paler greenish blue on the stomach, opalescent on the gillcovers. In shape he suggested a cross between dolphin, seal, and man. But the flukes, and the two flippers near his middle, were marvels of musculature with some prehensile capability. A fleshy dorsal fin grew above. Not far behind the head were two short, strong arms; except for vestigial webs, the hands were startlingly humanlike. The head was big and golden of eyes, blunt of smout, with quivering cilia flanking a mouth that had lips.

Abrams, Hauksberg and Flandry entered. ("You come too," the commander had said to the ensign. "You're in this thing ass deep.") The four marines on guard presented arms. The technicians straightened from their instruments.

"At ease," Abrams said. "Freely translated: get the hell back to work. How's she coming, Leong?"

"Encouraging, sir," the scientific chief answered. "Computation from neurological and encephalographic data shows he can definitely stand at least a half-intensity hypnoprobing without high probability of permanent lesion. We expect to have apparatus modified for underwater use in another couple of days."

Hauksberg went to the tank. The swimmer

moved toward him. Look met look; those were
beautiful eyes in there. Hauksberg was flushing
as he turned about. "D' you mean to torture that
bein'?" he demanded.

"A light hypnoprobing isn't painful, my
lord," Abrams said.

"You know what I mean. Psychological torture. 'Specially when he's in the hands of utter
aliens. Ever occur to you to talk with him?"

"That's easy? My lord, the Kursovikians have
tried for centuries. Our only advantages over
them are that we have a developed theory of
linguistics, and vocalizers to reproduce his kind
of sounds more accurately. From the Tigeries
and xenological records we have a trifle of his
language. But only a trifle. The early expeditions
investigated this race more thoroughly in the
Kimraig area, where the Merseians are now, no
doubt for just that reason. The cultural patterns
of Charlie here are completely unknown to us.
And he hasn't been exactly cooperative."

"Would you be, in his place?"

"Hope not. But my lord, we're in a hurry too.
His people may be planning a massive operation, like against settlements in the Chain. Or he
may up and die on us. We think he has an adequate diet and such, but how can we be certain?"

Hauksberg scowled. "You'll destroy any
chance of gettin' his cooperation, let alone his
trust."

"For negotiation purposes? So what have we
lost? But we won't necessarily alienate him forever. We don't know his psyche. He may well

figure ruthlessness is in the day's work. God knows Tigeries in small boats get short shrift from any Seatrolls they meet. And—" The great blue shape glided off to the end of the tank—"he looks pretty, but he is no kin of you or me or the landfolk."

"He thinks. He feels."

"Thinks and feels what? I don't know. I do know he isn't even a fish. He's homeothermic; his females give live birth and nurse their young. Under high atmospheric pressure, there's enough oxygen dissolved in water to support an active metabolism and a good brain. That must be why intelligence evolved in the seas: biological competition like you hardly ever find in the seas of Terra-type planets. But the environment is almost as strange to us as Jupiter."

"The Merseians get along with his kind."

"Uh-huh. They took time to learn everything we haven't. We've tried to xenologize ourselves, in regions the conflict hasn't reached so far, but the Merseians have always found out and arranged trouble."

"Found out how?" Hauksberg pounced. "By spies?"

"No, surveillance. 'Bout all that either side has available. If we could somehow get access to their undersea information—" Abrams snapped his mouth shut and pulled out a cigar.

Hauksberg eased. He smiled. "Please don't take me wrong Commander. Assure you I'm not some weepin' idealist. You can't make an omelet, et cet'ra. I merely object to breakin' every egg in sight. Rather messy, that." He

paused. "Won't bother you more today. But I
want a full report on this project to date, and
regular bulletins. I don't forbid hypnoprobin'
categorically, but I will not allow any form of
torture. And I'll be back." He couldn't quite
suppress a moue of distaste. "No, no, thanks
awf'lly but you needn't escort me out. Good day,
gentlemen."

The door closed on his elegance. Abrams went
into a conference with Leong. They talked low.
The hum, click, buzz of machines filled the
room, which was cold. Flandry stood staring at
the captive he had taken.

"A millo for 'em," Abrams said.

Flandry started. The older man had joined
him on cat feet. "Sir?"

"Your thoughts. What're you turning over in
your mind, besides the fair d'Io?"

Flandry blushed. "I was wondering, sir. Hau—
milord was right. You are pushing ahead ter-
ribly fast, aren't you?"

"Got to."

"No," said Flandry earnestly. "Pardon, sir,
but we could use divers and subs and probes to
scout the Zletovar. Charlie here has more value
in the long run, for study. I've read what I could
find about the Seatrolls. They *are* an unknown
quantity. You need a lot more information
before you can be sure that any given kind of
questioning will show results."

Beneath lowered bushy brows, behind a
tobacco cloud, Abrams regarded him. "Telling
me my business?" His tone was mild.

"No, sir. Certainly not. I—I've gotten plenty

of respect for you." The idea flamed. "Sir! You do have more information than you admit! A pipeline to—"

"Shut up." The voice stayed quiet, but Flandry gulped and snapped to an automatic brace. "Keep shut up. Understand?"

"Y-yes, sir."

Abrams glanced at his team. None of them had noticed. "Son," he murmured, "you surprise me. You really do. You're wasted among those flyboys. Ever considered transferring to the spyboys?"

Flandry bit his lip. "All right," Abrams said. "Tell uncle. Why don't you like the idea?"

"It—I mean—No, sir, I'm not suited."

"You look bundled to the ears to me. Give me a break. Talk honest. I don't mind being called a son of a bitch. I've got my birth certificate."

"Well—" Flandry rallied his courage. "This is a dirty business, sir."

"Hm. You mean for instance right here? Charlie?"

"Yes, sir. I . . . well, I sort of got sent to the Academy. Everybody took for granted I'd go. So did I. I was pretty young."

Abrams' mouth twitched upward.

"I've . . . started to wonder, though," Flandry stumbled. "Things I heard at the party . . . uh, Donna d'Io said—You know, sir, I wasn't scared in that sea action, and afterward it seemed like a grand, glorious victory. But now I—I've begun remembering the dead. One Tiger took a whole day to die. And Charlie, he doesn't so much as know what's going to happen to him!"

Abrams smoked awhile. "All beings are brothers, eh?" he said.

"No, sir, not exactly, but—"

"Not exactly? You know better'n that. They aren't! Not even all men are. Never have been. Sure, war is degrading. But there are worse degradations. Sure, peace is wonderful. But you can't always have peace, except in death, and you most definitely can't have a peace that isn't founded on hard common interest, that doesn't pay off for everybody concerned. Sure, the Empire is sick. But she's ours. She's all we've got. Son, the height of irresponsibility is to spread your love and loyalty so thin that you haven't got enough left for the few beings and the few institutions which rate it from you."

Flandry stood motionless.

"I know," Abrams said. "They rammed you through your education. You were supposed to learn what civilization is about, but there wasn't really time, they get so damned few cadets with promise these days. So here you are, nineteen years old, loaded to the hatches with technical information and condemned to make for yourself every philosophical mistake recorded in history. I'd like you to read some books I pack around in micro. Ancient stuff mostly, a smidgin of Aristotle, Machiavelli, Jefferson, Clausewitz, Jouvenel, Michaelis. But that'll take awhile. You just go back to quarters today. Sit. Think over what I said."

"Has the Fodaich not seen the report I filed?" asked Dwyr the Hook.

"Yes, of course," Runei answered. "But I want to inquire about certain details. Having gotten into the Terran base, even though your objective was too well guarded to burgle, why did you not wait for an opportunity?"

"The likelihood did not appear great, Fodaich. And dawn was coming. Someone might have addressed me, and my reply might have provoked suspicion. My orders were to avoid unnecessary risks. The decision to leave at once is justified in retrospect, since I did not find my vehicle in the canyon when I returned. A Terran patrol must have come upon it. Thus I had to travel overland to our hidden depot, and hence my delay in returning here."

"What about that other patrol you encountered on the way? How much did they see?"

"Very little, I believe, Fodaich. We were in thick forest, and they shot blindly when I failed to answer their challenge. They did, as you know, inflict considerable damage on me, and it is fortunate that I was then so close to my goal that I could crawl the rest of the way after escaping them."

"*Khr-r-r*," Runei sighed. "Well, the attempt was worth making. But this seems to make you supernumerary on Starkad, doesn't it?"

"I trust I may continue to serve in honor." Dwyr gathered nerve. "Fodaich, I did observe one thing from afar while in Highport, which may or may not be significant. Abrams himself walked downstreet in close conversation with a civilian who had several attendants—I suspect the delegate from Terra."

"Who is most wonderfully officious," Runei mused, "and who is proceeding on from here. Did you catch anything of what was said?"

"The noise level was high, Fodaich. With the help of aural amplification and focussing, I could identify a few words like 'Merseia.' My impression is that Abrams may be going with him. In such case, Abrams had better be kept under special watch."

"Yes." Runei stroked his chin. "A possibility. I shall consider it. Hold yourself in readiness for a quick departure."

Dwyr saluted and left. Runei sat alone. The whirr of ventilators filled his lair. Presently he nodded to himself, got out his chessboard, and pondered his next move. A smile touched his lips.

Chapter Six

Starkad rotated thrice more. Then the onslaught came.

Flandry was in Ujanka. The principal seaport of Kursoviki stood on Golden Bay, ringed by hills and slashed by the broad brown Pechaniki River. In the West Housing the Sisterhood kept headquarters. Northward and upward, the High Housing was occupied by the homes of the wealthy, each nestled into hectares of trained jungle where flowers and wings and venomous reptiles vied in coloring. But despite her position —not merely captain of the *Archer* but shareholder in a kin-corporation owning a whole fleet, and speaker for it among the Sisterhood— Dragoika lived in the ancient East Housing, on Shiv Alley itself.

"Here my mothers dwelt since the town was founded," she told her guest. "Here Chupa once feasted. Here the staircase ran with blood on the Day of the Gulch. There are too many ghosts for me to abandon." She chuckled, deep in her throat, and gestured around the stone-built room, at furs, carpets, furnishings, books, weapons, bronze vases and candelabra, goblets of glass and seashell souvenirs and plunder from across a quarter of the planet. "Also, too much stuff to move."

Flandry glanced out the third-floor window. A cobbled way twisted between tenements that could double as fortresses. A pair of cowled males slunk by, swords drawn; a drum thuttered; the yells and stampings and metal on metal of a brawl flared brief but loud. "What about robbers?" he asked.

Ferok grinned. "They've learned better."

He sprawled on a couch whose curves suggested a ship. Likewise did his skipper and Iguraz, a portly grizzled male who had charge of Seatraders' Castle. In the gloom of the chamber, their eyes and jewelry seemed to glow. The weather outside was bright but chill. Flandry was glad he had chosen to wear a thick coverall on his visit. They wouldn't appreciate Terran dress uniform anyhow.

"I don't understand you people," Dragoika said. She leaned forward and sniffed the mild narcotic smoke from a brazier. "Good to see you again, Dommaneek, but I *don't* understand you. What's wrong with a fight now and then? And —after personally defeating the vaz-Siravo—you come here to babble about making peace with them!"

Flandry turned. The murmur of his airpump seemed to grow in his head. "I was told to broach the idea," he replied.

"But you don't like it yourself?" Iguraz wondered. "Then why beneath heaven do you speak it?"

"Would you tolerate insubordination?" Flandry said.

"Not at sea," Dragoika admitted. "But land is different."

"Well, if nothing else, we vaz-Terran here find ourselves in a situation like sailors." Flandry tried to ease his nerves by pacing. His boots felt heavy.

"Why don't you simply wipe out the vaz-Siravo for us?" Ferok asked. "Shouldn't be hard if your powers are as claimed."

Dragoika surprised Flandry by lowering her tendrils and saying, "No such talk. Would you upset the world?" To the human: "The Sisterhood bears them no vast ill will. They must be kept at their distance like any other dangerous beasts. But if they would leave us alone there would be no occasion for battle."

"Perhaps they think the same," Flandry said. "Since first your people went to sea, you have troubled them."

"The oceans are wide. Let them stay clear of our islands."

"They cannot. Sunlight breeds life, so they need the shoals for food. Also, you go far out to chase the big animals and harvest weed. They have to have those things too." Flandry stopped, tried to run a hand through his hair, and struck his helmet. "I'm not against peace in the Zletovar myself. If nothing else, because the vaz-Merseian would be annoyed. They started this arming of one folk against another, you know. And they must be preparing some action here. What harm can it do to talk with the vaz-Siravo?"

"How do so?" Iguraz countered. "Any Toborko who went below'd be slaughtered out of hand, unless you equipped her to do the slaughtering herself."

"Be still," Dragoika ordered. "I asked you here because you have the records of what ships are in, and Ferok because he's Dommaneek's friend. But this is female talk."

The Tigeries took her reproof in good humor. Flandry explained: "The delegates would be my people. We don't want to alarm the seafolk unduly by arriving in one of our own craft. But we'll need a handy base. So we ask for ships of yours, a big enough fleet that attack on it is unlikely. Of course, the Sisterhood would have to ratify any terms we arrived at."

"That's not so easy," Dragoika said. "The Janjevar va-Radovik reaches far beyond Kursovikian waters. Which means, I suppose, that many different Siravo interests would also be involved in any general settlement." She rubbed her triangular chin. "Nonetheless . . . a local truce, if nothing else . . . hunh, needs thinking about—"

And then, from the castle, a horn blew.

Huge, brazen, bellows-driven, it howled across the city. The hills echoed. Birds stormed from trees. *Hoo-hoo! Fire, flood, or foe! To arms, to arms! Hoo, hoo-hoo, hoo-oo!*

"What the wreck?" Ferok was on his feet, snatching sword and shield from the wall, before Flandry had seen him move. Iguraz took his ponderous battleax. Dragoika crouched where she was and snarled. Bronze and crystal shivered.

"Attack?" Flandry cried among the horn-blasts. "But they can't!"

The picture unreeled for him. The mouth of Golden Bay was guarded by anchored hulks. Swimmers underwater might come fairly close, unseen by those garrisons, but never past. And supposing they did, they still had kilometers to go before they reached the docks, which with Seatraders' Castle commanded that whole face of Ujanka. They might, of course, come ashore well outside, as at Whitestrands, and march overland on their mechanical legs. The city was unwalled. But no, each outlying house was a defense post; and thousands of Tigeries would swarm from town to meet them; and—

Terran had worried about assaults on the archipelago colonies. Ujanka, though, had not seen war for hundreds of years, and that was with other Tigeries. . . . *Hoo, hoo!*

"We'll go look." Dragoika's gorgeous fur stood on end, her tail was rigid, her ears aquiver; but now she spoke as if suggesting dinner and flowed from her couch with no obvious haste. On the way, she slung a sword over her back.

Blaster in hand, Flandry followed her into a hall dominated by a contorted stone figure, three meters high, from the Ice Islands. Beyond an archway, a stair spiraled upward. His shoulders scraped the walls. Arrow slits gave some light. Ferok padded behind him, Iguraz wheezed in the rear.

They were halfway to the top when the world said *Crump!* and stones trembled. Dragoika was thrown back against Flandry. He caught her. It was like holding steel and rubber, sheathed in velvet. A rumble of collapsing masonry beat through his helmet. Screams came thin and remote.

"What's happened?" Iguraz bawled. Ferok cursed. Even then, Flandry noted some of his expressions for later use. If there was a later. Dragoika regained balance. "Thanks," she murmured, and stroked the human's arm. "Come." She bounded on.

They emerged on the house tower as a second explosion went off. That one was further away. But thunder rolled loud in Starkad's air. Flandry ran to the parapet. He stared across steeply pitched red tile roofs whose beam ends were carved with flowers and monster heads. Northward, beyond these old gray walls, the High Housing lifted emerald green, agleam with villas. He could see the Concourse pylon, where Pride's Way, the Upland Way, the Great East Road, and The Sun and Moons came together. Smoke made a pillar more tall.

"There!" Ferok yelled. He pointed to sea. Dragoika went to a telescope mounted under a canopy.

Flandry squinted. Light dazzled him off the water. He found the hulks, out past the Long Moles. They lay ablaze. Past them—Dragoika nodded grimly and pulled him to her telescope.

Where the bay broadened, between Whitestrands to west and Sorrow Cliff to east, a whale shape basked. Its hide was wet metal. A turret projected amidships; Flandry could just see that it stood open and held a few shapes not unlike men. Fore and aft were turrets more low, flat, with jutting tubes. As he looked, fire spat from one of those dragon snouts. A moment later, smoke puffed off the high square wall of Seatrader's Castle. Stones avalanched onto the wharf below. One of the ships which crowded the harbor was caught under them. Her mast reeled and broke, her hull settled. Noise rolled from waterfront to hills and back again.

"Lucifer! That's a submarine!"

And nothing like what he had fought. Yonder was a Merseian job, probably nuclear-propelled, surely Merseian crewed. She wasn't very big, some twenty meters in length, must have been assembled here on Starkad. Her guns, though of large caliber, were throwing chemical H.E. So the enemy wasn't introducing atomics into this war. (Yet. When somebody did, all hell would let out for noon.) But in this soup of an atmosphere, the shock waves were ample to knock down a city which had no defenses against them.

"We'll burn!" Ferok wailed.

On this planet, no one was ashamed to stand in terror of fire. Flandry raced through an assessment. Detested hours and years of psych drill at the Academy paid off. He knew rage and fear, his mouth was dry and his heart slammed, but emotion didn't get in the way of logic. Ujanka wouldn't go up fast. Over the centuries, stone and tile had replaced wood nearly everywhere. But if fire started among the ships, there went something like half the strength of Kursoviki. And not many shells were needed for that.

Dragoika had had the same thought. She

wheeled to glare across the Pechaniki, where the
Sisterhood centrum lifted a green copper dome
from the West Housing. Her mane fluttered
wild. "Why haven't they rung Quarters?"

"Surely none need reminding," Iguraz puffed.
To Flandry: "Law is that when aught may
threaten the ships, their crews are to report
aboard and take them out on the bay."

A shell trundled overhead. Its impact gouted
near Humpback Bridge.

"But today they may indeed forget,"
Dragoika said between her fangs. "They may
panic. Those tallywhackers yonder must've done
so, not to be hanging on the bell ropes now." She
started forward. "Best I go there myself. Ferok,
tell them not to await me on the *Archer*."

Flandry stopped her. She mewed anger.
"Apology-of-courage," he said. "Let's try calling first."

"Call—argh, yes, you've given 'em a radio,
haven't you? My brain's beaten flat."

Crash! Crash! The bombardment was increas-
ing. As yet it seemed almost random. The idea
must be to cause terror and conflagration as fast
as possible.

Flandry lifted wristcom to helmet speaker and
tuned the Sisters' waveband. His hope that
someone would be at the other end was not
great. He let out a breath when a female voice
replied, insect small beneath whistle and boom:
"Ey-ya, do you belong to the vaz-Terran? I
could not raise anyone of you."

*No doubt all switchboards're flooded with yammer
from our men in Ujanka,* Flandry thought. He

couldn't see their dome in the hills, but he could imagine the scene. Those were Navy too, of course—but engineers, technicians, hitherto concerned merely with providing a few gadgets and training Tigeries in the use of same. Nor was their staff large. Other regions, where the war was intense, claimed most of what Terra could offer. (Five thousand or so men get spread horribly thin across an entire world; and then a third of them are not technical but combat and Intelligence units, lest Runei feel free to gobble the whole mission.) Like him, the Ujanka team had sidearms and weaponless flitters: nothing else.

"Why haven't Quarters been rung?" Flandry demanded as if he'd known the law his whole life.

"But no one thought—"

"So start thinking!" Dragoika put her lips close to Flandry's wrist. Her bosom crowded against him. "I see no sign of craft readying to stand out."

"When that thing waits for them?"

"They'll be safer scattered than docked," Dragoika said. "Ring the call."

"Aye. But when do the vaz-Terran come?"

"Soon," Flandry said. He switched to the team band.

"I go now," Dragoika said.

"No, wait, I beg you. I may need you to . . . to help." *I would be so lonely on this tower*. Flandry worked the signal button with an unsteady forefinger. This microunit couldn't reach Highport unless the local 'caster relayed, but he could talk to someone in the dome, if anybody noticed a

signal light, if every circuit wasn't tied up—
Brrum! A female loped down Shiv Alley. Two
males followed, their young in their arms,
screaming.

"Ujanka Station, Lieutenant Kaiser."
Shellburst nearly drowned the Anglic words.
Concussion struck like a fist. The tower seemed
to sway.

"Flandry here." He remembered to overlook
naming his rank, and crisped his tone. "I'm
down on the east side. Have you seen what's on
the bay?"

"Sure have. A sub—"

"I know. Is help on the way?"

"No."

"What? But that thing's Merseian! It'll take
this town apart unless we strike."

"Citizen," said the voice raggedly, "I've just
signed off from HQ. Recon reports the greenskin
air fleet at hover in the stratosphere. Right over
your head. Our fliers are scrambled to cover
Highport. They're not going anywhere else."

Reckon they can't at that, Flandry thought. *Let a
general dogfight develop, and the result is up for grabs.
A Merseian could even break through and lay an egg on
our main base.*

"I understand Admiral Enriques is trying to
get hold of his opposite number and enter a
strenuous protest," Kaiser fleered.

"Never mind. What can you yourselves do?"

"Not a mucking thing, citizen. HQ did promise us a couple of transports equipped to spray
firefighting chemicals. They'll fly low, broad-
casting their identity. If the gatortails don't

shoot them regardless, they should get here in half an hour or so. Now, where are you? I'll dispatch a flitter."

"I have my own," Flandry said. "Stand by for further messages."

He snapped off his unit. From across the river began a high and striding peal.

"Well?" Dragoika's ruby eyes blazed at him.

He told her.

For a moment, her shoulders sagged. She straightened again. "We'll not go down politely. If a few ships with deck guns work close—"

"Not a chance," Flandry said. "That vessel's too well armored. Besides, she could sink you at twice your own range."

"I'll try anyhow." Dragoika clasped his hands. She smiled. "Farewell. Perhaps we'll meet in the Land of Trees Beyond."

"No!" It leaped from him. He didn't know why. His duty was to save himself for future use. His natural inclination was identical. But he wasn't about to let a bunch of smug Merseians send to the bottom these people he'd sailed with. Not if he could help it!

"Come on," he said. "To my flier."

Ferok stiffened. "I, flee?"

"Who talked about that? You've guns in this house, haven't you? Let's collect them and some assistants." Flandry clattered down the stairs.

He entered the alley with a slugthrower as well as his blaster. The three Tigeries followed, bearing several modern small arms between them. They ran into the Street Where They Fought and on toward Seatraders' Castle.

Crowds milled back and forth. No one had the civilized reflex of getting under cover when artillery spoke. But neither did many scuttle about blinded by terror. Panic would likeliest take the form of a mob rush to the waterfront, with weapons—swords and bows against pentanitro. Sailors shoved through the broil, purpose restored to them by the bells.

A shell smote close by. Flandry was hurled into a clothdealer's booth. He climbed to his feet with ears ringing, draped in multicolored tatters. Bodies were strewn between the walls. Blood oozed among the cobbles. The wounded ululated, most horribly, from beneath a heap of fallen stones.

Dragoika lurched toward him. Her black and orange fur was smeared with red. "Are you all right?" he shouted.

"Aye." She loped on. Ferok accompanied them. Iguraz lay with a smashed skull, but Ferok had gathered his guns.

By the time he reached the castle, Flandry was reeling. He entered the forecourt, sat down beside his flitter, and gasped. Dragoika called males down from the parapets and armed them. After a while, Flandry adjusted his pump. An upward shift in helmet pressure made his abused eardrums protest, but the extra oxygen restored some vitality.

They crowded into the flitter. It was a simple passenger vehicle which could hold a score or so if they filled seats and aisle and rear end. Flandry settled himself at the board and started the grav generators. Overloaded, the machine rose sluggishly. He kept low, nigh shaving the heads of the Tigeries outside, until he was across the river and past the docks and had a screen of forest between him and the bay.

"You're headed for Whitestrands," Dragoika protested.

"Of course," Flandry said. "We want the sun behind us."

She got the idea. Doubtless no one else did. They huddled together, fingered what guns they had, and muttered. He hoped their first airborne trip wouldn't demoralize them.

"When we set down," he said loudly, "everyone jump out. You will find open hatches on the deck. Try to seize them first. Otherwise the boat can submerge and drown you."

"Then their gunners will drown too," said a vindictive voice at his back.

"They'll have reserves." Flandry understood, suddenly and shatteringly, how insane his behavior was. If he didn't get shot down on approach, if he succeeded in landing, he still had one blaster and a few bullet projectors against how many Merseian firespitters? He almost turned around. But no, he couldn't, not in the presence of these beings. Moral cowardice, that's what was the matter with him.

At the beach he veered and kicked in emergency overpower. The vehicle raced barely above the water, still with grisly slowness. A gust threw spray across the windshield. The submarine lay gray, indistinct, and terrible.

"Yonder!" Dragoika screeched.

She pointed south. The sea churned with

dorsal fins. Fish-drawn catapult boats had begun to rise, dotting it as far as one could eye. *Of course,* trickled through the cellars of Flandry's awareness. *This has to be largely a Seatroll operation, partly to conserve Merseian facilities, partly to conserve the fiction. That sub's only an auxiliary . . . isn't it? Those are only advisors—well, volunteers this time—at the guns . . . aren't they? But once they've reduced Ujanka's defenses, the Seatrolls will clean the place out.*

I don't give a hiss what happens to Charlie.

An energy bolt tore through the thin fuselage. No one was hit. But he'd been seen.

But he was under the cannon. He was over the deck.

He stopped dead and lowered his wheels. A seat-of-the-pants shiver told him they had touched. Dragoika flung wide the door. Yelling, she led the rush.

Flandry held his flitter poised. These were the worst seconds, the unreal ones when death, which must not be real, nibbled around him. Perhaps ten Merseians were topside, in air helmets and black uniforms: three at either gun, three or four in the opened conning tower. For the moment, that tower was a shield between him and the after crew. The rest wielded blasters and machine pistols. Lightnings raged.

Dragoika had hit the deck, rolled, and shot from her belly. Her chatterbox spewed lead. Flame raked at her. Then Ferok was out, snapping with his own pistol. And more, and more.

The officers in the tower, sheltered below its bulwark, fired. And now the after crew dashed beneath them. Bolts and slugs seethed through the flitter. Flandry drew up his knees, hunched under the pilot board, and nearly prayed.

The last Tigery was out. Flandry stood the flitter upward. His luck had held; she was damaged but not crippled. (He noticed, vaguely, a burn on his arm.) In a wobbling arc, he went above the tower, turned sideways, hung onto his seat with one hand and fired out the open door with the other. Return burst missed him. However inadequate it was, he had some protection. He cleared the Merseians away.

An explosion rattled his teeth. Motor dead, the flitter crashed three meters down, onto the conning tower.

After a minute, Flandry was back to consciousness. He went on hands and knees across the buckled, tilted fuselage, took a quick peek, and dropped to the bridge deck. A body, still smoking, was in his path. He shoved it aside and looked over the bulwark. The dozen Tigeries who remained active had taken the forward gun and were using it for cover. They had stalled the second gang beneath Flandry. But reinforcements were boiling from the after hatch.

Flandry set his blaster to wide beam and shot. Again. Again. The crew must be small. He'd dropped—how many?—whoops, don't forget the hatch in the tower itself, up to this place he commanded! No, his flitter blocked the way. . . .

Silence thundered upon him. Only the wind and the slap-slap of water broke it, that and a steady sobbing from one Merseian who lay with his leg blasted off, bleeding to death. Satan on Saturn, they'd done it. They'd actually done it.

Flandry stared at his free hand, thinking in a
remote fashion how wonderful a machine it was,
look, he could flex the fingers.

Not much time to spare. He rose. A bullet
whanged from the bows. "Hold off there, you
tubehead! Me! Dragoika, are you alive?"

"Yes." She trod triumphant from behind the
gun. "What next?"

"Some of you get astern. Shoot anybody who
shows himself."

Dragoika drew her sword. "We'll go after
them."

"You'll do no such idiot thing," Flandry
stormed. "You'll have trouble enough keeping
them bottled."

"And you . . . now," she breathed ecstatically,
"you can turn these guns on the vaz-Siravo."

"Not that either," Flandry said. God, he was
tired! "First, I can't man something so heavy
alone and you don't know how to help. Second,
we don't want any heroic bastards who may be
left below to get the idea they can best serve the
cause by dunking the lot of us."

He tuned his communicator. Call the Navy
team to come get him and his people off. If they
were too scared of violating policy to flush out
this boat with anesthetic gas and take her for a
prize, he'd arrange her sinking personally. But
no doubt the situation would be accepted. Suc-
cesses don't bring courts-martial and policy is
the excuse you make up as you go along, if you
have any sense. Call the Sisterhood, too. Have
them peal the battle command. Once organized,
the Kursovikian ships could drive off the Seatroll

teers temporarily detached from duty with their
regular units. It is Terra which has long pro-
mulgated the doctrine that limited retaliation is
not a casus belli."

Hauksberg scowled. Speaking for the Empire,
he could not utter his full disapproval of that
principle. "Goes far back into our hist'ry, to the
era of international wars. We use it these days so
our people in remote parts of space'll have some
freedom of action when trouble develops, 'stead
of havin' to send couriers home askin' for orders.
Unfortunate. P'rhaps its abolition can be arranged, at least as between your government and
mine. But we'll want guarantees in exchange,
y'know."

"You are the diplomat, not I," Runei said.
"As of now, I chiefly want back any prisoners
you hold."

"Don't know if there were any survivors,"
Hauksberg said. He knew quite well there were
some, and that Abrams wouldn't release them
till they'd been interrogated at length, probably
hypnoprobed; and he suspected Runei knew he
knew. Most embarrassing. "I'll inquire, if you
wish, and urge—"

"Thank you," Runei said dryly. After a
minute: "Not to ask for military secrets, but
what will the next move be of your, *khraich,* allies?"

"Not allies. The Terran Empire is not a bellig-
erent."

"Spare me," Runei snorted. "I warn you, as I
have warned Admiral Enriques, that Merseia
won't stand idle if the aggressors try to destroy

what Merseia has helped create to ameliorate the lot of the sea people."

An opening! "Point o' fact," Hauksberg said, as casually as he was able, "with the assault on Ujanka repelled, we're tryin' to restrain the Kursovikians. They're hollerin' for vengeance and all that sort o' thing, but we've persuaded 'em to attempt negotiations."

A muscle jumped in Runei's jaw, the ebony eyes widened a millimeter, and he sat motionless for half a minute. "Indeed?" he said, flat-toned.

"Indeed." Hauksberg pursued the initiative he had gained. "A fleet'll depart very soon. We couldn't keep that secret from you, nor conceal the fact of our makin' contact with the Siravoans. So you'll be told officially, and I may's well tell you today, the fleet won't fight except in self-defense. I trust none o' those Merseian volunteers participate in any violence. If so, Terran forces would natur'lly have to intervene. But we hope to send envoys underwater, to discuss a truce with the idea of makin' permanent peace."

"So." Runei drummed his desktop.

"Our xenological information is limited," Hauksberg said. "And o' course we won't exactly get childlike trust at first. Be most helpful if you'd urge the, ah, Sixpoint to receive our delegation and listen to 'em."

"A joint commission, Terran and Merseian—"

"Not yet, Commandant. Please, not yet. These'll be nothin' but informal preliminary talks."

"What you mean," Runei said, "is that Admiral Enriques won't lend men to any dealings that involve Merseians."

Correct.

"No, no. Nothin' so ungracious. Nothin' but a desire to avoid complications. No reason why the sea people shouldn't keep you posted as to what goes on, eh? But we have to know where we stand with 'em; in fact, we have to know 'em much better before we can make sensible suggestions; and you, regrettably, decline to share your data."

"I am under orders," Runei said.

"Quite. Policy'll need to be modified on both sides before we can cooperate worth mentionin', let alone think about joint commissions. That sort o' problem is why I'm goin' on to Merseia."

"Those hoofs will stamp slowly."

"Hey? Oh. Oh, yes. We'd speak of wheels. Agreed, with the best will in the universe, neither government can end this conflict overnight. But we can make a start, you and us. We restrain the Kursovikians, you restrain the Sixpoint. All military operations suspended in the Zletovar till further notice. You've that much discretionary power, I'm sure."

"I do," Runei said. "You do. The natives may not agree. If they decide to move, either faction, I am bound to support the sea people."

Or if you tell them to move, Hauksberg thought. *You may. In which case Enriques will have no choice but to fight. However, I'll assume you're honest, that you'd also like to see this affair wound up before matters get out of hand. I have to assume that. Otherwise I can only go home and help Terra prepare for interstellar war.*

"You'll be gettin' official memoranda and such," he said. "This is preliminary chit-chat. But I'll stay on, myself, till we see how our try at a parley is shapin' up. Feel free to call on me at any time."

"Thank you. Good day, my lord."

"Good day, Com—Fodaich." Though they had been using Anglic, Hauksberg was rather proud of his Eriau.

The screen blanked. He lit a cigaret. Now what? Now you sit and wait, m' boy. You continue gathering reports, conducting interviews, making tours of inspection, but this is past the point of diminishing returns, among these iron-spined militarists who consider you a meddlesome ass. You'll see many an empty hour. Not much amusement here. Good thing you had the foresight to take Persis along.

He rose and drifted from the office to the living room. She sat there watching the animation. *Ondine* again—poor kid, the local tape library didn't give a wide selection. He lowered himself to the arm of her lounger and laid a hand on her shoulder. It was bare, in a low-cut blouse; the skin felt warm and smooth, and he caught a violet hint of perfume.

"Aren't you tired o' that thing?" he asked.

"No." She didn't quite take her eyes from it. Her voice was dark and her mouth not quite steady. "Wish I were, though."

"Why?"

"It frightens me. It reminds me how far we are from home, the strangeness, the— And we're going on."

Half human, the mermaid floated beneath seas which never were.

"Merseia's p'rhaps a touch more familiar,"

Hauksberg said. "They were already in-
dustrialized when humans discovered 'em. They
caught onto the idea of space travel fast."

"Does that make them anything like us? Does
it make us like . . . like ourselves?" She twisted
her fingers together. "People say 'hyperdrive'
and 'light-year' so casually. They don't understand. They can't or won't. Too shallow."

"Don't tell me you've mastered the theory,"
he jollied her.

"Oh, no. I haven't the brain. But I tried. A
series of quantum jumps which do not cross the
small intervening spaces, therefore do not
amount to a true velocity and are not bound by
the light-speed limitation . . . sounds nice and
scientific to you, doesn't it? You know what it
sounds like to me? Ghosts flitting forever in
darkness. And have you ever thought about a
light-year, one measly light-year, how *huge* it is?"

"Well, well." He stroked her hair. "You'll
have company."

"Your staff. Your servants. Little men with little minds. Routineers, yes-men, careerists
who've laid out their own futures on rails.
They're nothing, between me and the night. I'm
sick of them, anyway."

"You've me," he said.

She smiled a trifle. "Present company ex-
cepted. You're so often busy, though."

"We'll have two or three Navy chaps with us.
Might interest you. Diff'rent from courtiers and
bureaucrats."

She brightened further. "Who?"

"Well, Commander Abrams and I got talkin',

and next thing I knew I'd suggested he come
along as our expert on the waterfolk. We could
use one. Rather have that Ridenour fellow,
'course; he's the real authority, insofar as
Terra's got any. But on that account, he can't be
spared here." Hauksberg drew in a long tail of
smoke. "Obvious dangers involved. Abrams
wouldn't leave his post either, if he didn't think
this was a chance to gather more information
than he can on Starkad. Which could compromise our mission. I still don't know but what
I was cleverly maneuvered into co-optin' him."

"That old bear, manipulating you?" Persis
actually giggled.

"A shrewd bear. And ruthless. Fanatical,
almost. However, he can be useful, and I'll be
sure to keep a spot on him. Daresay he'll bring
an aide or two. Handsome young officers, hm?"

"You're handsome and young enough for me,
Mark." Persis rubbed her head against him.

Hauksberg chucked his cigaret at the nearest
disposal. "I'm not so frightfully busy, either."

The day was raw and overcast, with whitecaps
on a leaden sea. Wind piped in rigging; timbers
creaked; the *Archer* rocked. Astern lay the ac-
companying fleet, hove to. Banners snapped
from mastheads. One deck was covered by a
Terra-conditioned sealtent. But Dragoika's
vessel bore merely a tank and a handful of humans. She and her crew watched impassive as
Ridenour, the civilian head of xenological studies, went to release the Siravo.

He was a tall, sandy-haired man; within the

helmet, his face was intense. His fingers moved
across the console of the vocalizer attached to
one wall. Sounds boomed forth which otherwise
only a sea dweller's voice bladder could have
made.

The long body in the tank stirred. Those
curiously human lips opened. An answer could
be heard. John Ridenour nodded. "Very well,"
he said. "Let him go."

Flandry helped remove the cover. The prisoner arched his tail. In one dizzying leap he was
out and over the side. Water spouted across the
deck.

Ridenour went to the rail and stood staring
down. "So long, Evenfall," he said.

"That his real name?" Flandry asked.

"What the phrase means, roughly," the
xenologist answered. He straightened. "I don't
expect anyone'll show for some hours. But be
ready from 1500. I want to study my notes."

He walked to his cabin. Flandry's gaze fol-
lowed him. *How much does he know?* the ensign
wondered. *More'n he possibly could learn from our
Charlie, or from old records, that's for sure. Somehow
Abrams has arranged—Oh, God, the shells bursting in
Ujanka!*

He fled that thought and pulled his gaze back,
around the team who were to go undersea. A
couple of assistant xenologists; an engineer
ensign and four burly ratings with some previous
diving experience. They were almost more alien
to him than the Tigeries.

The glory of having turned the battle of
Golden Bay was blown away on this mordant

wind. So, too, was the intoxicating sequel: that
he, Dominic Flandry, was no longer a wet-eared
youngster but appreciated as he deserved, promised a citation, as the hero of all Kursoviki, the
one man who could talk the landfolk into at-
tempting peace. What that amounted to, in un-
romantic fact, was that he must go along with
the Terran envoys, so their mission would have
his full approval in Tigery eyes. And Ridenour
had told him curtly to keep out of the way.

Jan van Zuyl was luckier!

Well—Flandry put on his best nonchalance
and strolled to Dragoika. She regarded him
gravely. "I hate your going down," she said.

"Nonsense," he said. "Wonderful adventure.
I can't wait."

"Down where the bones of our mothers lie,
whom they drowned," she said. "Down where
there is no sun, no moons, no stars, only
blackness and cold sliding currents. Among enemies and horrors. Combat was better."

"I'll be back soon. This first dive is just to ask
if they'll let us erect a dome on the bottom. Once
that's done, your fleet can go home."

"How long will you be there yourself, in the
dome?"

"I don't know. I hope for not more than a few
days. If things look promising, I—" Flandry
preened—"won't be needed so much. They'll
need me more on land again."

"I will be gone by then," Dragoika said. "The
Archer still has an undelivered cargo, and the Sisterhood wants to take advantage of the truce
while it lasts."

"You'll return, won't you? Call me when you

do, and I'll flit straight to Ujanka." He patted
her hand.

She gripped his. "Someday you will depart
forever."

"Mm . . . this isn't my world."

"I would like to see yours," she said wistfully.
"The stories we hear, the pictures we see, like a
dream. Like the lost island. Perhaps it is in
truth?"

"I fear not." Flandry wondered why the Eden
motif was universal in the land cultures of
Starkad. Be interesting to know. Except for this
damned war, men could come here and really
study the planet. He thought he might like to
join them.

But no. There was little pure research, for
love, in the Empire any more. Outwardness had
died from the human spirit. Could that be because the Time of Troubles had brutalized civilization? Or was it simply that when he saw he
couldn't own the galaxy and consolidated what
little he had, man lost interest in anything
beyond himself? No doubt the ancient eagerness
could be regained. But first the Empire might
have to go under. And he was sworn to defend it.
*I better read more in those books of Abrams'. So far
they've mainly confused me.*

"You think high thoughts," Dragoika said.

He tried to laugh. "Contrariwise. I'm thinking
about food, fun, and females."

"Yes. Females." She stood quiet a while,
before she too laughed. "I can try to provide the
fun, anyhow. What say you to a game of
Yavolak?"

"I haven't yet straightened out those cursed

rules," Flandry said. "But if we can get a few players together, I have some cards with me and there's a Terran game called poker."

—A head rose sleek and blue from the waves. Flandry couldn't tell if it belonged to Evenfall or someone else. The flukes slapped thrice. "That's our signal," Ridenour said. "Let's go."

He spoke by radio. The team were encased in armor which was supposed to withstand pressures to a kilometer's depth. *Wish I hadn't thought of "supposed,"* Flandry regretted. He clumped across the deck and in his turn was lowered over the side. He had a last glimpse of Dragoika, waving. Then the hull was before his faceplate, and then green water. He cast loose, switched his communicator to sonic, and started the motor on his back. Trailing bubbles, he moved to join the others. For one who'd been trained in spacesuit maneuvers, underwater was simple. . . . Damn! He'd forgotten that friction would brake him.

"Follow me in close order," Ridenour's voice sounded in his earplugs. "And for God's sake, don't get trigger happy."

The being who was not a fish glided in advance. The water darkened. Lightbeams weren't needed, though, when they reached bottom; this was a shallow sea. Flandry whirred through a crepuscule that faded into sightlessness. Above him was a circle of dim radiance, like a frosted port. Below him was a forest. Long fronds rippled upward, green and brown and yellow. Massive boles trailed a mesh of filaments from their branches. Shellfish, often immense, covered with lesser shells, gripped lacy, delicately hued coraloid. A flock of crustaceans clanked—no other word would do—across a weed meadow. A thing like an eel wriggled over their heads. Tiny finned animals in rainbow stripes flitted among the sea trees. *Why, the place is beautiful!*

Charlie—no, Evenfall had directed the fleet to a spot in midsea where ships rarely passed. How he navigated was a mystery. But Shellgleam lay near.

Flandry had gathered that the vaz-Siravo of Zletovar lived in, and between, six cities more or less regularly spaced around a circle. Tidehome and Reefcastle were at the end of the Chain. The Kursovikians had long known about them; sometimes they raided them, dropping stones, and sometimes the cities were bases for attacks on Tigery craft. But Shellgleam, Vault, Crystal, and Outlier on the verge of that stupendous downfall of sea bottom called the Deeps—those had been unsuspected. Considering how inter-city traffic patterns must go, Flandry decided that the Sixpoint might as well be called the Davidstar. You couldn't make good translations anyway from a language so foreign.

A drumming noise resounded through the waters. A hundred or more swimmers came into view, in formation. They wore skull helmets and scaly leather corselets, they were armed with obsidian-headed spears, axes, and daggers. The guide exchanged words with their chief. They englobed the party and proceeded.

Now Flandry passed above agricultural (?) lands. He saw tended fields, fish penned in wicker domes, cylindrical woven houses anchored by rocks. A wagon passed not far away, a skin-covered torpedo shape with stabilizer fins, drawn by an elephant-sized fish which a Siravo led. Belike he traveled from some cave or depth, because he carried a lantern, a bladder filled with what were no doubt phosphorescent micro-organisms. As he approached town, Flandry saw a mill. It stood on an upthrust—go ahead and say "hill"—and a shaft ran vertically from an eccentric drive wheel. Aiming his laser light and adjusting his faceplate lens for telescopic vision, he made out a sphere at the other end, afloat on the surface. So, a tide motor.

Shellgleam hove in sight. The city looked frail, unstable, unreal: what a place to stage that ballet! In this weatherless world, walls and roofs need but give privacy; they were made of many-colored fabrics, loosely draped so they could move with currents, on poles which gave shapes soaring in fantastic curves. The higher levels were more broad than the lower. Lanterns glowed perpetually at the corners, against night's advent. With little need for ground trans-port, streets did not exist; but whether to control silt or to enjoy the sight, the builders had cov-ered the spaces between houses with gravel and gardens.

A crowd assembled. Flandry saw many females, holding infants to their breasts and slightly older offspring on leash. Few people wore clothes except for jewelry. They mur-mured, a low surf sound. But they were more quiet, better behaved, than Tigeries or humans.

In the middle of town, on another hill, stood a

building of dressed stone. It was rectangular, the main part roofless and colonnaded; but at the rear a tower equally wide thrust up and up, with a thick glass top just below the surface. If, as presumably was the case, it was similarly sealed further down, it should flood the interior with light. Though the architecture was altogether different, that whiteness reminded Flandry of Terra's Parthenon. He had seen the reconstruction once. . . . He was being taken thither.

A shape darkened the overhead luminance. Looking, he saw a fish team drawing a submarine. The escort was a troop of swimmers armed with Merseian-made guns. Suddenly he remembered he was among his enemies.

Chapter Eight

Once a dome was established outside town and equipped for the long-term living of men, Flandry expected to make rapid progress in Professor Abrams' Instant Philosophy of History Course. What else would there be to do, except practice the different varieties of thumbtwiddling, until HQ decided that sufficient of his prestige had rubbed off on Ridenour and ordered him back to Highport?

Instead, he found himself having the time of his life.

The sea people were every bit as interested in the Terrans as the Terrans in them. Perhaps more so; and after the horror stories the Merseians must have fed them, it was astonishing that they could make such an effort to get at the truth for themselves. But then, while bonny fighters at need and in some ways quite devoid of pity, they seemed less ferocious by nature than humans, Tigeries, or Merseians.

Ridenour and his colleagues were held to the Temple of Sky, where talk went on endlessly with the powers that were in the Davidstar. The xenologist groaned when his unoccupied followers were invited on a set of tours. "If you

were trained, my God, what you could learn!—
Well, we simply haven't got any more pro-
fessionals to use here, so you amateurs go ahead,
and if you don't observe in detail I'll personally
operate on you with a butter knife."

Thus Flandry and one or another companion
were often out for hours on end. Since none of
them understood the native language or Eriau,
their usual guide was Isinglass, who had some
command of Kursovikian and had also been
taught by the Merseians to operate a portable
vocalizer. (The land tongue had been gotten
gradually from prisoners. Flandry admired the
ingenuity of the methods by which their techno-
logically backward captors had kept them alive
for weeks, but otherwise he shuddered and
hoped with all his heart that the age-old strife
could indeed be ended.) Others whom he got to
know included Finbright, Byway, Zoomboy, and
the *weise Frau* Allhealer. They had total individ-
uality, you could no more characterize one of
them in a sentence than you could a human.

"We are glad you make this overture," Isinglass said on first acquaintance. "So glad that,
despite their helpfulness to us, we told the
Merseians to keep away while you are here."

"I have suspected we and the landfolk were
made pieces in a larger game," added Allhealer
through him. "Fortunate that you wish to resign
from it."

Flandry's cheeks burned inside his helmet. He
knew too well how little altruism was involved.
Scuttlebutt claimed Enriques had openly protested Hauksberg's proposal, and yielded only

when the viscount threatened to get him reassigned to Pluto. Abrams approved because
any chance at new facts was good, but he was
not sanguine.

Nor was Byway. "Peace with the Hunters is a
contradiction in terms. Shall the gilltooth swim
beside the tail-on-head? And as long as the green
strangers offer us assistance, we must take it.
Such is our duty to the cities and our dependents."

"Yet evidently, while they support us, their ad-
versaries are bound to support the Hunters,"
Finbright said. "Best might be that both sets of
foreigners withdrew and let the ancient balance
return."

"I know not," Byway argued. "Could we win
a final victory—"

"Be not so tempted by that as to overlook the
risk of a final defeat," Allhealer warned.

"To the Deeps with your bone-picking!"
Zoomboy exclaimed. "We'll be late for the thea-
ter." He shot off in an exuberant curve.

Flandry did not follow the drama which was
enacted in a faerie coraloid grotto. He gathered
it was a recently composed tragedy in the classic
mode. But the eldritch grace of movement, the
solemn music of voices, strings, percussion, the
utter balance of every element, touched his roots.
And the audience reacted with cries, surges back
and forth, at last a dance in honor of author and
cast.

To him, the sculptures and oil paintings he
was shown were abstract; but as such they were
more pleasing than anything Terra had pro-

duced for centuries. He looked at fishskin scrolls covered with writing in grease-based ink and did not comprehend. Yet they were so many that they must hold a deal of accumulated wisdom.

Then he got off into mathematics and science, and went nearly delirious. He was still so close to the days when such things had been unfolded for him like a flower that he could appreciate what had been done here.

For the people (he didn't like using the Kursovikian name "Siravo" in their own home, and could certainly never again call them Seatrolls) lived in a different conceptual universe from his. And thought they were handicapped—fireless save for volcanic outlets where glass was made as a precious material, metalless, unable to develop more than a rudimentary astronomy, the laws of motion and gravity and light propagation obscured for them by the surrounding water—they had thought their way through to ideas which not only made sense but which drove directly toward insights man had not had before Planck and Einstein.

To them, vision was not the dominant sense that it was for him. No eyes could look far undersea. Hence they were nearsighted by his standards, and the optical centers of their brains appeared to have slightly lower information-processing capability. On the other hand, their perception of tactile, thermal, kinesthetic, olfactory, and less familiar nuances was unbelievably delicate. The upper air was hostile to them; like humans vis-à-vis water, they could control but not kill an instinctive dread.

So they experienced space as relation rather than extension. For them, as a fact of daily life, it was unbounded but finite. Expeditions which circumnavigated the globe had simply given more weight and subtlety to that apprehension.

Reflecting this primitive awareness, undersea mathematics rejected infinity. A philosopher with whom Flandry talked via Isinglass asserted that it was empirically meaningless to speak of a number above factorial N, where N was the total of distinguishable particles in the universe. What could a large number count? Likewise, he recognized zero as a useful notion, corresponding to the null class, but not as a number. The least possible amount must be the inverse of the greatest. You could count from there, on to N!, but if you proceeded beyond, you would get decreasing quantities. The number axis was not linear but circular.

Flandry wasn't mathematician enough to decide if the system was entirely self-consistent. As far as he could tell, it was. It even went on to curious versions of negatives, irrationals, imaginaries, approximational calculus, differential geometry, theory of equations, and much else of whose Terran equivalents he was ignorant.

Physical theory fitted in. Space was regarded as quantized. Discontinuities between kinds of space were accepted. That might only be an elaboration of the everyday—the sharp distinction between water, solid ground, and air—but the idea of layered space accounted well for experimental data and closely paralleled the relativistic concept of a metric varying from point to point, as well as the wave-mechanical basis of atomistics and the hyperdrive.

Nor could time, in the thought of the People, be infinite. Tides, seasons, the rhythm of life all suggested a universe which would eventually return to its initial state and resume a cycle which it would be semantically empty to call endless. But having no means of measuring time with any precision, the philosophers had concluded that it was essentially immeasurable. They denied simultaneity; how could you say a distant event happened simultaneously with a near one, when news of the former must be brought by a swimmer whose average speed was unpredictable? Again the likeness to relativity was startling.

Biology was well developed in every macroscopic facet, including genetic laws. Physics proper, as opposed to its conceptual framework, was still early Newtonian, and chemistry little more than an embryo. But Judas on Jupiter, Flandry thought, give these fellows some equipment tailored for underwater use and watch them lift!

"Come along," Zoomboy said impatiently. "Wiggle a flipper. We're off to Reefcastle."

En route, Flandry did his unskilled best to get an outline of social structure. The fundamental Weltanschauung eluded him. You could say the People of the Davidstar were partly Apollonian and partly Dionysian, but those were mere metaphors which anthropology had long discarded and were worse than useless in dealing with nonhumans. Politics (if *that* word was applicable) looked simpler. Being more gregarious and ceremony-minded than most humans, and less impulsive, and finding travel easier than land animals do, the sea dwellers on Starkad tended to form large nations without strong rivalries.

The Zletovar culture was organized hieratically. Governors inherited their positions, as did People in most other walks (swims?) of life. On the individual level there existed a kind of serfdom, binding not to a piece of territory but to the person of the master. And females had that status with respect to their polygamous husbands.

Yet such expressions were misleading. The decision makers did not lord it over the rest. No formalities were used between classes. Merit brought promotion; so had Allhealer won her independence and considerable authority. Failure, especially the failure to meet one's obligation to dependents, brought demotion. For the system did nothing except apportion rights and duties.

Terra had known similar things, in theory. Practice had never worked out. Men were too greedy, too lazy. But it seemed to operate among the People. At least, Isinglass claimed it had been stable for many generations, and Flandry saw no evidence of discontent.

Reefcastle was nothing like Shellgleam. Here the houses were stone and coraloid, built into the skerries off a small island. The inhabitants were more brisk, less contemplative than their bottom-dwelling cousins; Isinglass scoffed at them as a bunch of wealth-grubbing traders. "But I must admit they have bravely borne an

undue share of trouble from the Hunters," he
added, "and they went in the van of our late attack: which took courage, when none knew
about the Merseian boat."

"None?" asked Flandry in surprise.

"I daresay the governors were told beforehand. Otherwise we knew only that when the
signal was given our leg-equipped troops were to
go ashore and lay waste what they could while
our swimmers sank the ships."

"Oh." Flandry did not describe his role in
frustrating that. He felt an enormous relief. If
Abrams had learned from Evenfall about the
planned bombardment, Abrams ought to have
arranged countermeasures. But since the information hadn't been there to obtain—Flandry
was glad to stop finding excuses for a man who
was rapidly becoming an idol.

The party went among the reefs beyond town
to see their tide pools. Surf roared, long wrinkled
azure-and-emerald billows which spouted white
under a brilliant sky. The People frolicked, leaping out of the waves, plunging recklessly through
channels where cross-currents ramped. Flandry
discarded the staleness of his armor for a plain
helmet and knew himself fully alive.

"We shall take you next to Outlier," Isinglass
said on the way home to Shellgleam. "It is something unique. Below its foundations the abyss
goes down into a night where fish and forests
glow. The rocks are gnawed by time and lividly
hued. The water tastes of volcano. But the silence—the silence!"

"I look forward," Flandry said.

"—? —. So. You scent a future perfume."

When he cycled through the airlock and entered the Terran dome, Flandry was almost repelled. This narrow, stinking, cheerless bubble, jammed with hairy bodies whose every motion was a jerk against weight! He started peeling off his undergarment to take a shower.

"How was your trip?" Ridenour asked.

"Wonderful," Flandry glowed.

"All right, I guess," said Ensign Quarles, who had been along. "Good to get back, though. How 'bout putting on a girlie tape for us?"

Ridenour flipped the switch of the recorder on his desk. "First things first," he said. "Let's have your report."

Flandry suppressed an obscenity. Adventures got spoiled by being reduced to data. Maybe he didn't really want to be a xenologist.

At the end, Ridenour grimaced. "Wish to blazes my part of the job were doing as well."

"Trouble?" Flandry asked, alarmed.

"Impasse. Problem is, the Kursovikians are too damned efficient. Their hunting, fishing, gathering do make serious inroads on resources, which are never as plentiful in the sea. The governors refuse any terms which don't involve the landfolk stopping exploitation. And of course the landfolk won't. They can't, without undermining their own economy and suffering famine. So I'm trying to persuade the Sixpoint to reject further Merseian aid. That way we might get the Zletovar out of the total-war mess. But they point out, very rightly, that what we've given the Kursovikians has upset the balance of power.

And how can we take our presents back? We'd antagonize them—which I don't imagine Runei's agents would be slow to take advantage of." Ridenour sighed. "I still have some hopes of arranging for a two-sided phaseout, but they've grown pretty dim."

"We can't start killing the People again!" Flandry protested.

"Can't we just?" Quarles said.

"After what we've seen, what they've done for us—"

"Grow up. We belong to the Empire, not some barnacle-bitten gang of xenos."

"You may be out of the matter anyhow, Flandry," Ridenour said. "Your orders came through several hours ago."

"Orders?"

"You report to Commander Abrams at Highport. An amphibian will pick you up at 0730 tomorrow, Terran clock. Special duty, I don't know what."

Abrams leaned back, put one foot on his battered desk, and drew hard on his cigar. "You'd really rather've stayed underwater?"

"For a while, sir," Flandry said from the edge of his chair. "I mean, well, besides being interesting, I felt I was accomplishing something. Information—friendship—" His voice trailed off.

"Modest young chap, aren't you? Describing yourself as 'interesting.'" Abrams blew a smoke ring. "Oh, sure, I see your point. Not a bad one. Were matters different, I wouldn't've hauled you topside. You might, though, ask what I have in mind for you."

"Sir?"

"Lord Hauksberg is continuing to Merseia in another couple days. I'm going along in an advisory capacity, my orders claim. I rate an aide. Want the job?"

Flandry goggled. His heart somersaulted. After a minute he noticed that his mouth hung open.

"Plain to see," Abrams continued, "my hope is to collect some intelligence. Nothing melodramatic; I hope I'm more competent than that. I'll keep my eyes and ears open. Nose, too. But none of our diplomats, attachés, trade-talk representatives, none of our sources has ever been very helpful. Merseia's too distant from Terra. Almost the only contact has been on the level of brute, chip-on-your-shoulder power. This may be a chance to circulate under fewer restrictions.

"So I ought to bring an experienced, proven man. But we can't spare one. You've shown yourself pretty tough and resourceful for a younker. A bit of practical experience in Intelligence will give you a mighty long leg up, if I do succeed in making you transfer. From your standpoint, you get off this miserable planet, travel in a luxury ship, see exotic Merseia, maybe other spots as well, probably get taken back to Terra and then probably not reassigned to Starkad even if you remain a flyboy—and make some highly useable contacts. How about it?"

"Y-y-yes, *sir!*" Flandry stammered.

Abrams' eyes crinkled. "Don't get above yourself, son. This won't be any pleasure cruise. I'll
expect you to forget about sleep and live on stim-
pills from now till departure, learning what an
aide of mine has to know. You'll be saddled with
everything from secretarial chores to keeping my
uniforms neat. En route, you'll take an elec-
trocram in the Eriau language and as much
Merseiology as your brain'll hold without ex-
ploding. I need hardly warn you that's no
carnival. Once we're there, if you're lucky you'll
grind through a drab list of duties. If you're un-
lucky—if things should go nova—you won't be a
plumed knight of the skies any longer, you'll be
a hunted animal, and if they take you alive their
style of quizzing won't leave you any personality
worth having. Think about that."

Flandry didn't. His one regret was that he'd
likely never see Dragoika again, and it was a
passing twinge. "Sir," he declaimed, "you've got
yourself an aide."

Chapter Nine

The *Dronning Margrete* was not of a size to land safely on a planet. Her auxiliaries were small spaceships in their own right. Officially belonging to Ny Kalmar, in practice a yacht for whoever was the current viscount, she did sometimes travel in the Imperial service: a vast improvement with respect to comfort over any Navy vessel. Now she departed her orbit around Starkad and accelerated outward on gravitics. Before long she was into clear enough space that she could switch over to hyperdrive and outpace light. Despite her mass, with her engine power and phase frequency, top pseudospeed equalled that of a Planet class warcraft. The sun she left behind was soon dwindled to another star, and then to nothing. Had the viewscreens not compensated for aberration and Doppler effect, the universe would have looked distorted beyond recognition.

Yet the constellations changed but slowly. Days and nights passed while she fled through the marches. Only once was routine broken, when alarms sounded. They were followed immediately by the All Clear. Her force screens, warding off radiation and interstellar atoms, had for a microsecond brushed a larger piece of matter, a pebble estimated at five grams. Though contact with the hull would have been damaging, given the difference in kinetic velocities, and though such meteoroids occur in the galaxy to the total of perhaps 10^{50}, the likelihood of collision was too small to worry about. Once, also, another vessel passed within a light-year and thus its "wake" was detected. The pattern indicated it was Ymirite, crewed by hydrogen breathers whose civilization was nearly irrelevant to man or Merseian. They trafficked quite heavily in these parts. Nonetheless this sign of life was the subject of excited conversation. So big is the cosmos.

There came at last the time when Hauksberg and Abrams sat talking far into the middle watch. Hitherto their relationship had been distant and correct. But with journey's end approaching they saw a mutual need to understand each other better. The viscount invited the commander to dinner *à deux* in his private suite. His chef transcended himself for the occasion and his butler spent considerable time choosing wines. Afterward, at the cognac stage of things, the butler saw he could get away with simply leaving the bottle on the table plus another in reserve, and went off to bed.

The ship whispered, powerplant, ventilators, a rare hail when two crewmen on duty passed in the corridor outside. Light glowed soft off pictures and drapes. A heathery scent in the air underlay curling smoke. After Starkad, the Terran weight maintained by the gravitors was good;

Abrams still relished a sense of lightness and often in his sleep had flying dreams.

"Pioneer types, eh?" Hauksberg kindled a fresh cheroot. "Sounds int'restin'. Really must visit Dayan someday."

"You wouldn't find much there in your line," Abrams grunted. "Ordinary people."

"And what they've carved for themselves out of howlin' wilderness. I know." The blond head nodded. "Natural you should be a little chauvinistic, with such a background. But's a dangerous attitude."

"More dangerous to sit and wait for an enemy," Abrams said around his own cigar. "I got a wife and kids and a million cousins. My duty to them is to keep the Merseians at a long arm's length."

"No. Your duty is to help make that unnecess'ry."

"Great, if the Merseians'll cooperate."

"Why shouldn't they? No, wait." Hauksberg lifted a hand. "Let me finish. I'm not int'rested in who started the trouble. That's childish. Fact is, there we were, *the* great power among oxygen breathers in the known galaxy. S'pose they'd been? Wouldn't you've plumped for man acquirin' a comparable empire? Otherwise we'd've been at their mercy. As was, they didn't want to be at our mercy. So, by the time we took real notice, Merseia'd picked up sufficient real estate to alarm us. We reacted, propaganda, alliances, diplomacy, economic maneuvers, subversion, outright armed clashes now and then. Which was bound to confirm their poor opinion of our intentions. They re-reacted, heightenin' our fears. Positive feedback. Got to be stopped."

"I've heard this before," Abrams said. "I don't believe a word of it. Maybe memories of Assyria, Rome, and Germany are built into my chromosomes, I dunno. Fact is, if Merseia wanted a real *détente* she could have one today. We're no longer interested in expansion. Terra is old and fat. Merseia is young and full of beans. She hankers for the universe. We stand in the way. Therefore we have to be eaten. Everything else is dessert."

"Come, come," Hauksberg said. "They're not stupid. A galactic government is impossible. It'd collapse under its own weight. We've everything we can do to control what we have, and we don't control tightly. Local self-government is so strong, most places, that I see actual feudalism evolvin' within the Imperial structure. Can't the Merseians look ahead?"

"Oh, Lord, yes. Can they ever. But I don't imagine they want to copy us. The Roidhunate is not like the Empire."

"Well, the electors of the landed clans do pick their supreme chief from the one landless one, but that's a detail."

"Yes, from the Vach Urdiolch. It's not a detail. It reflects their whole concept of society. What they have in mind for their far future is a set of autonomous Merseian-ruled regions. The race, not the nation, counts with them. Which makes them a hell of a lot more dangerous than simple imperialists like us, who only want to be top dogs and admit other species have an equal right to exist. Anyway, so I think on the basis of what information is available. While on Merseia I hope to read a lot of their philosophers."

Hauksberg smiled. "Be my guest. Be theirs. Long's you don't get zealous and upset things with any cloak-and-dagger stuff, you're welcome aboard." The smile faded. "Make trouble and I'll break you."

Abrams looked into the blue eyes. They were suddenly very cold and steady. It grew on him that Hauksberg was not at all the fop he pretended to be.

"Thanks for warning me," the officer of Intelligence said. "But damnation!" His fist smote the table. "The Merseians didn't come to Starkad because their hearts bled for the poor oppressed seafolk. Nor do I think they stumbled in by mistake and are looking for any face-saving excuse to pull out again. They figure on a real payoff there."

"F'r instance?"

"How the devil should I know? I swear none of their own personnel on Starkad do. Doubtless just a hatful of higher-ups on Merseia itself have any idea what the grand strategy is. But those boys see it in clockwork detail."

"Valuable minerals undersea, p'rhaps?"

"Now you must realize that's ridiculous. Likewise any notion that the seafolk may possess a great secret like being universal telepaths. If Starkad per se had something useful, the Merseians could have gotten it more quietly. If it's a base they're after, say for the purpose of pressuring Betelgeuse, then there are plenty of better planets in that general volume. No, they for sure want a showdown."

"I've speculated along those lines," Hauksberg said thoughtfully. "S'pose some fanatical militarists among 'em plan on a decisive clash with Terra. That'd have to be built up to. If nothin' else, lines of communication are so long that neither power could hope to mount a direct attack on the other. So if they escalate things on an intrinsically worthless Starkad— well, eventually there could be a confrontation. And out where no useful planet got damaged."

"Could be," Abrams said. "In fact, it's sort of a working hypothesis for me. But it don't smell right somehow."

"I aim to warn them," Hauksberg said. "Informally and privately, to keep pride and such from complicatin' matters. If we can discover who the reasonable elements are in their government, we can cooperate with those—most discreetly—to freeze the warhawks out."

"Trouble is," Abrams aid, "the whole bunch of them are reasonable. But they don't reason on the same basis as us."

"No, you're the unreasonable one, old chap. You've gotten paranoid on the subject." Hauksberg refilled their glasses, a clear gurgle through the stillness. "Have another drink while I explain to you the error of your ways."

The officers' lounge was deserted. Persis had commandeered from the bar a demi of port but had not turned on the fluoros. Here in the veranda, enough light came through the viewport which stretched from deck to overhead. It was soft and shadowy, caressed a cheek or a lock of hair and vanished into susurrant dark.

Stars were the source, uncountable throngs of them, white, blue, yellow, green, red, cold and unwinking against an absolute night. And the Milky Way was a shining smoke and the nebulae and the sister galaxies glimmered at vision's edge. That was a terrible beauty.

Flandry was far too conscious of her eyes and of the shape enclosed by thin, slightly phosphorescent pajamas, where she faced him in her lounger. He sat stiff on his. "Yes," he said, "yonder bright one, you're right, Donna, a nova. What . . . uh . . . what Saxo's slated to become before long."

"Really?" Her attentiveness flattered him.

"Yes. F-type, you know. Evolves faster than the less massive suns like Sol, and goes off the main sequence more spectacularly. The red giant stage like Betelgeuse is short—then bang."

"But those poor natives!"

Flandry made a forced-sounding chuckle. "Don't worry, Donna. It won't happen for almost a billion years, according to every spectroscopic indication. Plenty of time to evacuate the planet."

"A billion years." She shivered a little. "Too big a number. A billion years ago, we were still fish in the Terran seas, weren't we? All the numbers are too big out here."

"I, uh, guess I'm more used to them." His nonchalance didn't quite come off.

He could barely see how her lips curved upward. "I'm sure you are," she said. "Maybe you can help me learn to feel the same way."

His tunic collar was open but felt tight anyhow. "Betelgeuse is an interesting case," he said. "The star expanded slowly by mortal standards. The autochthons could develop an industrial culture and move out to Alfzar and the planets beyond. They didn't hit on the hyperdrive by themselves, but they had a high-powered interplanetary society when Terrans arrived. If we hadn't provided a better means, they'd have left the system altogether in sublight ships. No real rush. Betelgeuse won't be so swollen that Alfzar becomes uninhabitable for another million years or better. But they had their plans in train. A fascinating species, the Betelgeuseans."

"True." Persis took a sip of wine, then leaned forward. One leg, glimmering silky in the starlight, brushed his. "However," she said, "I didn't lock onto you after dinner in hopes of a lecture."

"Why, uh, what can I do for you, Donna? Glad to, if—" Flandry drained his own goblet with a gulp. His pulse racketed.

"Talk to me. About yourself. You're too shy."

"About me?" he squeaked. "Whatever for? I mean, I'm nobody."

"You're the first young hero I've met. The others, at home, they're old and gray and crusted with decorations. You might as well try to make conversation with Mount Narpa. Frankly, I'm lonesome on this trip. You're the single one I could relax and feel human with. And you've hardly shown your nose outside your office."

"Uh, Donna, Commander Abrams has kept

me busy. I didn't want to be unsociable, but, well, this is the first time he'd told me I could go off duty except to sleep. Uh, Lord Hauksberg-''

Persis shurgged. "He doesn't understand. All right, he's been good to me and without him I'd probably be an underpaid dancer on Luna yet. But he does not understand."

Flandry opened his mouth, decided to close it again, and recharged his goblet.

"Let's get acquainted," Persis said gently. "We exist for such a short time at best. Why were you on Starkad?"

"Orders, Donna."

"That's no answer. You could simply have done the minimum and guarded your neck. Most of them seem to. You must have some belief in what you're doing."

"Well—I don't know, Donna. Never could keep out of a good scrap, I suppose."

She sighed. "I thought better of you, Dominic."

"Beg pardon?"

"Cynicism is boringly fashionable. I didn't think you would be afraid to say mankind is worth fighting for."

Flandry winced. She had touched a nerve. "Sort of thing's been said too often, Donna. The words have gone all hollow. I . . . I do like some ancient words. '. . . the best fortress is to be found in the love of the people.' From Machiavelli."

"Who? Never mind. I don't care what some dead Irishman said. I want to know what you care about. You are the future. What did Terra give you, for you to offer your life in return?"

"Well, uh, places to live. Protection. Education."

"Stingy gifts," she said. "You were poor?"

"Not really, Donna. Illegitimate son of a petty nobleman. He sent me to good schools and finally the Naval Academy."

"But you were scarcely ever at home?"

"No. Couldn't be. I mean, my mother was in opera then. She had her career to think of. My father's a scholar, an encyclopedist, and, uh, everything else is sort of incidental to him. That's the way he's made. They did their duty by me. I can't complain, Donna."

"At least you won't." She touched his hand. "My name is Persis."

Flandry swallowed.

"What a hard, harsh life you've had," she mused. "And still you'll fight for the Empire."

"Really, it wasn't bad . . . Persis."

"Good. You progress." This time her hand lingered.

"I mean, well, we had fun between classes and drills. I'm afraid I set some kind of record for demerits. And later, a couple of training cruises, the damnedest things happened."

She leaned closer. "Tell me."

He spun out the yarns as amusingly as he was able.

She cocked her head at him. "You were right fluent there," she said. "Why are you backward with me?"

He retreated into his lounger. "I—I, you see,

never had a chance to, uh, learn how to, well, behave in circumstances like—"

She was so near that beneath perfume he caught the odor of herself. Her eyes were half closed, lips parted. "Now's your chance," she whispered. "You weren't afraid of anything else, were you?"

Later, in his cabin, she raised herself to one hand and regarded him for a long moment. Her hair spilled across his shoulder. "And I thought I was your first," she said.

"Why, Persis!" he grinned.

"I felt so—And every minute this evening you knew exactly what you were doing."

"I had to take action," he said. "I'm in love with you. How could I help being?"

"Do you expect me to believe that? Oh, hell, just for this voyage I will. Come here again."

Chapter Ten

Ardaig, the original capital, had grown to surround that bay where the River Oiss poured into the Wilwidh Ocean; and its hinterland was now a megalopolis eastward to the Hun foothills. Nonetheless it retained a flavor of antiquity. Its citizens were more tradition-minded, ceremonies, leisurely than most. It was the cultural and artistic center of Merseia. Though the Grand Council still met here annually, and Castle Afon was still the Roidhun's official primary residence, the bulk of government business was transacted in antipodal Tridaig. The co-capital was young, technology-oriented, brawling with traffic and life, seething with schemes and occasional violence. Hence there had been surprise when Brechdan Ironrede wanted the new Navy offices built in Ardaig.

He did not encounter much opposition. Not only did he preside over the Grand Council; in the space service he had attained fleet admiral's rank before succeeding to Handship of the Vach Ynvory, and the Navy remained his special love and expertise. Characteristically, he had offered little justification for his choice. This was his will, therefore let it be done.

In fact he could not even to himself have given fully logical reasons. Economics, regional balance, any such argument was rebuttable. He appreciated being within a short flit of Dhangodhan's serenity but hoped and believed that had not influenced him. In some obscure fashion he simply knew it was right that the instruments of Merseia's destiny should have roots in Merseia's eternal city.

And thus the tower arose, tier upon gleaming tier until at dawn its shadow engulfed Afon. Aircraft swarmed around the upper flanges like seabirds. After dark its windows were a constellation of goblin eyes and the beacon on top a torch that frightened stars away. But Admiralty House did not clash with the battlements, dome roofs, and craggy spires of the old quarter. Brechdan had seen to that. Rather, it was a culmination of them, their answer to the modern skyline. Its uppermost floor, decked by nothing except a level of traffic control automata, was his own eyrie.

A while after a certain sunset he was there in his secretorium. Besides himself, three living creatures were allowed entry. Passing through an unoccupied antechamber before which was posted a guard, they would put eyes and hands to scanner plates in the armored door. Under positive identification, it would open until they had stepped through. Were more than one present, all must be identified first. The rule was enforced by alarms and robotic blasters.

The vault behind was fitted with spaceship-type air recyclers and thermostats. Walls, floor,

ceiling were a sable against which Brechdan's
black uniform nigh vanished, the medals he wore
tonight glittering doubly fierce. The furnishing
was usual for an office—desk, communicators,
computer, dictoscribe. But in the center a beau-
tifully grained wooden pedestal supported an
opalescent box.

He walked thither and activated a second recognition circuit. A hum and swirl of dim colors
told him that power had gone on. His fingers
moved above the console. Photoelectric cells
fired commands to the memory unit. Electromagnetic fields interacted with distorted
molecules. Information was compared, evaluated, and assembled. In a nanosecond or two,
the data he wanted—ultrasecret, available to
none but him and his three closest, most trusted
colleagues—flashed onto a screen.

Brechdan had seen the report before, but on
an interstellar scale (every planet a complete
world, old and infinitely complex) an overlord
was doing extraordinarily well if he could remember that a specific detail was known let
alone the fact itself. A sizeable party in the
Council wanted to install more decision-making
machines on that account. He had resisted them.
Why ape the Terrans? Look what a state their
dominions had gotten into. Personal government, to the greatest extent possible, was less
stable but more flexible. Unwise to bind oneself
to a single approach, in this unknowable universe.

"*Khraich.*" He switched his tail. Shwylt was
entirely correct, the matter must be attended to

without delay. An unimaginative provincial governor was missing a radium opportunity to bring one more planetary system into the power of the race.

And yet—He sought his desk. Sensing his absence, the data file went blank. He stabbed a communicator button. On sealed and scrambled circuit, his call flew across a third of the globe.

Shwylt Shipsbane growled. "You woke me. Couldn't you pick a decent hour?"

"Which would be an indecent one for me," Brechdan laughed. "This Therayn business won't wait on our joint convenience. I have checked, and we'd best get a fleet out there as fast as may be, together with a suitable replacement for Gadrol."

"Easy to say. But Gadrol will resent that, not without justice, and he has powerful friends. Then there are the Terrans. They'll hear about our seizure, and even though it's taken place on the opposite frontier to them, they'll react. We have to get a prognostication of what they'll do and a computation of how that'll affect events on Starkad. I've alerted Lifrith and Priadwyr. The sooner the four of us can meet on this problem, the better."

"I can't, though. The Terran delegation arrived today. I must attend a welcoming festival tonight."

"What?" Shwylt's jaws snapped together. "One of *their* stupid rites? Are you serious?"

"Quite. Afterward I must remain available to them. In Terran symbology, it would be grave indeed if the, gr-r-rum, the prime minister of

Merseia snubbed the special representative of his Majesty."

"But the whole thing is such a farce!"

"They don't know that. If we disillusion them promptly we'll accelerate matters off schedule. Besides, by encouraging their hopes for a Starkadian settlement we can soften the emotional impact of our occupying Therayn. Which means I shall have to prolong these talks more than I originally intended. Finally, I want some personal acquaintance with the significant members of this group."

Shwylt rubbed the spines on his head. "You have the strangest taste in friends."

"Like you?" Brechdan jibed. "See here. The plan for Starkad is anything but a road we need merely walk at a precalculated pace. It has to be watched, nurtured, modified according to new developments, almost day by day. Something unforeseeable—a brilliant Terran move, a loss of morale among them, a change in attitude by the natives themselves—anything could throw off the timing and negate our whole strategy. The more subliminal data we possess, the better our judgments. For we do have to operate on their emotions as well as their military logic, and they are an alien race. We need empathy with them. In their phrase, we must play by ear."

Shwylt looked harshly out of the screen. "I suspect you actually like them."

"Why, that's no secret," Brechdan said. "They were magnificent once. They could be again. I would love to see them our willing subjects." His scarred features drooped a little.

"Unlikely, of course. They're not that kind of species. We may be forced to exterminate."

"What about Therayn?" Shwylt demanded.

"You three take charge," Brechdan said. "I'll advise from time to time, but you will have full authority. After the postseizure configuration has stabilized enough for evaluation, we can all meet and discuss how this will affect Starkad."

He did not add he would back them against an outraged Council, risking his own position, if they should make some ruinous error. That went without saying.

"As you wish," nodded Shwylt. "Hunt well."

"Hunt well." Brechdan broke the circuit.

For a space he sat quiet. The day had been long for him. His bones felt stiff and his tail ached from the weight on it. Yes, he thought, one grows old; at first the thing merely creeps forward, a dulling of sense and a waning of strength, nothing that enzyme therapy can't handle—then suddenly, overnight, you are borne on a current so fast that the landscape blurs, and you hear the cataract roar ahead of you.

Dearly desired he to flit home, breathe the purity which blew around Dhangodhan's towers, chat over a hot cup with Elwych and tumble to bed. But they awaited him at the Terran Embassy; and afterward he must return hither and meet with . . . who was that agent waiting down in Intelligence? . . . Dwyr the Hook, aye; and then he might as well bunk here for what remained of the night.

He squared his shoulders, swallowed a stim-pill, and left the vault.

His Admiralty worked around the clock. He heard its buzz, click, foot-shuffle, mutter through the shut anteroom door. Because he really had not time for exchanging salutes according to rank and clan with every officer, technician, and guard, he seldom passed that way. Another door opened directly on his main suite of offices. Opposite, a third door gave on a private corridor which ran black and straight to the landing flange.

When he stepped out onto that, the air was cool and damp. The roof screened the beacon from him and he saw clearly over Ardaig.

It was not a Terran city and knew nothing of hectic many-colored blaze after dark. Ground vehicles were confined to a few avenues, otherwise tubeways; the streets were for pedestrians and gwydh riders. Recreation was largely at home or in ancient theaters and sports fields. Shops—as contrasted to mercantile centers with communicator and delivery systems—were small enterprises, closed at this hour, which had been in the same house and the same family for generations. Tridaig shouted. Ardaig murmured, beneath a low salt wind. Luminous pavements wove their web over the hills, trapping lit windows; aircraft made moving lanterns above; spotlights on Afon simply heightened its austerity. Two of the four moons were aloft, Neihevin and Seith. The bay glowed and sparkled under them.

Brechdan's driver folded arms and bowed. Illogical, retaining that old gaffer when this aircar had a robopilot. But his family had always served the Ynvorys. Guards made their clashing salute and entered the vehicle too. It purred off.

The stimulant took hold. Brechdan felt renewed eagerness. What might he not uncover tonight? Relax, he told himself, *keep patience, wait for the one gem to appear from a dungheap of formalisms. . . . If we must exterminate the Terrans, we will at least have rid the universe of much empty chatter.*

His destination was another offense, a compound of residences and offices in the garish bubble style of the Imperium four hundred years ago. Then Merseia was an up-and-coming planet, worth a legation but in no position to dictate architecture or site. Qgoth Heights lay well outside Ardaig. Later the city grew around them and the legation became an embassy and Merseia could deny requests for expanded facilities.

Brechdan walked the entranceway alone, between rosebushes. He did admire that forlorn defiance. A slave took his cloak, a butler tall as himself announced him to the company. The usual pack of civilians in fancy dress, service attaches in uniform—no, yonder stood the newcomers. Lord Oliveira of Ganymede, Imperial Ambassador to his Supremacy the Roidhun, scurried forth. He was a thin and fussy man whose abilities had on a memorable occasion given Brechdan a disconcerting surprise.

"Welcome, Councillor," he said in Eriau, executing a Terran style bow. "We are delighted you could come." He escorted his guest across the parquet floor. "May I present his Majesty's envoy, Lord Markus Hauksberg, Viscount of Ny Kalmar?"

"I am honored, sir." (Languid manner belied by physical condition, eyes that watched closely from beneath the lids, good grasp of language.)

". . . Commander Max Abrams."

"The Hand of the Vach Ynvory is my shield." (Dense accent, but fluent; words and gestures precisely right, dignified greeting of one near in rank to his master who is your equal. Stout frame, gray-shot hair, big nose, military carriage. So this was the fellow reported by courier to be coming along from Starkad. Handle with care.)

Introductions proceeded. Brechdan soon judged that none but Hauksberg and Abrams were worth more than routine attention. The latter's aide, Flandry, looked alert; but he was young and very junior.

A trumpet blew the At Ease. Oliveira was being especially courteous in following local custom. But as this also meant females were excluded, most of his staff couldn't think what to do next. They stood about in dismal little groups, trying to make talk with their Merseian counterparts.

Brechdan accepted a glass of arthberry wine and declined further refreshment. He circulated for what he believed was a decent minimum time —let the Terrans know that he could observe their rituals when he chose—before he zeroed in on Lord Hauksberg.

"I trust your journey here was enjoyable," he began.

"A bit dull, sir," the viscount replied, "until your naval escort joined us. Must say they put on a grand show; and the honor guard after we landed was better yet. Hope no one minded my taping the spectacle."

"Certainly not, provided you stopped before entering Afon."

"Haw! Your, ah, foreign minister is a bit stiff, isn't he? But he was quite pleasant when I offered my credentials, and promised me an early presentation to his Supremacy."

Brechdan took Hauksberg's arm and strolled him toward a corner. Everyone got the hint; the party plodded on at a distance from where they two sat down below an abominable portrait of the Emperor.

"And how was Starkad?" Brechdan asked.

"Speaking for myself, sir, grim and fascinating," Hauksberg said. "Were you ever there?"

"No." Sometimes Brechdan was tempted to pay a visit. By the God, it was long since he had been on a planet unraped by civilization! Impossible, however, at any rate for the next few years when Starkad's importance must be underplayed. Conceivably near the end— He decided that he hoped a visit would not be called for. Easier to make use of a world which was a set of reports than one whose people had been seen in their own lives.

"Well, scarcely in your sphere of interest, eh, sir?" Hauksberg said. "We are bemused by, ah, Merseia's endeavors."

"The Roidhunate has explained over and over."

"Of course. Of course. But mean to say, sir, if you wish to practice charity, as you obviously do, well, aren't there equal needs closer to home? The Grand Council's first duty is to Merseia. I would be the last to accuse you of neglecting your duty."

Brechdan shrugged. "Another mercantile base would be useful in the Betelgeuse region. Starkad is not ideal, either in location or characteristics, but it is acceptable. If at the same time we can gain the gratitude of a talented and deserving species, that tips the balance." He sharpened his gaze. "Your government's reaction was distressing."

"Predictable, though." Hauksberg sprawled deeper into his antique chromeplated chair. "To build confidence on both sides, until a true general agreement can be reached—" mercifully, he did not say "between our great races"—"the inter-imperial buffer space must remain inviolate. I might add, sir, that the landfolk are no less deserving than the seafolk. Meaningless quibble, who was the initial aggressor. His Majesty's government feels morally bound to help the landfolk before their cultures go under."

"Now who is ignoring needs close to home?" Brechdan asked dryly.

Hauksberg grew earnest. "Sir, the conflict can be ended. You must have received reports of our efforts to negotiate peace in the Zletovar area. If Merseia would join her good offices to ours, a planet-wide arrangement could be made. And as for bases there, why should we not establish one together? A long stride toward real friendship, wouldn't you say?"

"Forgive possible rudeness," Brechdan parried, "but I am curious why your pacific mision includes the chief of Intelligence operations on Starkad."

"As an advisor, sir," Hauksberg said with less enthusiasm. "Simply an advisor who knows more about the natives than anyone else who was available. Would you like to speak with him?" He raised an arm and called in Anglic, which Brechdan understood better than was publicly admitted: "Max! I say, Max, come over here for a bit, will you?"

Commander Abrams disengaged himself from an assistant secretary (Brechdan sympathized; that fellow was the dreariest of Oliveira's entire retinue) and saluted the Councillor. "May I serve the Hand?"

"Never mind ceremony, Max," Hauksberg said in Eriau. "We're not talking business tonight. Merely sounding each other out away from protocol and recorders. Please explain your intentions here."

"Give what facts I have and my opinions for whatever they are worth, if anyone asks," Abrams drawled. "I don't expect I'll be called on very often."

"Then why did you come, Commander?" Brechdan gave him his title, which he had not bothered to do for Hauksberg.

"Well, Hand, I did hope to ask a good many questions."

"Sit down," Hauksberg invited.

Abrams said, "With the Hand's leave?"

Brechdan touched a finger to his brow, feeling sure the other would understand. He felt a higher and higher regard for this man, which meant Abrams must be watched closer than anyone else.

The officer plumped his broad bottom into a chair. "I thank the Hand." He lifted a glass of whisky-and-soda to them, sipped, and said: "We really know so little on Terra about you. I couldn't tell you how many Merseiological volumes are in the archives, but no matter; they can't possibly contain more than a fraction of the truth. Could well be we misinterpret you on any number of important points."

"You have your Embassy," Brechdan reminded him. "The staff includes xenologists."

"Not enough, Hand. Not by a cometary orbit. And in any event, most of what they do learn is irrelevant at my level. With your permission, I'd like to talk freely with a lot of different Merseians. Please keep those talks surveyed, to avoid any appearance of evil." Brechdan and Abrams exchanged a grin. "Also, I'd like access to your libraries, journals, whatever is public information as far as you're concerned but may not have reached Terra."

"Have you any specific problems in mind? I will help if I can."

"The Hand is most gracious. I'll mention just one typical point. It puzzles me, I've ransacked our files and turned researchers loose on it myself, and still haven't found an answer. How did Merseia come upon Starkad in the first place?"

Brechdan stiffened. "Exploring the region," he said curtly. "Unclaimed space is free to all ships."

"But suddenly, Hand, there you were, active on the confounded planet. Precisely how did you happen to get interested?"

Brechdan took a moment to organize his reply. "Your people went through that region rather superficially in the old days," he said. "We are less eager for commercial profit than the Polesotechnic League was, and more eager for knowledge, so we mounted a systematic survey. The entry for Saxo, in your pilot's manual, made Starkad seem worth thorough study. After all, we too are attracted by planets with free oxygen and liquid water, be they ever so inhospitable otherwise. We found a situation which needed correction, and proceeded to send a mission. Inevitably, ships in the Betelgeuse trade noted frequent wakes near Saxo. Terran units investigated, and the present unhappy state of affairs developed."

"Hm." Abrams looked into his glass. "I thank the Hand. But it'd be nice to have more details. Maybe, buried somewhere among them, is a clue to something our side has misunderstood—semantic and cultural barrier, not so?"

"I doubt that," Brechdan said. "You are welcome to conduct inquiries, but on this subject you will waste your energy. There may not even be a record of the first several Merseian expeditions to the Saxo vicinity. We are not as concerned to put everything on tape as you."

Sensing his coldness, Hauksberg hastened to change the subject. Conversation petered out in banalities. Brechdan made his excuses and departed before midnight.

A good opponent, Abrams, he thought. *Too good for my peace of mind. He is definitely the one on whom to concentrate attention.*

Or is he? Would a genuinely competent spy look formidable? He could be a—yes, they call it a stalking horse—for someone or something else. Then again, that may be what he wants me to think.

Brechdan chuckled. This regression could go on forever. And it was not his business to play watchbeast. The supply of security officers was ample. Every move that every Terran made, outside the Embassy which they kept bugproof with annoying ingenuity, was observed as a matter of course.

Still, he was about to see in person an individual Intelligence agent, one who was important enough to have been sent especially to Starkad and especially returned when wily old Runei decided he could be more valuable at home. Dwyr the Hook might carry information worthy of the Council president's direct hearing. After which Brechdan could give him fresh orders. . . .

In the icy fluorescence of an otherwise empty office, the thing waited. Once it had been Merseian and young. The lower face remained, as a mask rebuilt by surgery; part of the torso; left arm and right stump. The rest was machine.

Its biped frame executed a surprisingly smooth salute. At such close quarters Brechdan, who had keen ears, could barely discern the hum from within. Power coursed out of capacitors which need not be recharged for several days, even under strenuous use: out through microminiaturized assemblies that together formed a body. "Service to my overlord." A faint metal tone rang in the voice.

Brechdan responded in honor. He did not know if he would have had the courage to stay alive so amputated. "Well met, Arlech Dwyr. At ease."

"The Hand of the Vach Ynvory desired my presence?"

"Yes, yes." Brechdan waved impatiently. "Let us have no more etiquette. I'm fed to the occiput with it. Apology that I kept you waiting, but before I could talk meaningfully about those Terrans I must needs encounter them for myself. Now then, you worked on the staff of Fodaich Runei's Intelligence corps as well as in the field, did you not? So you are conversant both with collated data and with the problems of gathering information in the first place. Good. Tell me in your own words why you were ordered back."

"Hand," said the voice, "as an operative I was useful but not indispensable. The one mission which I and no other might have carried out, failed: to burgle the office of the Terran chief of Intelligence."

"You expected success?" Brechdan hadn't known Dwyr was that good.

"Yes, Hand. I can be equipped with electromagnetic sensors and transducers, to feel out a hidden circuit. In addition, I have developed an empathy with machines. I can be aware, on a level below consciousness, of what they are about to do, and adjust my behavior accordingly. It is analogous to my former perception, the normal one, of nuances in expression, tone,

stance on the part of fellow Merseians whom I
knew intimately. Thus I could have opened the
door without triggering an alarm. Unfortunate-
ly, and unexpectedly, living guards were posted.
In physical strength, speed, and agility, this
body is inferior to what I formerly had. I could
not have killed them unbeknownst to their
mates."

"Do you think Abrams knows about you?"
Brechdan asked sharply.

"No, Hand. Evidence indicates he is ultra-
cautious by habit. Those Terrans who damaged
me later in the jungle got no good look at me. I
did glimpse Abrams in companionship with the
other, Hauksberg. This led us to suspect early
that he would accompany the delegation to
Merseia, no doubt in the hope of conducting espionage. Because of my special capabilities, and
my acquaintance with Abrams' working methods, Fodaich Runei felt I should go ahead of the
Terrans and await ther arrival."

"*Khraich*. Yes. Correct." Brechdan forced
himself to look at Dwyr as he would at a fully
alive being. "You can be put into other bodies,
can you not?"

"Yes, Hand," came from the blank visage.
"Vehicles, weapons, detectors, machine tools,
anything designed to receive my organic compo-
nent and my essential prostheses. I do not take
long to familiarize myself with their use. Under
his Supremacy, I stand at your orders."

"You will have work," Brechdan said. "In
truth you will. I know not what as yet. You may
even be asked to burgle the envoy's ship in orbit.

For a beginning, however, I think we must plan
a program against our friend Abrams. He will
expect the usual devices; you may give him a
surprise. If you do, you shall not go unhonored."

Dwyr the Hook waited to hear further.

Brechdan could not forebear taking a minute
for plain fleshly comradeship. "How were you
hurt?" he asked.

"In the conquest of Janair, Hand. A nuclear
blast. The field hospital kept me alive and sent
me to base for regeneration. But the surgeons
there found that the radiation had too much de-
ranged my cellular chemistry. At that point I requested death. They explained that techniques
newly learned from Gorrazan gave hope of an
alternative, which might make my service quite
precious. They were correct."

Brechdan was momentarily startled. This
didn't sound right—Well, he was no biomedic.

His spirits darkened. Why pretend pity? You
can't be friends with the dead. And Dwyr was
dead, in bone, sinew, glands, gonads, guts,
everything but a brain which had nothing left
except the single-mindedness of a machine. So,
use him. That was what machines were for.

Brechdan took a turn around the room, hands
behind back, tail unrestful, scar throbbing.
"Good," he said. "Let us discuss procedure."

Chapter Eleven

"Oh, no," Abrams had said. "I thank most humbly the government of his Supremacy for this generous offer, but would not dream of causing such needless trouble and expense. True, the Embassy cannot spare me an airboat. However, the ship we came in, *Dronning Margrete,* has a number of auxiliaries now idle. I can use one of them."

"The Commander's courtesy is appreciated," bowed the official at the other end of the vidiphone line. "Regrettably, though, law permits no one not of Merseian race to operate within the Korychan System a vessel possessing hyperdrive capabilities. The Commander will remember that a Merseian pilot and engineer boarded his Lordship's vessel for the last sublight leg of the journey here. Is my information correct that the auxiliaries of his Lordship's so impressive vessel possess hyperdrives in addition to gravitics?"

"They do, distinguished colleague. But the two largest carry an airboat apiece as their own auxiliaries. I am sure Lord Hauksberg won't mind lending me one of those for my personal transporation. There is no reason to bother your department."

"But there is!" The Merseian threw up his hands in quite a manlike gesture of horror. "The Commander, no less than his Lordship, is a guest of his Supremacy. We cannot disgrace his Supremacy by failing to show what hospitality lies within our power. A vessel will arrive tomorrow for the Commander's personal use. The delay is merely so that it may be furnished comfortably for Terrans and the controls modified to a Terran pattern. The boat can sleep six, and we will stock its galley with whatever is desired and available here. It has full aerial capability, has been checked out for orbital use, and could no doubt reach the outermost moon at need. I beg for the Commander's acceptance."

"Distinguished colleague, I in turn beg that you, under his Supremacy, accept my sincerest thanks," Abrams beamed.

The beam turned into a guffaw as soon as he had cut the circuit. Of course the Merseians weren't going to let him travel around unescorted—not unless they could bug his transportation. And of course they would expect him to look for eavesdropping gimmicks and find any of the usual sorts. Therefore he really needn't conduct that tedious search.

Nonetheless, he did. Negligence would have been out of character. To those who delivered his beautiful new flier he explained that he set technicians swarming through her to make certain that everything was understood about her operation; different cultures, different engineering, don't y' know. The routine disclaimer was met by the routine pretense of believing it. The air-

boat carried no spy gadgets apart from the one
he had been hoping for. He found this by the
simple expedient of waiting till he was alone
aboard and then asking. The method of its con-
cealment filled him with admiration.

But thereafter he ran into a stone wall—or,
rather, a pot of glue. Days came and went, the
long thirty-seven-hour days of Merseia. He lost
one after another by being summoned to the
chamber in Castle Afon where Hauksberg and
staff conferred with Brechdan's puppets. Usually
the summons was at the request of a Merseian,
who wanted elucidation of some utterly trivial
question about Starkad. Having explained,
Abrams couldn't leave. Protocol forbade. He
must sit there while talk droned on, inquiries,
harangues, haggles over points which a child
could see were unessential—oh, yes, these greenskins had a fine art of making negotiations in-
terminable.

Abrams said as much to Hauksberg, once
when they were back at the Embassy. "I know,"
the viscount snapped. He was turning gaunt and
hollow-eyed. "They're so suspicious of us. Well,
we're partly to blame for that, eh? Got to show
good faith. While we talk, we don't fight."

"They fight on Starkad," Abrams grumbled
around his cigar. "Terra won't wait on Brechdan's comma-counting forever."

"I'll dispatch a courier presently, to report
and explain. We are gettin' somewhere, don't
forget. They're definitely int'rested in establish-
in' a system for continuous medium-level conference between the governments."

"Yah. A great big gorgeous idea which'll give political leverage to our accommodationists at home for as many years as Brechdan feels like carrying on discussions about it. I thought we came here to settle the Starkad issue."

"I thought I was the head of this mission," Hauksberg retorted. "That'll do, Commander." He yawned and stretched stiffly. "One more drink and ho for bed. Lord Emp'ror, but I'm tired!"

On days when he was not immobilized, Abrams ground through his library research and his interviews. The Merseians were most courteous and helpful. They flooded him with books and periodicals. Officers and officials would talk to him for hours on end. That was the trouble. Aside from whatever feel he might be getting for the basic setup, he learned precisely nothing of value.

Which was a kind of indicator too, he admitted. The lack of hard information about early Merseian journeys to the Saxo region might be due to sloppiness about record keeping as Brechdan had said. But a check of other planets showed that they were, as a rule, better documented. Starkad appeared to have some secret importance. *So what else is new?*

At first Abrams had Flandry to help out. Then an invitation arrived. In the cause of better understanding between races, as well as hospitality, would Ensign Flandry like to tour the planet in company with some young Merseians whose rank corresponded more or less to his?

"Would you?" Abrams asked.

"Why—" Flandry straightened at his desk. "Hell, yes. Right now I feel as if every library in the universe should be bombed. But you need me here . . . I suppose."

"I do. This is a baldpated ruse to cripple me still worse. However, you can go."

"You *mean* that?" Flandry gasped.

"Sure. We're stalled here. You just might discover something."

"Thank you, sir!" Flandry rocketed out of his chair.

"Whoa there, son. Won't be any vacation for you. You've got to play the decadent Terran nogoodnik. Mustn't disappoint their expectations. Besides, it improves your chances. Keep your eyes and ears open, sure, but forget the rule about keeping your mouth shut. Babble. Ask questions. Foolish ones, mainly; and be damned sure not to get so inquisitive they suspect you of playing spy."

Flandry frowned. "Uh . . . sir, I'd look odd if I didn't grab after information. Thing to do, I should guess, is be clumsy and obvious about it."

"Good. You catch on fast. I wish you were experienced, but—Nu, everybody has to start sometime, and I'm afraid you will not run into anything too big for a pup to handle. So go get yourself some experience."

Abrams watched the boy bustle off, and a sigh gusted from him. By and large, after winking at a few things, he felt he'd have been proud to have Dominic Flandry for a son. Though not likely to hit any pay dirt, this trip would further test the ensign's competence. If he proved out well, then probably he must be thrown to the wolves by Abrams' own hand.

Because events could not be left on dead zero as long as Brechdan wished. The situation right now carried potentials which only a traitor would fail to exploit. Nonetheless, the way matters had developed, with the mission detained on Merseia for an indefinite period, Abrams could not exploit them as he had originally schemed. The classically neat operation he had had in mind must be turned into an explosion.

And Flandry was the fuse.

Like almost every intelligent species, the Merseians had in their past evolved thousands of languages and cultures, Finally, as in the case of Terra, one came to dominate the others and slowly absorb them into itself. But the process had not gone as far on Merseia. The laws and customs of the lands bordering the Wilwidh Ocean were still a mere overlay on some parts of the planet. Eriau was the common tongue, but there were still those who were less at home in it than in the languages they had learned from their mothers.

Perhaps this was why Lannawar Belgis had never risen above yqan—CPO, Flandry translated—and was at the moment a sort of batman to the group. He couldn't even pronounce his rating correctly. The sound rendered by *q*, approximately *kdh* where *dh* = *th* as in "the," gave him almost as much trouble as it did an Anglic speaker. Or perhaps he just wasn't ambitious.

For certainly he was able, as his huge fund of stories from his years in space attested. He was also a likeable old chap.

He sat relaxed with the Terran and Tachwyr the Dark, whose rank of mei answered somewhat to lieutenant j.g. Flandry was getting used to the interplay of formality and ease between officers and enlisted personnel in the Merseian service. Instead of the mutual aloofness on Terran ships, there was an intimacy which the seniors led but did not rigidly control, a sort of perpetual dance.

"Aye, foreseers," Lannawar rumbled, "yon was a strange orb and glad I was to see the last of it. Yet somehow, I know not, ours was never a lucky ship afterward. Nothing went ever wholly right, you track me? Speaking naught against captain nor crew, I was glad for transfer to the *Bedh-Ivrich*. Her skipper was Runei the Wanderer, and far did he take us on explores."

Tachwayr's tailtip jerked and he opened his mouth. Someone was always around to keep a brake on Lannawar's garrulousness. Flandry, who had sat half drowsing, surged to alertness. He beat Tachwyr by a millisecond in exclaiming: "Runei? The same who is now Fodaich on Starkad?"

"Why . . . aye, believe so, foreseer." Eyes squinched in the tattooed face across the table. A green hand scratched the paunch where the undress tunic bulged open. "Not as I know much. Heard naught of Starkad ere they told me why you Terrans is come."

Flandry's mind went into such furious action that he felt each of the several levels on which it

was operating. He had to grab whatever lead
chance had offered him after so many fruitless
days; he must fend off Tachwyr's efforts to
wrench the lead away from him, for a minute or
two anyhow; at the same time, he must maintain
his role. (Decadent, as Abrams had suggested,
and this he had enjoyed living up to whenever
his escorts took him to some place of amusement. But not fatuous; he had quickly seen that
he'd get further if they respected him a little and
were not bored by his company. He was naïve,
wide-eyed, pathetically hoping to accomplish
something for Mother Terra, simultaneously im-
pressed by what he saw here. In wry moments he
admitted to himself that this was hardly a faked
character.) On lower levels of consciousness, excitement opened the sensory floodgates.

Once more he noticed the background. They
sat, with a bench for him, in a marble pergola
intricately arabesqued and onion-domed.
Tankards of bitter ale stood before them.
Merseian food and drink were nourishing to a
Terran, and often tasty. They had entered this
hilltop restaurant (which was also a shrine, run
by the devotees of a very ancient faith) for the
view and for a rest after walking around in
Dalgorad. That community nestled below them,
half hidden by lambent flowers and deep-green
fronds, a few small modern buildings and many
hollowed-out trees which had housed untold
generations of a civilized society. Past the airport
lay a breath of red sand. An ocean so blue it was
nearly black cast breakers ashore; their booming
drifted faint to Flandry on a wind that smelled
cinnamon. Korych shone overhead with sub-

tropical fierceness, but the moons Wythna and Lythyr were discernible, like ghosts.

Interior sensations: muscles drawn tight in thighs and belly, bloodbeat in the eardrums, chill in the palms. No feeling of excess weight; Merseian gravity was only a few percent above Terra's. Merseian air, water, biochemistry, animal and plant life, were close parallels to what man had evolved among. By the standards of either world, the other was beautiful.

Which made the two races enemies. They wanted the same kind of real estate.

"So Runei himself was not concerned with the original missions to Starkad?" Flandry asked.

"No, foreseer. We surveyed beyond Rigel." Lannawar reached for his tankard.

"I imagine, though," Flandry prompted, "from time to time when space explorers got together, as it might be in a tavern, you'd swap yarns?"

"Aye, aye. What else? 'Cept when we was told to keep our hatches dogged about where we'd been. Not easy, foreseer, believe you me 'tis not, when you could outbrag the crew of 'em save 'tis a Naval secret."

"You must have heard a lot about the Betelgeuse region, regardless."

Lannawar raised his tankard. Thereby he missed noticing Tachwyr's frown. But he did break the thread, and the officer caught the raveled end deftly.

"Are you really interested in anecdotes, Ensign? I fear that our good Yqan has nothing else to give you."

"Well, yes, Mei, I am interested in anything

about the Betelgeuse sector," Flandry said. "After all, it borders on our Empire. I've already served there, on Starkad, and I daresay I will again. So I'd be grateful for whatever you care to tell me." Lannawar came up for air. "If you yourself, Yqan, were never there, perhaps you know someone who was. I ask for no secrets, of course, only stories."

"Khr-r-r-." Lannawar wiped foam off his chin. "Not many about. Not many what have fared yonderways. They're either back in space, or they've died. Was old Ralgo Tamuar, my barracks friend in training days. He was there aplenty. How he could lie! But he retired to one of the colonies, let me see now, which one?"

"Yqan Belgis." Tachwyr spoke quietly, with no special inflection, but Lannawar stiffened. "I think best we leave this subject. The Starkadian situation is an unfortunate one. We are trying to be friends with our guest, and I hope we are succeeding, but to dwell on the dispute makes a needless obstacle." To Flandry, with sardonicism: "I trust the ensign agrees?"

"As you wish," the Terran mumbled.

Damn, damn, and damn to the power of hell! He'd been on a scent. He could swear he'd been. He felt nauseated with frustration.

Some draughts of ale soothed him. He'd never been idiot enough to imagine himself making any spectacular discoveries or pulling off any dazzling coups on this junket. (Well, certain daydreams, but you couldn't really count that.) What he had obtained now was—a hint which tended to confirm that the early Merseian ex-

peditions to Starkad had found a big and strange
thing. As a result, secrecy had come down like a
candlesnuffer. Officers and crews who knew, or
might suspect, the truth were snatched from
sight. Murdered? No, surely not. The Merseians
were not the antlike monsters which Terran
propaganda depicted. They'd never have come
as far as this, or be as dangerous as they were,
had that been the case. To shut a spacefarer's
mouth, you reassigned him or retired him to an
exile which might well be comfortable and which
he himself might never realize was an exile.

Even for the post of Starkadian commandant,
Brechdan had been careful to pick an officer who
knew nothing beforehand about his post, and
could not since have been told the hidden truth.
Why . . . aside from those exploratory personnel
who no longer counted, perhaps only half a
dozen beings in the universe knew!

Obviously Tachwyr didn't. He and his fellows
had simply been ordered to keep Flandry off certain topics.

The Terran believed they were honest, most of
them, in their friendliness toward him and their
expressed wish that today's discord could be resolved. They were good chaps. He felt more akin
to them than to many humans.

In spite of which, they served the enemy, the
real enemy. Brechdan Ironrede and his Grand
Council, who had put something monstrous in
motion. Wind and surfbeat sounded all at once
like the noise of an oncoming machine.

*I haven't found anything Abrams doesn't already sus-
pect,* Flandry thought. *But I have got for him a bit*

more proof. God! Four days to go before I can get back and give it to him.

His mouth still felt dry. "How about another round?" he said.

"We're going for a ride," Abrams said.

"Sir?" Flandry blinked.

"Little pleasure trip. Don't you think I deserve one too? A run to Gethwyd Forest, say, that's an unrestricted area."

Flandry looked past his boss's burly form, out the window to the compound. A garden robot whickered among the roses, struggling to maintain the microecology they required. A secretary on the diplomatic staff stood outside one of the residence bubbles, flirting boredly with the assistant naval attaché's wife. Beyond them, Ardaig's modern towers shouldered brutally skyward. The afternoon was hot and quiet.

"Uh . . . sir—" Flandry hesitated.

"When you 'sir' me in private these days, you want something," Abrams said. "Carry on."

"Well, uh, could we invite Donna d'Io?" Beneath those crow's-footed eyes, Flandry felt himself blush. He tried to control it, which made matters worse. "She, uh, must be rather lonesome when his Lordship and aides are out of town."

Abrams grinned. "What, I'm not decorative enough for you? Sorry. It wouldn't look right. Let's go."

Flandry stared at him. He knew the man by now. At least, he could spot when something unadmitted lurked under the skin. His spine tingled. Having reported on his trip, he'd expected a return to desk work, dullness occasionally relieved after dark. But action must be starting at last. However much he had grumbled, however sarcastic he had waxed about the glamorous life in romantic alien capitals, he wasn't sure he liked the change.

"Very good, sir," he said.

They left the office and crossed aboveground to the garages. The Merseian technies reported periodically to inspect the luxury boat lent Abrams, but today a lone human was on duty. Envious, he floated the long blue teardrop out into the sunlight. Abrams and Flandry boarded, sealed the door, and found chairs in the saloon. "Gethwyd Forest, main parking area," Abrams said. "Five hundred KPH. Any altitude will do."

The machine communicated with other machines. Clearance was granted and lane assigned. The boat rose noiselessly. On Terra, its path could have been monitored, but the haughty chieftains of Merseia had not allowed that sort of capability to be built in for possible use against them. Traffic control outside of restricted sections was automatic and anonymous. Unless they shadowed a boat, or bugged it somehow, security officers were unable to keep it under surveillance. Abrams had remarked that he liked that, on principle as well as because his own convenience was served.

He groped in his tunic for a cigar. "We could have a drink," he suggested. "Whisky and water for me."

Flandry got it, with a stiff cognac for himself.

By the time he returned from the bar, they were leveled off at about six kilometers and headed north. They would take a couple of hours, at this ambling pace, to reach the preserve which the Vach Dathyr had opened to the public. Flandry had been there before, on a holiday excursion Oliveira arranged for Hauksberg and company. He remembered great solemn trees, gold-feathered birds, the smell of humus and the wild taste of a spring. Most vividly he remembered sunflecks patterned across Persis' thin gown. Now he saw the planet's curve through a broad viewport, the ocean gleaming westward, the megalopolitan maze giving way to fields and isolated castles.

"Sit down," Abrams said. His hand chopped at a lounger. Smoke hazed him where he sprawled.

Flandry lowered himself. He wet his lips. "You've business with me, haven't you?" he said.

"Right on the first guess! To win your Junior Spy badge and pocket decoder, tell me what an elephant is."

"Huh, sir?"

"An elephant is a mouse built to government specifications. Or else a mouse is a transistorized elephant." Abrams didn't look jovial. He was delaying.

Flandry took a nervous sip. "If it's confidential," he asked, "should we be here?"

"Safer than the Embassy. That's only probably debugged, not certainly, and old-fashioned listening at doors hasn't ever quite gone out of style."

"But a Merseian runabout—"

"We're safe. Take my word." Abrams glared at the cigar he rolled between his fingers. "Son, I need you for a job of work and I need you bad. Could be dangerous and sure to be nasty. Are you game?"

Flandry's heart bumped. "I'd better be, hadn't I?"

Abrams cocked his head at the other. "Not bad repartee for a nineteen-year-old. But do you mean it, down in your bones?"

"Yes, sir." *I think so.*

"I believe you. I have to." Abrams took a drink and a long drag. Abruptly:

"Look here, let's review the circumstances as she stands. I reckon you have the innate common sense to see what's written on your eyeballs, that Brechdan hasn't got the slightest intention of settling the squabble on Starkad. I thought for a while, maybe he figured to offer us peace there in exchange for some other thing he really wants. But if that were the case, he wouldn't have thrown a triple gee field onto the parley the way he has. He'd have come to the point with the unavoidable minimum of waste motion. Merseians don't take a human's glee in forensics. If Brechdan wanted to strike a bargain, Hauksberg would be home on Terra right now with a preliminary report.

"Instead, Brechdan's talkboys have stalled, with one quibble and irrelevancy after another. Even Hauksberg's getting a gutful. Which I think is the reason Brechdan personally invited him and aides to Dhangodhan for a week or two of shootin' and fishin'. Partly because that

makes one more delay by itself; partly to smooth
our viscount's feelings with a 'gesture of good
will.'" The quotes were virtually audible. "I
was invited too, but begged off on ground of
wanting to continue my researches. If he'd
thought of it, Brechdan'd likely have broken custom and asked Donna Persis, as an added in-
ducement for staying in the mountains a while.
Unless, hm, he's provided a little variety for his
guests. There are humans in Merseians service,
you know."

Flandry nodded. For a second he felt disappointment. Hauksberg's absence when he returned had seemed to provide a still better opportunity than Hauksberg's frequent exhaustion
in Ardaig. But excitement caught him. Never
mind Persis. She was splendid recreation, but
that was all.

"I might be tempted to think like his
Lordship, Brechdan is fundamentally sincere,"
he said. "The average Merseian is, I'm sure."

"Sure you're sure. And you're right. Fat lot of
difference that makes."

"But anyhow, Starkad *is* too important.
Haven't you told that idi—Lord Hauksberg so?"

"I finally got tired of telling him," Abrams
said. "What have I got to argue from except a
prejudice based on experiences he's never
shared?"

"I wonder why Brechdan agreed to receive a
delegation in the first place."

"Oh, easier to accept than refuse, I suppose.
Or it might have suited his plans very well. He
doesn't want total war yet. I do believe he orig-

inally intended to send us packing in fairly
short order. What hints I've gathered suggest
that another issue has arisen—that he's planning quite a different move, not really germane
to Starkad—and figures to put a better face on it
by acting mild toward us. God alone knows how
long we'll be kept here. Could be weeks more."

Abrams leaned forward. "And meanwhile,"
he continued, "anything could happen. I came
with some hopes of pulling off a hell of a good
stunt just before we left. And it did look hopeful
at first, too. Could give us the truth about
Starkad. Well, things have dragged on, con-
figurations have changed, my opportunity may
vanish. We've got to act soon, or our chance of
acting at all will be mighty poor."

This is it, Flandry thought, and a part of him
jeered at the banality, while he waited with
hardheld breath.

"I don't want to tell you more than I've got
to," Abrams said. "Just this: I've learned where
Brechdan's ultrasecret file is. That wasn't hard;
everybody knows about it. But I think I can get
an agent in there. The next and worst problem
will be to get the information out, and not have
the fact we're doing so be known.

"I dare not wait till we all go home. That gives
too much time for too many things to go wrong.
Nor can I leave beforehand by myself. I'm too
damn conspicuous. It'd look too much as if I'd
finished whatever I set out to do. Hauksberg
himself might forbid me to go, precisely because
he suspected I was going to queer his pea-ea-
eace mission. Or else . . . I'd be piloted out of the

system by Merseians. Brechdan's bully boys could arrange an unfortunate accident merely as a precaution. They could even spirit me off to a hynoprobe room, and what happened to me there wouldn't matter a hoot-let compared to what'd happen to our forces later. I'm not being melodramatic, son. Those are the unbuttered facts of life."

Flandry sat still. "You want me to convey the data out, if you get them," he said.

"Ah, you do know what an elephant is."

"You must have a pretty efficient pipeline to Merseian HQ."

"I've seen worse," Abrams said rather smugly.

"Couldn't have been developed in advance." Flandry spoke word by word. Realization was freezing him. "Had it been, why should you yourself come here? Must be something you got hold of on Starkad, and hadn't a chance to instruct anyone about that you trusted and who could be spared."

"Let's get down to business," Abrams said fast.

"No. I want to finish this."

"You?"

Flandry stared past Abrams like a blind man. "If the contact was that good," he said, "I think you got a warning about the submarine attack on Ujanka. And you didn't tell. There was no preparation. Except for a fluke, the city would have been destroyed." He rose. "I saw Tigeries killed in the streets."

"Sit down!"

"One mortar planted on a wharf would have gotten that boat." Flandry started to walk away. His voice lifted. "Males and females and little cubs, blown apart, buried alive under rubble, and you did nothing!"

Abrams surged to his feet and came after him. "Hold on, there," he barked.

Flandry whirled on him. "Why the obscenity should I?"

Abrams grabbed the boy's wrists. Flandry tried to break free. Abrams held him where he was. Rage rode across the dark Chaldean face. "You listen to me," Abrams said. "I did know. I knew the consequences of keeping silent. When you saved that town, I went down on my knees before God. I'd've done it before you if you could've understood. But suppose I had acted. Runei is no man's fool. He'd have guessed I had a source, and there was exactly one possibility, and after he looked into that my pipeline would've been broken like a dry stick. And I was already developing it as a line into Brechdan's own files. Into the truth about Starkad. How many lives might that save? Not only human. Tigery, Siravo, hell, Merseian! Use your brains, Dom. You must have a couple of cells clicking together between those ears. Sure, this is a filthy game. But it has one point of practicality which is also a point of honor. You don't compromise your sources. You don't!"

Flandry struggled for air. Abrams let him go. Flandry went back to his lounger, collapsed in it, and drank deep. Abrams stood waiting.

Flandry looked up. "I'm sorry, sir," he got

out. "Overwrought, I guess."

"No excuses needed." Abrams clapped his shoulder. "You had to learn sometime. Might as well be now. And you know, you give me a tinge of hope. I'd begun to wonder if anybody was left on our side who played the game for anything but its own foul sake. When you get some rank— Well, we'll see."

He sat down too. Silence lay between them for a while.

"I'm all right now, sir," Flandry ventured.

"Good," Abrams grunted. "You'll need whatever all rightness you can muster. The best way I can see to get that information out soon involves a pretty dirty trick too. Also a humiliating one. I'd like to think you can hit on a better idea, but I've tried and failed."

Flandry gulped. "What is it?"

Abrams approached the core gingerly. "The problem is this," he said. "I do believe we can raid that file unbeknownst. Especially now while Brechdan is away, and the three others who I've found have access to that certain room. But even so, it'd look too funny if anyone left right after who didn't have a plausible reason. You can have one."

Flandry braced himself. "What?"

"Well . . . if Lord Hauksberg caught you *in flagrante delicto* with his toothsome traveling companion—"

That would have unbraced a far more sophisticated person. Flandry leaped from his seat. "Sir!"

"Down, boy. Don't tell me the mice haven't been playing while the cat's elsewhere. You've been so crafty that I don't think anybody else guesses, even in our gossipy little enclave. Which augurs well for your career in Intelligence. But son, I work close to you. When you report draggle-tailed on mornings after I noticed Lord Hauksberg was dead tired and took a hypnotic; when I can't sleep and want to get some work done in the middle of the night and you aren't in your room; when you and she keep swapping glances—Must I spell every word? No matter. I don't condemn you. If I weren't an old man with some eccentric ideas about my marriage, I'd be jealous.

"But this does give us our chance. All we need do is keep Persis from knowing when her lord and master is coming back. She don't mix much with the rest of the compound—can't say I blame her—and you can provide the distraction to make sure. Then the message sent ahead—which won't be to her personally anyhow, only to alert the servants in the expectation they'll tell everyone—I'll see to it that the word doesn't reach her. For the rest, let nature take its course."

"No!" Flandry raged.

"Have no fears for her," Abrams said. "She may suffer no more than a scolding. Lord Hauksberg is pretty tolerant. Anyway, he ought to be. If she does lose her position . . . our corps has a slush fund. She can be supported in reasonable style on Terra till she hooks someone else. I really don't have the impression she'd be heartbroken at having to trade Lord Hauksberg in on a newer model."

"But—" Confound that blush! Flandry stared

at the deck. His fists beat on his knees. "She trusts me. I can't."

"I said this was a dirty business. Do you flatter yourself she's in love with you?"

"Well—uh—"

"You do. I wouldn't. But supposing she is, a psych treatment for something that simple is cheap, and she's cool enough to get one. I've spent more time worrying about you."

"What about me?" asked Flandry miserably.

"Lord Hauksberg has to retaliate on you. Whatever his private feelings, he can't let something like this go by; because the whole compound, hell, eventually all Terra is going to know, if you handle the scene right. He figures on dispatching a courier home a day or two after he gets back from Dhangodhan, with a progress report. You'll go on the same boat, in disgrace, charged with some crime like disrespect for hereditary authority.

"Somewhere along the line—I'll have to work out the details as we go—my agent will nobble the information and slip it to me. I'll pass it to you. Once on Terra, you'll use a word I'll give you to get the ear of a certain man. Afterward— son, you're in. You shouldn't be fumbly-diddling this way. You should be licking my boots for such an opportunity to get noticed by men who count. My boots need polishing."

Flandry shifted, looked away, out to the clouds which drifted across the green and brown face of Merseia. The motor hum pervaded his skull.

"What about you?" he asked finally. "And the rest?"

"We'll stay here till the farce is over."

"But . . . no, wait, sir . . . so many things could go wrong. Deadly wrong."

"I know. That's the risk you take."

"You more." Flandry swung back to Abrams. "I might get free without a hitch. But if later there's any suspicion—"

"They won't bother Persis," Abrams said. "She's not worth the trouble. Nor Hauksberg. He's an accredited diplomat, and arresting him would damn near be an act of war."

"But you, sir! You may be accredited to him, but—"

"Don't fret," Abrams said. "I aim to die of advanced senile decay. If that starts looking un- likely, I've got my blaster. I won't get taken alive and I won't go out of the cosmos alone. Now: are you game?"

It took Flandry's entire strength to nod.

Chapter Twelve

Two days later, Abrams departed the Embassy again in his boat. Ahead, on the ocean's rim, smoldered a remnant of sunset. The streets of Ardaig glowed ever more visible as dusk deepened into night. Windows blinked to life, the Admiralty beacon flared like a sudden red sun. Traffic was heavy, and the flier's robopilot must keep signals constantly flickering between itself, others, and the nearest routing stations. The computers in all stations were still more tightly linked, by a web of data exchange. Its nexus was Central Control, where the total pattern was evaluated and the three-dimensional grid of airlanes adjusted from minute to minute for optimum flow.

Into this endless pulsation, it was easy to inject a suitably heterodyned and scrambled message. None but sender and recipient would know. Nothing less than a major job of stochastic analysis could reveal to an outsider that occasional talk had passed (and even then, would not show what the talk had been about). Neither the boat nor the Terran Embassy possessed the equipment for that.

From the darkness where he lay, Dwyr the

Hook willed a message forth. Not sent: willed, as one wills a normal voice to speak; for his nerve endings meshed directly with the circuits of the vessel and he felt the tides in the electronic sea which filled Ardaig like a living creature feeling the tides in its own blood.

"Prime Observer Three to Intelligence Division Thirteen." A string of code symbols followed. "Prepare to receive report."

Kilometers away, a Merseian tautened at his desk. He was among the few who knew about Dwyr; they alternated shifts around the clock. Thus far nothing of great interest had been revealed to them. But that was good. It proved the Terran agent, whom they had been warned was dangerous, had accomplished nothing. "Division Thirteen to Prime Three. Dhech on duty. Report."

"Abrams has boarded alone and instructed the 'pilot to take him to the following location." Dwyr specified. He identified the place as being in a hill suburb, but no more; Ardaig was not his town.

"Ah, yes," Dhech nodded. "Fodaich Qwynn's home. We knew already Abrams was going there tonight."

"Shall I expect anything to happen?" Dwyr asked.

"No, you'll be parked for several hours, I'm sure, and return him to the Embassy. He's been after Qwynn for some time for an invitation, so they could talk privately and at length about certain questions of mutual interest. Today he pressed so hard that Qwynn found it impossible not to invite him for tonight without open discourtesy."

"Is that significant?"

"Hardly. We judge Abrams makes haste simply because he got word that his chief will return tomorrow with the Hand of the Vach Ynvory, great protector of us all. Thereafter he can expect once more to be enmeshed in diplomatic maneuverings. This may be his last chance to see Qwynn."

"I could leave the boat and spy upon them," Dwyr offered.

"No need. Qwynn is discreet, and will make his own report to us. If Abrams hopes to pick up a useful crumb, he will be disappointed. Quite likely, though, his interest is academic. He appears to have abandoned any plans he may have entertained for conducting espionage."

"He has certainly done nothing suspicious under my surveillance," Dwyr said, "in a boat designed to make him think it ideal for hatching plots. I will be glad when he leaves. This has been a drab assignment."

"Honor to you for taking it," Dhech said. "No one else could have endured so long." A burst of distortion made him start. "What's that?"

"Some trouble with the communicator," said Dwyr, who had willed the malfunction. "It had better be checked soon. I might lose touch with you."

"We'll think of some excuse to send a technician over in a day or so. Hunt well."

"Hunt well." Dwyr broke the connection. Through the circuits, which included scanners, he observed both outside and inside the hull. The boat was slanting down toward its destination. Abrams had risen and donned a formal cloak. Dwyr activated a speaker. "I have contacted Division Thirteen," he said. "They are quite unsuspicious. I planted the idea that my sender may go blank, in case for some reason they try to call me while I am absent."

"Good lad." Abrams' tones were likewise calm, but he took a last nervous pull on his cigar and stubbed it out viciously. "Now remember, I'll stay put for several hours. Should give you ample time to do your job and slip back into this shell. But if anything goes wrong, I repeat, what matters is the information. Since we can't arrange a safe drop, and since mine host tonight will have plenty of retainers to arrest me, in emergency you get hold of Ensign Flandry and tell him. You recall he should be in Lord Hauksberg's suite, or else his own room; and I've mapped the Embassy for you. Now also, make damn sure the phone here is hooked to the 'pilot, so you or he can call this boat to him. I haven't told him about you, but I have told him to trust absolutely whoever has the key word. You remember?"

"Yes, of course. *Meshuggah*. What does it mean?"

"Never mind." Abrams grinned.

"What about rescuing you?"

"Don't. You'd come to grief for certain. Besides, my personal chances are better if I invoke diplomatic immunity. I hope, though, our stunt will go off without a hitch." Abrams looked about. "I can't see you, Dwyr, and I can't shake your hand, but I'd sure like to. And one day I plan to." The boat grounded. "Good luck."

Dwyr's electronic gaze followed the stocky figure out, down the ramp and across the small parking strip in the garden. A pair of clan members saluted the Terran and followed him toward the mansion. A screen of trees soon hid them. No one else was in view. Shadows lay heavy around the boat.

Let us commence, Dwyr thought. His decision was altogether unperturbed. Once he would have tasted fear, felt his heart thud, clutched to him the beloved images of wife and young and their home upon far Tanis. Courage would have followed, sense of high purpose, joy of proving his maleness by a leap between the horns of death—thus did you know yourself wholly alive! But those things had departed with his body. He could no longer recollect how they felt. The one emotion which never left him, like an unhealing wound, was the wish to know all emotions again.

He had a few. Workmanship gave a cerebral pleasure. Hate and fury could still burn . . . though cold, cold. He wondered if they were not mere habits, engraved in the synapses of his brain.

He stirred in the womblike cubicle where he lay. Circuit by circuit, his living arm disconnected his machine parts from the boat. For a moment he was totally cut off. How many hours till sensory deprivation broke down his sanity? He had been kept supplied with impressions of the world, and asleep he never dreamed. But suppose he stayed where he was, in this lightless, soundless, currentless nothing. When he began to hallucinate, would he imagine himself back on Tanis? Or would Sivilla his wife come to him?

Nonsense. The objective was that he come to her, whole. He opened a panel and glided forth. The systems that kept him functional were mounted in a tiny gravsled. His first task would be to exchange it for a more versatile body.

Emerging, he floated low, keeping to the bushes and shadows. Stars were plainer to see here, away from the city web and the beacon flare which lay at the foot of these hills. He noted the sun of Tanis, where Merseians had made their homes among mountains and forests, where Sivilla lived yet with their children. She thought him dead, but they told him she had not remarried and the children were growing up well.

Was that another lie?

The problem of weaving his way unseen into the city occupied a bare fragment of Dwyr's attention. His artificial senses were designed for this kind of task, and he had a decade of experience with them. Mostly he was remembering.

"I was reluctant to leave," he had confessed to Abrams on Starkad. "I was happy. What was the conquest of Janair to me? They spoke of the glory of the race. I saw nothing except that other race, crushed, burned, enslaved as we advanced. I would have fought for my liberty as they did for theirs. Instead, being required to do my military service, I was fighting to rob them of their

birthright. Do not misunderstand. I stayed loyal
to my Roidhun and my people. It was they who
betrayed me."

"They sure as the seventh hell did," Abrams
said.

That was after the revelation which knocked
Dwyr's universe apart. "What?" Abrams had
roared. "You could not be regenerated? Impossible!"

"But radiation damage to the cells—"

"With that kind of radiation damage, you'd've
been dead. The basic gene pattern governs the
organism throughout life. If everything mutated
at once, life would have to stop. And the regeneration process uses the chromosomes for a
chemical template. No, they saw their chance to
make a unique tool out of you, and lied. I suppose they must've planted an unconscious men-
tal block too, so you'd never think to study basic
biomedicine for yourself, and avoid situations
where somebody might tell you. God! I've seen
some vile tricks in my time, but this one takes the
purple shaft, with pineapple clusters."

"You can heal me?" Dwyr screamed.

"Our chemosurgeons can. But slow down.
Let's think a bit. I could order the job done on
you, and would as a matter of ethics. Still, you'd
be cut off from your family. What we ought to do
is smuggle them out also. We could resettle you
on an Imperial planet. And I haven't the authority to arrange that. Not unless you rate it. Which
you could, by serving as a double agent."

"To you too, then, I am nothing but a tool."

"Easy. I didn't say that. I just said that get-

ting back your family won't come cheap. It'll involve some risk to the crew who fetch them.
You've got to earn a claim on us. Willing?"

Oh, very willing!

As he darted between towers, Dwyr was no
more conspicuous than a nightbird. He could
easily reach the place assigned him, on an upper
level of a control station where only computers
dwelt, without being noticed. That had been arranged on Brechdan Ironrede's own command.
The secret of Dwyr's existence was worth taking
trouble to preserve. A recognition lock opened
for him and he glided into a room crowded with
his bodies and attachments. There was nothing
else; an amputated personality did not carry
around the little treasures of a mortal.

He had already chosen what to take. After de-
taching from the sled, he hitched himself to the
biped body which lay stretched out like a metal
corpse. For those moments he was without any
senses but sight, hearing, a dim touch and
kinesthesia, a jab of pain through what remained
of his tissues. He was glad when he had finished
making the new connections.

Rising, he lumbered about and gathered what
else he would need and fastened it on: special
tools and sensors, a gravity impeller, a blaster.
How weak and awkward he was. He much preferred being a vehicle or a gun. Metal and plastic
did not substitute well for cells, nerves, muscles,
the marvelous structure which was bone. But tonight an unspecialized shape was required.

Last came some disguise. He could not pass
for Merseian (after what had been done to him)

but he could look like a spacesuited human or
Iskeled. The latter race had long ago become re-
signed to the domination of his, and furnished
many loyal personnel. No few had been granted
Merseian citizenship. It had less significance
than the corresponding honor did for Terra, but
it carried certain valuable privileges.

Ready. Dwyr left his room and took to the air
again, openly this time. Admiralty House grew
before him, a gaunt mountain where caves
glared and the beacon made a volcano spout. A
sound of machines mumbled through the sky he
clove. He sensed their radiation as a glow, a
tone, a rising wave. Soaring, he approached the
forbidden zone and spoke, on a tight beam, those
passwords Brechdan had given him. "Absolute
security," he added. "My presence is to be kept
secret."

When he landed on the flange, an officer had
joined the sentries. "What is your business on
this level?" the Merseian demanded. "Our protector the Hand is not in Ardaig."

"I know," Dwyr said. "I am at his direct orders, to conduct some business inside. That is as
much as I am allowed to tell you. You and these
males will admit me, and let me out in a while,
and forget I was ever here. It is not to be men-
tioned to anyone in any circumstances. The matter is sealed."

"Under what code?"

"Triple Star."

The officer saluted. "Pass."

Dwyr went down the corridor. It echoed a little to his footfalls. When he reached the ante-

room, he heard the buzz of work in the offices
beyond; but he stood alone at the door of the
vault. He had never seen this place. However,
the layout was no secret and had been easy to
obtain.

The door itself, though—He approached with
immense care, every sensor at full amplification.
The scanners saw he was not authorized to go
by, and might trigger an alarm. No. Nothing.
After all, people did use this route on certain er-
rands. He removed the false glove on his robot
arm and extended tendrils to the plates.

They reacted. By induction, his artificial neu-
rones felt how signals moved into a comparison
unit and were rejected. So now he must feed in
pulses which would be interpreted as the right
eye and hand patterns. Slowly . . . slowly, micro-
metric exactitude, growing into the assembly,
feeling with it, calling forth the response he
wanted, a seduction which stirred instincts until
his machine heart and lungs moved rapidly and
he was lost to the exterior world . . . *there!*

The door opened, ponderous and silent. He
trod through. It closed behind him. In a black
chamber, he confronted a thing which shone like
opal.

Except for possessing a recognition trigger of
its own, the molecular file was no different from
numerous others he had seen. Still full of oneness
with the flow of electrons and intermeshed fields,
still half in a dream, he activated it. The operation code was unknown to him, but he detected
that not much information was stored here.
Stood to reason, the thought trickled at the back

of his awareness. No individual could single-handedly steer an empire. The secrets which Brechdan reserved for himself and his three comrades must be few, however tremendous. He, Dwyr the Hook, need not carry on a lengthy random search before he got the notes on Starkad.

Eidhafor: Report on another Hand who often opposed Brechdan in Council; data which could be used, at need, to break him.

Maxwell Crawford: Ha, the Terran Emperor's governor of the Arachnean System was in Merseian pay. A sleeper, kept in reserve.

Therayn: So that was what preoccupied Brechdan's friends. Abrams was evidently right; Hauksberg was being delayed so as to be present, influenceable, when the news broke.

Starkad!

Onto the screen flashed a set of numbers. 0.17847,3° 14' 22" .591, 1818 h.3264. . . . Dwyr memorized them automatically, while he stood rigid with shock. Something had happened in the file. An impulse had passed. Its transient radiation had given his nerves a split second's wispy shiver. Might be nothing. But better finish up and get out fast!

The screen blanked. Dwyr's fingers moved with blurring speed. The numbers returned. Why—they were the whole secret. They were what Starkad was about. And he didn't know what they meant.

Let Abrams solve this riddle. Dwyr's task was done. Almost.

He went toward the door. It opened and he stepped into the antechamber. The door behind, to the main offices, was agape. A guard waited, blaster poised. Two more were hurrying toward him. Desk workers scuttled from their path.

"What is the matter?" Dwyr rapped. Because he could not feel terror or dismay, a blue flame of wrath sheeted through him.

Sweat glistened on the guard's forehead and ran down over the brow ridges. "You were in his secretorium," he whispered.

So terrible is the magic in those numbers that the machine has had one extra geas laid upon it. When they are brought forth, it calls for help.

"I am authorized," Dwyr said. "How else do you think I could enter?"

He did not really believe his burglary could long remain unknown. Too many had seen. But he might gain a few hours. His voice belled. "No one is to speak of this to anyone else whatsoever, not even among yourselves. The business is sealed under a code which the officer of the night knows. He can explain its significance to you. Let me pass."

"No." The blaster trembled.

"Do you wish to be charged with insubordination?"

"I . . . I must take that risk, foreseer. We all must. You are under arrest until the Hand clears you in person."

Dwyr's motors snarled. He drew his own gun as he flung himself aside. Fire and thunder broke free. The Merseian collapsed in a seared heap. But he had shot first. Dwyr's living arm was blasted off.

He did not go into shock. He was not that

alive. Pain flooded him, he staggered for a moment in blindness. Then the homeostats in his prostheses reacted. Chemical stimulation poured from tubes into veins. Electronic impulses at the control of a microcomputer joined the nerve currents, damped out agony, forced the flesh to stop bleeding. Dwyr whirled and ran.

The others came behind him. Guns crashed anew. He staggered from their impact. Looking down, he saw a hole drilled in him from back to breast. The energy beam must have wrecked some part of the mechanism which kept his brain alive. What part, he didn't know. Not the circulation, for he continued moving. The filtration system, the purifier, the osmotic balancer? He'd find out soon enough. *Crash!* His left leg went immobile. He fell. The clatter was loud in the corridor. Why hadn't he remembered his impeller? He willed the negagravity field to go on. Still he lay like a stone. The Merseians pounded near, shouting. He flipped the manual switch and rose.

The door to the flange stood shut. At top speed, he tore the panels asunder. A firebolt from a guard rainbowed off his armor. Out . . . over the verge . . . down toward shadow!

And shadows were closing in on him. His machinery must indeed have been struck in a vital spot. It would be good to die. No, not yet. He must hang on a while longer. Get by secret ways to the Terran Embassy; Abrams was too far, and effectively a prisoner in any event. Get to the Embassy—don't faint!—find this Flandry—how it roared in his head—summon the airboat—the

fact that his identity was unknown to his
pursuers until they called Brechdan would help
—try for an escape—if you must faint, hide
yourself first, and do not die, do not die—perhaps Flandry can save you. If nothing else, you
will have revenged yourself a little if you find
him. Darkness and great rushing waters. . . .

Dwyr the Hook fled alone over the night city.

Chapter Thirteen

That afternoon, Abrams had entered the office where Flandry was at work. He closed the door and said, "All right, son, you can knock off."

"Glad to," Flandry said. Preparing a series of transcribed interviews for the computer was not his idea of sport, especially when the chance of anything worthwhile being buried in them hovered near zero. He shoved the papers across his desk, leaned back, and tensed cramped muscles against each other. "How come?"

"Lord Hauksberg's valet just called the majordomo here. They're returning tomorrow morning. Figure to arrive about Period Four, which'd be fourteen or fifteen hundred Thursday, Terran Prime Meridian."

Flandry sucked in a breath, wheeled his chair about, and stared up at his chief. "Tonight—?"

"Uh-huh," Abrams nodded. "I won't be around. For reasons you don't need to know, except that I want attention focused my way, I'm going to wangle me an invite to a local Poo-Bah."

"And a partial alibi, if events go sour." Flandry spoke with only the top half of his mind engaged. The rest strove to check pulse, lungs, perspiration, tension. It had been one thing to dash impulsively against a Merseian watercraft. It would be quite another to play against incalculable risks, under rules that would change minute by minute, in cold blood, for *x* many hours.

He glanced at his chrono. Persis was doubtless asleep. Unlike Navy men, who were trained to adapt to nonterrestrial diurnal periods by juggling watches, the Embassy civilians split Merseia's rotation time into two short, complete "days." She followed the practice. "I suppose I'm to stand by in reserve," Flandry said. "Another reason for our separating."

"Smart boy," Abrams said. "You deserve a pat and a dog biscuit. I hope your lady fair will provide the same."

"I still hate to . . . to use her this way."

"In your position, I'd enjoy every second. Besides, don't forget your friends on Starkad. They're being shot at."

"Y-yes." Flandry rose. "What about, uh, emergency procedure?"

"Be on tap, either in her place or yours. Our agent will identify himself by a word I'll think of. He may look funny, but trust him. I can't give you specific orders. Among other reasons, I don't like saying even this much here, however unbuggable we're alleged to be. Do whatever seems best. Don't act too damned fast. Even if the gaff's been blown, you might yet manage to ride out the aftermath. But don't hesitate too long, either. If you must move, then: no heroics, no rescues, no consideration for any living soul.

Plain get that information out!"

"Aye, aye, sir."

"Sounds more like 'I-yi-yi, sir!'," Abrams laughed. He seemed at ease. "Let's hope the whole operation proves dull and sordid. Good ones are, you know. Shall we review a few details?"

—Later, when twilight stole across the city, Flandry made his way to the principal guest suite. The corridor was deserted. Ideally, Lord Hauksberg should come upon his impudence as a complete surprise. That way, the viscount would be easier to provoke into rage. However, if this didn't work—if Persis learned he was expected and shooed Flandry out—the scandal must be leaked to the entire compound. He had a scheme for arranging that.

He chimed on the door. After a while, her voice came drowsy. "Who's there?" He waved at the scanner. "Oh. What is it, Ensign?"

"May I come in, Donna?"

She stopped to throw on a robe. Her hair was tumbled and she was charmingly flushed. He entered and closed the door. "We needn't be so careful," he said. "Nobody watching. My boss is gone for the night and a good part of tomorrow." He laid hands on her waist. "I couldn't pass up the chance."

"Nor I." She kissed him at great length.

"Why don't we simply hide in here?" he suggested.

"I'd adore to. But Lord Oliveira—"

"Call the butler. Explain you're indisposed and want to be alone till tomorrow. Hm?"

"Not very polite. Hell, I'll do it. We have so little time, darling."

Flandry stood in back of the vidiphone while she talked. If the butler should mention that Hauksberg was due in, he must commence Plan B. But that didn't happen, as curt as Persis was. She ordered food and drink 'chuted here and switched off. He deactivated the instrument. "I don't want any distractions," he explained.

"What wonderful ideas you have," she smiled.

"Right now I have still better ones."

"Me too." Persis rejoined him.

Her thoughts included refreshments. The Embassy larder was lavishly stocked, and the suite had a small server to prepare meals which she knew well how to program. They began with eggs Benedict, caviar, akvavit, and champagne. Some hours later followed Perigordian duck, with trimmings, and Bordeaux. Flandry's soul expanded. "My God," he gusted, "where has this sort of thing been all my life?"

Persis chuckled. "I believe I have launched you on a new career. You have the makings of a gourmet first class."

"So, two causes why I shall never forget you."

"Only two?"

"No, I'm being foolish. Aleph-null causes at the minimum. Beauty, brains, charm—Well, why'm I just talking?"

"You have to rest sometime. And I do love to hear you talk."

"Hn? I'm not much in that line. After the people and places you've known—"

"What places?" she said with a quick,

astonishing bitterness. "Before this trip, I was
never further than Luna. And the people, the
articulate, expensive, brittle people, their in-
trigues and gossip, the shadow shows that are
their adventures, the words they live by—words,
nothing but words, on and on and on—No,
Dominic my dearest, you've made me realize
what I was missing. You've pulled down a wall
for me that was shutting off the universe."

Did I do you any favor? He dared not let conscience stir, he drowned it in the fullness of this
moment.

They were lying side by side, savoring an ancient piece of music, when the door recognized
Lord Hauksberg and admitted him.

"Persis? I say, where—Great Emperor!"

He stopped cold in the bedroom archway.
Persis smothered a scream and snatched for her
robe. Flandry jumped to his feet. *But it's still
dark! What's happened?*

The blond man looked altogether different in
green hunting clothes and belted blaster. Sun
and wind had darkened his face. For an instant
that visage was fluid with surprise. Then the
lines congealed. The eyes flared like blue stars.
He clapped hand to weapon butt. "Well, well,"
he said.

"Mark—" Persis reached out.

He ignored her. "So you're the indisposition
she had," he said to Flandry.

Here we go. Off schedule, but lift gravs anyway. The
boy felt blood course thickly, sweat trickle down
ribs; worse than fear, he was aware how ludi-

crous he must look. He achieved a grin. "No, my
lord. You are."

"What d'you mean?"

"You weren't being man enough." Flandry's
belly grew stiff, confronting that gun. Strange to
hear Mozart lilting on in the background.

The blaster stayed sheathed. Hauksberg
moved only to breathe. "How long's this been
between you?"

"It was my fault, Mark," Persis cried. "All
mine." Tears whipped over her cheeks.

"No, my sweet, I insist," Flandry said. "My
idea entirely. I must say, my lord, you weren't
nice to arrive unannounced. Now what?"

"Now you're under nobleman's arrest, you
whelp," Hauksberg said. "Put on some clothes.
Go to your quarters and stay there."

Flandry scrambled to obey. On the surface,
everything had gone smoothly, more so than expected. Too much more so. Hauksberg's tone
was not furious; it was almost absentminded.

Persis groped toward him. "I tell you, Mark,
I'm to blame," she wept. "Let him alone. Do
what you want to me, but not him!"

Hauksberg shoved her away. "Stop blub-
berin'," he snapped. "D' you think I care a pip
on a 'scope about your peccadillos, at a time like
this?"

"What's happened?" Flandry asked sharply.

Hauksberg turned and looked at him, up and
down, silent for an entire minute. "Wonder if
you really don't know," he said at the end.
"Wonder quite a lot."

"My lord, I don't!" Flandry's mind rocked.

Something *was* wrong.

"When word came to Dhangodhan, natur'lly we flitted straight back," Hauksberg said. "They're after Abrams this minute, on my authority. But you—what was your part?"

I've got to get out. Abrams' agent has to be able to reach me. "I don't know anything, my lord. I'll report to my room."

"Stop!"

Persis sat on the bed, face in hands, and sobbed. She wasn't loud.

"Stay right here," Hauksberg said. "Not a step, understand?" His gun came free. He edged from the chamber, keeping Flandry in sight, and went to the phone. "Hm. Turned off, eh?" He flipped the switch. "Lord Oliveira."

Silence lay thick while the phone hunted through its various scanner outlets. The screen flickered, the ambassador looked forth. "Hauksberg! What the devil?"

"Just returned," said the viscount. "We heard of an attempt to rifle Premier Brechdan's files. May have been a successful attempt, too; and the agent escaped. The premier accused me of havin' a finger in it. Obvious thought. Somebody wants to sabotage my mission."

"I—" Oliveira collected himself. "Not necessarily. Terra isn't the only rival Merseia has."

"So I pointed out. Prepare to do likewise at length when you're notified officially. But we've got to show good faith. I've deputed the Merseians to arrest Commander Abrams. He'll be fetched back here. Place him under guard."

"Lord Hauksberg! He's an Imperial officer,

and accredited to the diplomatic corps."

"He'll be detained by Terrans. By virtue of
my commission from his Majesty, I'm assumin'
command. No back talk if you don't want to be
relieved of your position."

Oliveira whitened but bowed. "Very good, my
lord. I must ask for this in properly recorded
form."

"You'll have it when I get the chance. Next,
this young fella Flandry, Abrams' assistant.
Happens I've got him on deck. Think I'll quiz
him a while myself. But have a couple of men
march him to detention when I give the word.
Meanwhile, alert your staff, start preparin'
plans, explanations, and disclaimers, and stand
by for a visit from Brechdan's foreign office."

Hauksberg cut the circuit. "Enough," he said.
"C'mon out and start talkin', you."

Flandry went. Nightmare hammered at him.
In the back of his head ran the thought: *Abrams
was right. You don't really want drama in these things.*
What'll happen to him?
To me? To Persis? To Terra?

"Sit down." Hauksberg pointed his gun at a
lounger and swung the barrel back at once. With
his free hand he pulled a flat case from his tunic
pocket. He appeared a little relaxed; had he
begun to enjoy the tableau?

Flandry lowered himself. *Psychological disadvan-
tage, looking upward. Yes we underestimated his
Lordship badly.* Persis stood in the archway, red-
eyed, hugging herself and gulping.

Hauksberg flipped open the case—an unruly
part of Flandry noticed how the chased silver

shone beneath the fluoroceiling—and stuck a cheroot between his teeth. "What's your role in this performance?" he asked.

"Nothing, my lord." Flandry stammered. "I don't know—I mean, if—if I were concerned, would I have been here tonight?"

"Might." Hauksberg returned the case and extracted a lighter. His glance flickered to Persis. "What about you, m' love?"

"I don't know anything," she whispered. "And neither does he. I swear it."

"Inclined to believe you." The lighter scritted and flared. "In this case, though, you've been rather cynic'lly used."

"He wouldn't!"

"Hm." Hauksberg dropped the lighter on a table and blew smoke from his nostrils. "Could be you both were duped. We'll find that out when Abrams is probed."

"You can't!" Flandry shouted. "He's an officer!"

"They certainly can on Terra, my boy. I'd order it done this very hour, and risk the repercussions, if we had the equipment. 'Course, the Merseians do. If necess'ry, I'll risk a much bigger blowback and turn him over to them. My mission's too important for legal pettifoggin'. You might save the lot of us a deal of grief by tellin' all, Ensign. If your testimony goes to prove we Terrans are not involved—d' you see?"

Give him a story, any story, whatever gets you away. Flandry's brain was frozen. "How could we have arranged the job?" he fumbled. "You saw what kind of surveillance we've been under."

"Ever hear about agents provocateurs? I never

believed Abrams came along for a ride."
Hauksberg switched the phone to Record. "Begin at the beginnin', continue to the end, and stop. Why'd Abrams co-opt you in the first place?"

"Well, I—that is, he needed an aide." *What actually did happen? Everything was so gradual. Step by step. I never really did decide to go into Intelligence. But somehow, here I am.*

Persis squared her shoulders. "Dominic had proven himself on Starkad," she said wretchedly. "Fighting for the Empire."

"Fine, sonorous phrase." Hauksberg tapped the ash from his cheroot. "Are you really infatuated with this lout? No matter. P'rhaps you can see anyhow that I'm workin' for the Empire myself. Work sounds less romantic than fight, but's a bit more useful in the long haul, eh? Go on, Flandry. What'd Abrams tell you he meant to accomplish?"

"He . . . he hoped to learn things. He never denied that. But spying, no. He's not stupid, my lord." *He's simply been outwitted.* "I ask you, how could he arrange trouble?"

"Leave the questions to me. When'd you first get together with Persis, and why?

"We—I—" Seeing the anguish upon her, Flandry knew in full what it meant to make an implement of a sentient being. "My fault. Don't listen to her. On the way—"

The door opened. There was no more warning than when Hauksberg had entered. But the thing which glided through, surely the lock was not keyed to that!

Persis shrieked. Hauksberg sprang back with

an oath. The thing, seared and twisted metal, blood starting afresh from the cauterized fragment of an arm, skin drawn tight and gray across bones in what was left of a face, rattled to the floor.

"Ensign Flandry," it called. The voice had volume yet, but no control, wavering across the scale and wholly without tone. Light came and went in the scanners which were eyes.

Flandry's jaws locked. Abrams' agent? Abrams' hope, wrecked and dying at his feet?

"Go on," Hauksberg breathed. The blaster crouched in his fist. "Talk to him."

Flandry shook his head till the sweat-drenched hair flew.

"Talk, I say," Hauksberg commanded. "Or I'll kill you and most surely give Abrams to the Merseians."

The creature which lay and bled before the now shut main door did not seem to notice. "Ensign Flandry. Which one is you? Hurry. *Meshuggah*. He told me to say *meshuggah*."

Flandry moved without thinking, from his lounger, down on his knees in the blood. "I'm here," he whispered.

"Listen." The head rolled, the eyes flickered more and more dimly, a servomotor rattled dry bearings inside the broken shell. "Memorize. In the Starkad file, these numbers."

As they coughed forth, one after the next in the duodecimals of Eriau, Flandry's training reacted. He need not understand, and did not; he asked for no repetitions; each phoneme was burned into his brain.

"Is that everything?" he asked with someone else's throat.

"Aye. The whole." A hand of metal tendrils groped until he clasped it. "Will you remember my name? I was Dwyr of Tanis, once called the Merry. They made me into this. I was planted in your airboat. Commander Abrams sent me. That is why he left this place, to release me unobserved. But an alarm order was on the Starkad reel. I was ruined in escaping. I would have come sooner to you but I kept fainting. You must phone for the boat and . . . escape, I think. Remember Dwyr."

"We will always remember."

"Good. Now let me die. If you open the main plate you can turn off my heart." The words wobbled insanely, but they were clear enough. "I cannot hold Sivilla long in my brain. It is poisoned and oxygen starved. The cells are going out, one by one. Turn off my heart."

Flandry disengaged the tendrils around his hand and reached for the hinged plate. He didn't see very well, nor could he smell the oil and scorched insulation.

"Hold off," Hauksberg said. Flandry didn't hear him. Hauksberg stepped close and kicked him. "Get away from there, I say. We want him alive."

Flandry lurched erect. "You can't."

"Can and will." Hauksberg's lips were drawn back, his chest rose and fell, the cheroot had dropped from his mouth into the spreading blood. "Great Emperor! I see the whole thing. Abrams had this double agent. He'd get the information, it'd be passed on to you, and you'd go home in disgrace when I caught you with Persis." He took a moment to give the girl a look of triumph. "You follow, my dear? You were nothin' but an object."

She strained away from them, one hand to her mouth, the other fending off the world. "Sivilla, Sivilla," came from the floor. "Oh, hurry!"

Hauksberg backed toward the phone. "We'll call a medic. I think if we're fast we can save this chap."

"But don't you understand?" Flandry implored. "Those numbers—there *is* something about Starkad—your mission never had a chance. We've got to let our people know!"

"Let me worry 'bout that," Hauksberg said. "You face a charge of treason."

"For trying to bail out the Empire?"

"For tryin' to sabotage an official delegation. Tryin' to make your own policy, you and Abrams. Think you're his Majesty? You'll learn better." Flandry took a step forward. The gun jerked. "Stand back! Soon blast you as not, y' know." Hauksberg's free hand reached for the phone.

Flandry stood over Dwyr, in a private Judgment Day.

Persis ran across the floor. "Mark, no!"

"Get away." Hauksberg held his gun on the boy.

Persis flung her arms around him. Suddenly her hands closed on his right wrist. She threw herself down, dragging the blaster with her. "Nicky!" she screamed.

Flandry sprang. Hauksberg hit Persis with his fist. She took the blow on her skull and hung on. Flandry arrived. Hauksberg struck at him. Flandry batted the hand aside with one arm. His other, stiff-fingered, drove into the solar plexus. Hauksberg doubled. Flandry chopped him behind the ear. He fell in a heap.

Flandry scooped up the blaster and punched the phone controls. "Airboat to Embassy," he ordered in Eriau.

Turning he strode back to Dwyr, knelt, and opened the frontal plate. Was this the switch he wanted? He undid its safety lock. "Good-bye, my friend," he said.

"One moment," wavered from the machine. "I lost her. So much darkness. Noise. . . . Now."

Flandry pulled the switch. The lights went out in the eyes and Dwyr lay still.

Persis sprawled by Hauksberg, shaken with crying. Flandry returned and raised her. "I'll have to make a dash," he said. "Might not finish it. Do you want to come?"

She clung to him. "Yes, yes, yes. They'd have killed you."

He embraced her one-armed, his other hand holding the blaster on Hauksberg, who stirred and choked. Wonder broke upon him like morning. "Why did you help me?" he asked low.

"I don't know. Take me away from here!"

"Well . . . you may have done something great for the human race. If that information really is important. It has to be. Go put on a dress and shoes. Comb your hair. Find me a clean pair of pants. These are all bloody. Be quick." She gripped him tighter and sobbed. He slapped her "Quick, I said! Or I'll have to leave you behind."

She ran. He nudged Hauksberg with his foot. "Up, my lord."

Hauksberg crawled to a stance. "You're crazy," he gasped. "Do you seriously expect to escape?"

"I seriously expect to try. Give me that holster belt." Flandry clipped it on. "We'll walk to the boat. If anyone asks, you're satisfied with my story, I've given you news which can't wait, and we're off to report in person to the Merseian authorities. At the first sign of trouble, I'll start shooting my way through, and you'll get the first bolt. Clear?"

Hauksberg rubbed the bruise behind his ear and glared.

With action upon him, Flandry lost every doubt. Adrenalin sang in his veins. Never had he perceived more sharply—this over-elegant room, the bloodshot eyes in front of him, the lovely sway of Persis re-entering in a fire-red gown, odors of sweat and anger, sigh of a ventilator, heat in his skin, muscle sliding across muscle, the angle of his elbow where he aimed the gun, by eternity, he was alive!

Having changed pants, he said, "Out we go. You first, my lord. Me a pace behind, as fits my rank. Persis next to you. Watch his face, darling. He might try to signal with it. If he blows a distress rocket from his nose, tell me and I'll kill him."

Her lips trembled. "No. You can't do that. Not to Mark."

"He'd've done it to me. We're committed, and not to any very genteel game. If he behaves himself he'll live, maybe. March."

As they left, Flandry saluted that which lay on the floor.

But he did not forget to screen the view of it with his body on his way out to the corridor, until the door shut behind him. Around a corner, they met a couple of young staffmen headed in their direction. "Is everything well, my lord?" one asked. Flandry's fingers twitched near his sheathed gun. He cleared his throat loudly.

Hauksberg made a nod. "Bound for Afon," he said. "Immediately. With these people."

"Confidential material in the suite," Flandry added. "Don't go in, and make sure nobody else does."

He was conscious of their stares, like bullets hitting his back. Could he indeed bluff his way clear? Probably. This is no police or military center, wasn't geared to violence, only created violence for others to quell. His danger lay beyond the compound. Surely, by now, the place was staked out. Dwyr had wrought a miracle in entering unseen.

They were stopped again in the lobby, and again got past on words. Outside, the garden lay aflash with dew under Lythyr and a sickle Neihevin. The air was cool. It quivered with distant machine sounds. Abrams' speedster had arrived. *O God, I have to leave him behind!* It sat on the parking strip, door open. Flandry urged Hauksberg and Persis aboard. He closed the door and waved on the lights. "Sit down at the console," he ordered his prisoner. "Persis, bring a towel from the head. My lord, we're about to talk our way through their security cordon. Will they believe we're harmlessly bound for Dhangodhan?"

Hauksberg's face contorted. "When Brechdan isn't here? Don't be ridiculous. C'mon, end the comedy, surrender and make things easier for yourself."

"Well, we'll do it the hard way. When we're challenged, tell 'em we're headed back to your ship to fetch some stuff we need to show Brechdan in connection with this episode."

"D'you dream they'll swallow that?"

"I think they might. Merseians aren't as rule-bound as Terrans. To them, it's in character for a boss noble to act on his own, without filing twenty different certificates first. If they don't believe us, I'll cut out the safety locks and ram a flier of theirs; so be good." Persis gave Flandry the towel. "I'm going to tie your hands. Cooperate or I'll slug you."

He grew conscious, then, of what power meant, how it worked. You kept the initiative. The other fellow's instinct was to obey, unless he was trained in self-mastery. But you dared not slack off the pressure for a second. Hauksberg slumped in his seat and gave no trouble.

"You won't hurt him, Nicky?" Persis begged.

"Not if I can avoid it. Haven't we troubles enough?" Flandry took the manual-pilot chair. The boat swung aloft.

A buzz came from the console. Flandry closed that circuit. A uniformed Merseian looked from the vidscreen. He could see nothing but their upper bodies. "Halt!" he ordered. "Security."

Flandry nudged Hauksberg. The viscount said, "Ah . . . we must go to my ship—" No human would have accepted a tale so lamely delivered. Nor would a Merseian educated in the subtleties of human behavior. But this was merely an officer of planetary police, assigned here because he happened to be on duty at the time of emergency. Flandry had counted on that.

"I shall check," said the green visage.

"Don't you realize?" Hauksberg snapped. "I am a diplomat. Escort us if you like. But you have no right to detain us. Move along, pilot."

Flandry gunned the gravs. The boat mounted. Ardaig fell away beneath, a glittering web, a spot of light. Turning in the after viewscreen, Flandry saw two black objects circle about and trail him. They were smaller than this vessel, but they were armed and armored.

"Nice work, there at the end, my lord," he said.

Hauksberg was rapidly regaining equilibrium. "You've done rather well yourself," he answered. "I begin to see why Abrams thinks you've potentialities."

"Thanks." Flandry concentrated on gaining speed. The counteracceleration field was not quite in tune; he felt a tug weight that, uncompensated, would have left him hardly able to breathe.

"But it won't tick, y' know," Hauksberg continued. "Messages are flyin' back and forth. Our escort'll get an order to make us turn back."

"I trust not. If I were them, I'd remember

Queen Maggy was declared harmless by her Merseian pilot. I'd alert my forces, but otherwise watch to see what you did. After all, Brechdan must be convinced you're sincere."

Ardaig was lost. Mountains gleamed in moonlight, and high plains, and cloud cover blanketing the planet in white. The wail of air grew thin and died. Stars trod forth, wintry clear.

"More I think about it," Hauksberg said, "more I'd like to have you on the right side. Peace needs able men even worse'n war does."

"Let's establish peace first, huh?" Flandry's fingers rattled computer keys. As a matter of routine, he had memorized the six elements of the spaceship's orbit around Merseia. Perturbation wouldn't have made much difference yet.

"That's what I'm tryin' for. We can have it, I tell you. You've listened to that fanatic Abrams. Give me a turn."

"Sure." Flandry spoke with half his attention. "Start by explaining why Brechdan keeps secrets about Starkad."

"D' you imagine we've no secrets? Brechdan has to defend himself. If we let mutual fear and hate build up, of course we'll get the big war."

"If we let Terra be painted into a corner, I agree, my lord, the planet incinerators will fly."

"Ever look at it from the Merseian viewpoint?"

"I didn't say it's wise to leave them with no out but to try and destroy us." Flandry shrugged. "That's for the statesmen, though, I'm told. I only work here. Please shut up and let me figure my approach curve."

Korych flamed over the edge of the world. That sunrise was gold and amethyst, beneath a million stars.

The communicator buzzed anew. "Foreseer," said the Merseian, "you may board your ship for a limited time provided we accompany you."

"Regrets," Hauksberg said. "But quite impossible. I'm after material which is for the eyes of Protector Brechdan alone. You are welcome to board as soon as I have it in this boat, and escort me straight to Castle Afon."

"I shall convey the foreseer's word to my superiors and relay their decision." Blankoff.

"You're wonderful," Persis said.

Hauksberg barked a laugh. "Don't fancy this impetuous young hero of yours includin' me in his Divine Wind dive." Seriously: "I s'pose you figure to escape in an auxiliary. Out of the question. Space patrol'll overhaul you long before you can go hyper."

"Not if I go hyper right away," Flandry said.

"But—snakes alive, boy! You know what the concentration of matter is, this near a sun. If a microjump lands you by a pebble, even—"

"Chance we take. Odds favor us, especially if we head out normally to the ecliptic plane."

"You'll be in detection range for a light-year. A ship with more legs can run you down. And will."

"You won't be there," Flandry said. "Dog your hatch. I'm busy."

The minutes passed. He scarcely noticed when the call came, agreeing that Hauksberg's party might board alone. He did reconstruct the reasoning behind that agreement. *Dronning Margrete* was unarmed and empty. Two or three men could not start her up in less than hours. Long before then, warcraft would be on hand to blast her. Hauksberg must be honest. Let him have his way and see what he produced.

The great tapered cylinder swam into sight. Flandry contacted the machines within and made rendezvous on instruments and trained senses. A boatlock gaped wide. He slid through. The lock closed, air rushed into the turret, he killed his motor and stood up. "I'll have to secure you, my lord," he said. "They'll find you when they enter."

Hauksberg regarded him. "You'll not reconsider?" he asked. "Terra shouldn't lose one like you."

"No. Sorry."

"Warn you, you'll be outlawed. I don't aim to sit idle and let you proceed. After what's happened, the best way I can show my bona fides is to cooperate with the Merseians in headin' you off."

Flandry touched his blaster. Hauksberg nodded. "You can delay matters a trifle by killin' me," he said.

"Have no fears. Persis, another three or four towels. Lie down on the deck, my lord."

Hauksberg did as he was told. Looking at the girl, he said: "Don't involve yourself. Stay with me. I'll tell 'em you were a prisoner too. Hate to waste women."

"They are in short supply hereabouts," Flandry agreed. "You'd better do it, Persis."

She stood quiet for a little. "Do you mean you forgive me, Mark?" she asked.

"Well, yes," Hauksberg said.

She bent and kissed him lightly. "I think I believe you. But no, thanks. I've made my choice."

"After the way your boy friend's treated you?"

"He had to. I have to believe that." Persis helped bind Hauksberg fast.

She and Flandry left the boat. The passageways glowed and echoed as they trotted. They hadn't far to go until they entered another turret. The slim hull of a main auxiliary loomed over them. Flandry knew the model: a lovely thing, tough and versatile, with fuel and supplies for a journey of several hundred parsecs. Swift, too; not that she could outpace a regular warcraft, but a stern chase is a long chase and he had some ideas about what to do if the enemy came near.

He made a quick check of systems. Back in the control room, he found Persis in the copilot's seat. "Will I bother you?" she asked timidly.

"Contrariwise," he said. "Keep silent, though, till we're in hyperdrive."

"I will," she promised. "I'm not a complete null, Nicky. You learn how to survive when you're a low-caste dancer. Different from space, of course. But this is the first time I've done anything for anyone but myself. Feels good. Scary, yes, but good."

He ran a hand across the tangled dark hair, smooth cheek and delicate profile, until his fingers tilted her chin and he bestowed his own kiss on her. "Thanks more'n I can say," he murmured. "I was doing this mainly on account of Max Abrams. It'd have been cold, riding alone with his ghost. Now I've got you to live for."

He seated himself. At his touch, the engine woke. "Here we go," he said.

Chapter Fourteen

Dawn broke over Ardaig, and from the tower on Eidh Hill kettledrums spoke their ancient prayer. Admiralty House cast its shadow across the Oiss, blue upon the mists that still hid early river traffic. Inland the shadow was black, engulfing Castle Afon.

Yet Brechdan Ironrede chose to receive the Terrans there instead of in his new eyrie. *He's shaken*, Abrams thought. *He's rallying quick, but he needs the help of his ancestors.*

Entering the audience chamber, a human was at first dazed, as if he had walked into a dream. He needed a moment to make sense of what he saw. The proportions of long, flagged floor, high walls, narrow windows arched at both top and bottom, sawtoothed vaulting overhead, were wrong by every Terran canon and nonetheless had a rightness of their own. The mask helmets on suits of armor grinned like demons. The patterns of faded tapestries and rustling battle banners held no human symbology. For this was Old Wilwidh, before the machine came to impose universal sameness. It was the wellspring of Merseia. You had to see a place like this if you would understand, in your bones, that Merseians would never be kin to you.

I wish my ancestors were around. Approaching the dais beside a silent Hauksberg, his boots resounding hollow, bitter incense in his nostrils, Abrams conjured up Dayan in his head. *I too have a place in the cosmos. Let me not forget.*

Black-robed beneath a dragon carved in black wood, The Hand of Vach Ynvory waited. The men bowed to him. He lifted a short spear and crashed it down in salute. Brusquely, he said: "This is an evil thing that has happened."

"What news, sir?" Hauksberg asked. His eyes were sunken and a tic moved one corner of his mouth.

"At latest report, a destroyer had locked detectors on Flandry's hyperwake. It can catch him, but time will be required, and meanwhile both craft have gone beyond detection range."

"The Protector is assured anew of my profoundest regrets. I am preferring charges against this malefactor. Should he be caught alive, he may be treated as a common pirate."

Yah, Abrams thought. *Dragged under a hypnoprobe and wrung dry. Well, he doesn't have any vital military secrets, and testimony about me can't get me in any deeper than I am. But please, let him be killed outright.*

"My lord," he said, "to you and the Hand I formally protest. Dominic Flandry holds an Imperial commission. At a minimum the law entitles him to a court-martial. Nor can his diplomatic immunity be removed by fiat."

"He was not accredited by his Majesty's government, but myself," Hauksberg snapped.

"The same applies to you, Abrams."

"Be still," Brechdan ordered him. Hauksberg gaped unbelieving at the massive green countenance. Brechdan's look was on Abrams. "Commander," the Merseian said, "when you were seized last night, you insisted that you had information I must personally hear. Having been told of this, I acceded. Do you wish to talk with me alone?"

Hang on, here we go. I boasted to Dom once, they wouldn't take me in any condition to blab, and they'd pay for whatever they got. Nu, here I am, whole-skinned and disarmed. If I'm to justify my brag, these poor wits will have to keep me out of the interrogation cell. "I thank the Hand," Abrams said, "but the matter concerns Lord Hauksberg also."

"Speak freely. Today is no time for circumlocutions."

Abram's heart thudded but he held his words steady. "Point of law, Hand. By the Covenant of Alfzar, Merseia confirmed her acceptance of the rules of war and diplomacy which evolved on Terra. They evolved, and you took them over, for the excellent reason that they work. Now if you wish to declare us personae non gratae and deport us, his Majesty's government will have no grounds for complaint. But taking any other action against any one of us, no matter what the source of our accreditation, is ground for breaking off relations, if not for war."

"Diplomatic personnel have no right to engage in espionage," Brechdan said.

"No, Hand. Neither is the government to which they are sent supposed to spy on them.

And in fact, Dwyr the Hook was planted on me
as a spy. Scarcely a friendly act, Hand, the more
so when urgent negotiations are under way. It
happened his sympathies were with Terra—"

Brechdan's smile was bleak. "I do not believe
it merely happened, Commander. I have the dis-
tinct impression that you maneuvered to get him
posted where he would be in contact with you.
Compliments on your skill."

"Hand, his Majesty's government will deny
any such allegation."

"How dare you speak for the Empire?"
Hauksberg exploded.

"How dare you, my lord?" Abrams replied. "I
am only offering a prediction. But will the Hand
not agree it is probably correct?"

Brechdan rubbed his chin. "Charge and
counter-charge, denial and counter-denial . . .
yes, no doubt. What do you expect the Empire to
maintain?"

"That rests with the Policy Board, Hand, and
how it decides will depend on a number of factors, including mood. If Merseia takes a course
which looks reasonable in Terran eyes, Terra is
apt to respond in kind."

"I presume a reasonable course for us includes
dropping charges against yourself," Brechdan
said dryly.

Abrams lifted his shoulders and spread his
palms. "What else? Shall we say that Dwyr and
Flandry acted on impulse, without my knowledge? Isn't it wise to refrain from involving the
honor of entire planets?"

"Khraich. Yes. The point is well taken.
Though frankly, I am disappointed in you. I

would stand by a subordinate."

"Hand, what happens to him is outside your control or mine. He and his pursuer have gone past communication range. It may sound pompous, but I want to save myself for further service to the Empire."

"We'll see about that," Hauksberg said venomously.

"I told you to be silent," Brechdan said. "No, Commander, on Merseia your word is not pompous at all." He inclined his head. "I salute you. Lord Hauksberg will oblige me by considering you innocent."

"Sir," the viscount protested, "surely he must be confined to the Embassy grounds for the duration of our stay. What happens to him on his return will lie with his service and his government."

"I do request the commander to remain within the compound," Brechdan said. He leaned forward. "Now, delegate, comes your turn. If you are willing to continue present discussions, so are we. But there are certain preconditions. By some accident, Flandry might yet escape, and he does carry military secrets. We must therefore dispatch a fast courier to the nearest Terran regional headquarters, with messages from us both. If Terra disowns him and cooperates with Merseia in his capture or destruction, then Terra has proven her desire for peaceful relations and the Grand Council of His Supremacy will be glad to adjust its policies accordingly. Will you lend your efforts to this end?"

"Of course, sir! Of course!"

"The Terran Empire is far away, though,"
Brechdan continued. "I don't imagine Flandry
would make for it. Our patrols will cover the
likeliest routes, as insurance. But the nearest human installation is on Starkad, and if somehow
he eludes our destroyer, I think it probable he
will go either there or to Betelgeuse. The region
is vast and little known. Thus our scouts would
have a very poor chance of intercepting him—
until he is quite near his destination. Hence, if he
should escape, I shall wish to guard the ap-
proaches. But as my government has no more
desire than yours to escalate the conflict, your
commandant on Starkad must be told that these
units are no menace to him and he need not send
for reinforcements. Rather, he must cooperate.
Will you prepare such orders for him?"

"At once, sir," Hauksberg said. Hope was re-
vitalizing him. He paid no attention to Abrams'
stare.

"Belike this will all prove unnecessary,"
Brechdan said. "The destroyer estimated she
would overtake Flandry in three days. She will
need little longer to report back. At such time we
can feel easy, and so can his Majesty's government. But for certainty's sake, we had best get
straight to work. Please accompany me to the
adjacent office." He rose. For a second he locked
eyes with Abrams. "Commander," he said,
"your young man makes me proud to be a sentient creature. What might our united races not
accomplish? Hunt well."

Abrams could not speak. His throat was too
thick with unshed tears. He bowed and left. At

the door, Merseian guards fell in, one either side of him.

Stars crowded the viewscreens, unmercifully brilliant against infinite night. The spaceboat thrummed with her haste.

Flandry and Persis returned from their labor. She had been giving him tools, meals, anything she could that seemed to fit his request, "Just keep feeding me and fanning me." In a shapeless coverall, hair caught under a scarf, a smear of grease on her nose, she was somehow more desirable than ever before. Or was that simply because death coursed near?

The Merseian destroyer had called the demand to stop long ago, an age ago, when she pulled within range of a hypervibration 'cast. Flandry refused. "Then prepare your minds for the God," said her captain, and cut off. Moment by moment, hour by hour, he had crept in on the boat, until instruments shouted his presence.

Persis caught Flandry's hand. Her own touch was cold. "I don't understand," she said in a thin voice. "You told me he can track us by our wake. But space is so big. Why can't we go sublight and let him hunt for us?"

"He's too close," Flandry said. "He was already too close when we first knew he was on our trail. If we cut the secondaries, he'd have a pretty good idea of our location, and need only cast about a small volume of space till he picked up the neutrino emission of our powerplant."

"Couldn't we turn that off too?"

"We'd die inside a day. Everything depends

on it. Odds-on bet whether we suffocated or froze. If we had suspended-animation equipment—But we don't. This is no warcraft, not even an exploratory vessel. It's just the biggest lifeboat-cum-gig *Queen Maggy* could tote."

They moved toward the control room. "What's going to happen?" she asked.

"In theory, you mean?" He was grateful for a chance to talk. The alternative would have been that silence which pressed in on the hull. "Well, look. We travel faster than light by making a great many quantum jumps per second, which don't cross the intervening space. You might say we're not in the real universe most of the time, though we are so often that we can't notice any difference. Our friend has to phase in. That is, he has to adjust his jumps to the same frequency and the same phase angle as ours. This makes each ship a completely solid object to the other, as if they were moving sublight, under ordinary gravitic drive at a true velocity."

"But you said something about the field."

"Oh, that. Well, what makes us quantum-jump is a pulsating force-field generated by the secondary engine. The field encloses us and reaches out through a certain radius. How big a radius, and how much mass it can affect, depends on the generator's power. A big ship can lay alongside a smaller one and envelop her and literally drag her at a resultant pseudospeed. Which is how you carry out most capture and boarding operations. But a destroyer isn't that large in relation to us. She does have to come so close that our fields overlap. Otherwise her beams and artillery can't touch us."

"Why don't we change phase?"

"Standard procedure in an engagement. I'm sure our friends expect us to try it. But one party can change as fast as another, and runs a continuous computation to predict the pattern of the opposition's maneuvers. Sooner or later, the two will be back in phase long enough for a weapon to hit. We're not set up to do it nearly as well as he is. No, our solitary chance is the thing we've been working on."

She pressed against him. He felt how she trembled. "Nicky, I'm afraid."

"Think I'm not?" Both pairs of lips were dry when they touched. "Come on, let's to our posts. We'll know in a few minutes. If we go out—Persis, I couldn't ask for a better traveling companion." As they sat down, Flandry added, because he dared not stay serious: "Though we wouldn't be together long. You're ticketed for heaven, my destination's doubtless the other way."

She gripped his hand again. "Mine too. You won't escape me th-th-that easily."

Alarms blared. A shadow crossed the stars. It thickened as phasing improved. Now it was a torpedo outline, still transparent; now the gun turrets and missile launchers showed clear; now all but the brightest stars were occulted. Flandry laid an eye to the crosshairs of his improvised fire-control scope. His finger rested on a button. Wires ran aft from it.

The Merseian destroyer became wholly real to him. Starlight glimmered off metal. He knew how thin that metal was. Force screens warded off solid matter, and nothing protected against nuclear energies: nothing but speed to get out of their way, which demanded low mass. Nevertheless he felt as if a dinosaur stalked him.

The destroyer edged nearer, swelling in the screens. She moved leisurely, knowing her prey was weaponless, alert only for evasive tactics. Flandry's right hand went to the drive controls. So . . . so . . . he was zeroed a trifle forward of the section where he knew her engines must be.

A gauge flickered. Hyperfields were making their first tenuous contact. In a second it would be sufficiently firm for a missile or a firebolt to cross from one hull to another. Persis, reading the board as he had taught her, yelled, "Go!"

Flandry snapped on a braking vector. Lacking the instruments and computers of a man-of-war, he had estimated for himself what the thrust should be. He pressed the button.

In the screen, the destroyer shot forward in relation to him. From an open hatch in his boat plunged the auxiliary's auxiliary, a craft meant for atmosphere but propellable anywhere on gravity beams. Fields joined almost at the instant it transitted them. At high relative velocity, both pseudo and kinetic, it smote.

Flandry did not see what happened. He had shifted phase immediately, and concentrated on getting the hell out of the neighborhood. If everything worked as hoped, his airboat ripped the Merseian plates, ruinously at kilometers per second. Fragments howled in air, flesh, engine connections. The destroyer was not destroyed. Repair would be possible, after so feeble a blow.

But before the ship was operational again, he would be outside detection range. If he zigzagged, he would scarcely be findable.

He hurtled among the stars. A clock counted one minute, two, three, five. He began to stop fighting for breath. Persis gave way to tears. After ten minutes he felt free to run on automatic, lean over and hold her.

"We did it," he whispered. "Satan in Sirius! One miserable gig took a navy vessel."

Then he must leap from his seat, caper and crow till the boat rang. "We won! Ta-ran-tu-la! We won! Break out the champagne! This thing must have champagne among the rations! God is too good for anything else!" He hauled Persis up and danced her over the deck. "Come on, you! We won! Swing your lady! I gloat, I gloat, I gloat!"

Eventually he calmed down. By that time Persis had command of herself. She disengaged from him so she could warn: "We've a long way to Starkad, darling, and danger at the end of the trip."

"Ah," said Ensign Dominic Flandry, "but you forget, this is the beginning of the trip."

A smile crept over her mouth. "Precisely what do you mean, sir?"

He answered with a leer. "That it *is* a long way to Starkad."

Chapter Fifteen

Saxo glittered white among the myriads. But it was still so far that others outshone it. Brightest stood Betelgeuse. Flandry's gaze fell on that crimson spark and lingered. He sat at the pilot board, chin in hand, for many minutes; and only the throb of the engine and murmur of the ventilators were heard.

Persis entered the control room. During the passage she had tried to improvise a few glamorous changes of garment from the clothes in stock, but they were too resolutely utilitarian. So mostly, as now, she settled for a pair of shorts, and those mostly for the pockets. Her hair swept loose, dark-bright as space; a lock tickled him when she bent over his shoulder, and he sensed its faint sunny odor, and her own. But this time he made no response.

"Trouble, darling?" she asked.

" 'It ain't the work, it's them damn decisions,' " he quoted absently.

"You mean which way to go?"

"Yes. Here's where we settle the question. Saxo or Betelgeuse?"

He had threshed the arguments out till she knew them by heart, but he went on anyhow: "Got to be one or the other. We're not set up to lie doggo on some undiscovered planet. The Empire's too far; every day of travel piles up chances for a Merseian to spot our wake. They'll have sent couriers in all directions—every kind of ship that could outrun our skulker's course—soon's they learned we escaped. Maybe before, even. Their units must be scouring these parts.

"Saxo's the closer. Against heading there is the consideration they can keep a pretty sharp watch on it without openly using warcraft in the system. Any big, fast merchantmen could gobble us, and the crew come aboard with sidearms. However, if we were in call range, I might raise Terran HQ on Starkad and pass on the information we're carrying. Then we might hope the Merseians would see no further gain in damaging us. But the whole thing is awful iffy.

"Now Betelgeuse is an unaligned power, and very jealous of her neutrality. Foreign patrols will have to keep their distance, spread so thin we might well slip through. Once on Alfzar, we could report to the Terran ambassador. *But* the Betelgeuseans won't let us enter their system secretly. They maintain their own patrols. We'd have to go through traffic procedures, starting beyond orbital radius of the outermost planet. And the Merseians can monitor those com channels. A raider could dash in quick-like and blast us."

"They wouldn't dare," Persis said.

"Sweetheart, they'd dare practically anything, and apologize later. You don't know what's at stake."

She sat down beside him. "Because you won't tell me."

"Right."

He had gnawed his way to the truth. Hour upon hour, as they fled through Merseia's dominions, he hunched with paper, penstyl, calculator, and toiled. Their flight involved nothing dramatic. It simply meandered through regions where one could assume their enemies rarely came. Why should beings with manlike biological requirements go from a dim red dwarf star to a planetless blue giant to a dying Cepheid variable? Flandry had ample time for his labors.

Persis was complaining about that when the revelation came. "You might talk to me."

"I do," he muttered, not lifting his eyes from the desk. "I make love to you as well. Both with pleasure. But not right now, please!"

She flopped into a seat. "Do you recall what we have aboard for entertainment?" she said. "Four animations: a Martian travelogue, a comedian routine, a speech by the Emperor, and a Cynthian opera on the twenty-tone scale. Two novels: *Outlaw Blastman* and *Planet of Sin*. I have them memorized. They come back to me in my dreams. Then there's a flute, which I can't play, and a set of operation manuals."

"M-hm." He tried putting Brechdan's figures in a different sequence. It had been easy to translate from Merseian to Terran arithmetic. But what the devil did the symbols refer to? Angles, times, several quantities with no dimensions specified . . . rotation? Of what? Not of Brechdan; no such luck.

A nonhuman could have been similarly puzzled by something from Terra, such as a periodic table of isotopes. He wouldn't have known which properties out of many were listed, nor the standardized order in which quantum numbers were given, nor the fact that logarithms were to the base ten unless e was explicit, nor a lot of other things he'd need to know before he could guess what the table signified.

"You don't have to solve the problem," Persis sulked. "You told me yourself, an expert can see the meaning at a glance. You're just having fun."

Flandry raised his head, irritated. "Might be hellish important for us to know. Give us some idea what to expect. How in the name of Copros can Starkad matter so much? One lonesome planet!"

And the idea came to him.

He grew so rigid, he stared so wildly out into the universe, that Persis was frightened. "Nicky, what's wrong?" He didn't hear. With a convulsive motion, he grabbed a fresh sheet of paper and started scrawling. Finished, he stared at the result. Sweat stood on his brow. He rose, went into the control room, returned with a reel which threaded into his microreader. Again he wrote, copying off numbers. His fingers danced on the desk computer. Persis held herself moveless.

Until at last he nodded. "That's it," he said in a cold small voice. "Has to be."

"What is?" she could then ask.

He twisted around in his chair. His eyes took a second to focus on her. Something had changed in his face. He was almost a stranger.

"I can't tell you," he said.

"Why not?"

"We might get captured alive. They'd probe you and find you knew. If they didn't murder you out of hand, they'd wipe your brain—which to my taste is worse."

He took a lighter from his pocket and burned every paper on the desk and swept the ashes into a disposal. Afterward he shook himself, like a dog that has come near drowning, and went to her.

"Sorry," he smiled. "Kind of a shock for me there. But I'm all right now. And I really will pay attention to you, from here on in."

She enjoyed the rest of the voyage, even after she had identified the change in him, the thing which had gone and would never quite come back. Youth.

The detector alarm buzzed. Persis drew a gasp and caught Flandry's arm. He tore her loose, reaching for the main hyperdrive switch.

But he didn't pull it, returning them to normal state and kinetic velocity. His knuckles stood white on the handle. A pulse fluttered in his throat. "I forgot what I'd already decided," he said. "We don't have an especially good detector. If she's a warship, we were spotted some time ago."

"But this time she can't be headed straight at us." Her tone was fairly level. She had grown somewhat used to being hunted. "We have a big sphere to hide in."

"Uh-huh. We'll try that if necessary. But first

let's see which way yonder fellow is bound." He changed course. Stars wheeled in the viewports, otherwise there was no sensation. "If we can find a track on which the intensity stays constant, we'll be running parallel to him and he isn't trying to intercept." Saxo burned dead ahead. "S'pose he's going there—"

Minutes crawled. Flandry let himself relax. His coverall was wet. "Whew! What I hoped. Destination, Saxo. And if he's steered on a more or less direct line, as is probable, then he's come from the Empire."

He got busy, calculating, grumbling about rotten civilian instrumentation. "Yes, we can meet him. Let's go."

"But he could be Merseian," Persis objected. "He needn't have come from a Terran planet."

"Chance we take. The odds aren't bad. He's slower than us, which suggests a merchant vessel." Flandry set the new path, leaned back and stretched. A grin spread across his features. "My dilemma's been solved for me. We're off to Starkad."

"Why? How?"

"Didn't mention it before, for fear of raising false hopes in you. When I'd rather raise something else. But I came here first, instead of directly to Saxo or Betelgeuse, because this is the way Terran ships pass, carrying men and supplies to Starkad and returning home. If we can hitch a ride . . . you see?"

Eagerness blossomed in her and died again. "Why couldn't we have found one going home?"

"Be glad we found any whatsoever. Besides,

this way we deliver our news a lot sooner." Flandry rechecked his figures. "We'll be in call range in an hour. If he should prove to be Merseian, chances are we can outspeed and lose him." He rose. "I decree a good stiff drink."

Persis held her hands up. They trembled. "We do need something for our nerves," she agreed, "but there are psychochemicals aboard."

"Whisky's more fun. Speaking of fun, we have an hour."

She rumpled his hair. "You're impossible."

"No," he said. "Merely improbable."

The ship was the freighter *Rieskessel,* registered on Nova Germania but operating out of the Imperial frontier world Irumclaw. She was a huge, potbellied, ungainly and unkempt thing, with a huge, potbellied, ungainly and unkempt captain. He bellowed a not quite sober welcome when Flandry and Persis came aboard.

"Oh, ho, ho, ho! Humans! So soon I did not expect seeing humans. And never this gorgeous." One hairy hand engulfed Flandry's, the other chucked Persis under the chin. "Otto Brummelmann is me."

Flandry looked past the bald, wildly bearded head, down the passageway from the airlock. Corroded metal shuddered to the drone of an ill-tuned engine. A pair of multi-limbed beings with shiny blue integuments stared back from their labor; they were actually swabbing by hand. The lights were reddish orange, the air held a metallic tang and was chilly enough for his breath to smoke. "Are you the only Terran, sir?" he asked.

"Not Terran. Not me. Germanian. But for years now on Irumclaw. My owners want Irumclagian spacehands, they come cheaper. No human language do I hear from end to end of a trip. They can't pronounce." Brummelmann kept his little eyes on Persis, who had donned her one gown and tugged at his own soiled tunic in an effort at getting some wrinkles out. "Lonely, lonely. How nice to find you. First we secure your boat, next we go for drinks in my cabin, right?"

"We'd better have a private talk immediately, sir," Flandry said. "Our boat—no, let's wait till we're alone."

"You wait. I be alone with the little lady, right? Ho, ho, ho!" Brummelmann swept a paw across her. She shrank back in distaste.

On the way, the captain was stopped by a crew member who had some question. Flandry took the chance to hiss in Persis' ear: "Don't offend him. This is fantastic luck."

"This?" Her nose wrinkled.

"Yes. Think. No matter what happens, none of these xenos'll give us away. They can't. All we have to do is stay on the good side of the skipper, and that shouldn't be hard."

He had seen pigpens, in historical dramas, better kept up than Brummelmann's cabin. The Germanian filled three mugs, ignoring coffee stains, with a liquid that sank fangs into stomachs. His got half emptied on the first gulp. "So!" he belched. "We talk. Who sent you to deep space in a gig?"

Persis took the remotest corner. Flandry stayed near Brummelmann, studying him. The man was a failure, a bum, an alcoholic wreck. Doubtless he kept his job because the owners insisted on a human captain and couldn't get anyone else at the salary they wanted to pay. Didn't matter greatly, as long as the mate had some competence. For the most part, antiquated though her systems must be, the ship ran herself.

"You are bound for Starkad, aren't you, sir?" Flandry asked.

"Yes, yes. My company has a Naval contract. Irumclaw is a transshipment point. This trip we carry food and construction equipment. I hope we go on another run soon. Not much pleasure in Highport. But we was to talk about you."

"I can't say anything except that I'm on a special mission. It's vital for me to reach Highport secretly. If Donna d'Io and I can ride down with you, and you haven't radioed the fact ahead, you'll have done the Empire a tremendous service."

"Special mission . . . with a lady?" Brummelmann dug a blackrimmed thumb into Flandry's ribs. "I can guess what sort of mission. Ho, ho, ho!"

"I rescued her," Flandry said patiently. "That's why we were in a boat. A Merseian attack. The war's sharpening. I have urgent information for Admiral Enriques."

Brummelmann's laughter chocked off. Behind the matted whiskers, that reached to his navel, he swallowed. "Attack, you said? But no, the Merseians, they have never bothered civilian ships."

"Nor should they bother this one, Captain. Not if they don't know I'm aboard."

Brummelmann wiped his pate. Probably he thought of himself as being in the high, wild tradition of early space-faring days. But now his daydreams had orbited. "My owners," he said weakly. "I have obligation to my owners. I am responsible for their ship."

"Your first duty is to the Empire." Flandry considered taking over at blaster point. No; not unless he must; too chancy. "And all you need do is approach Starkad in the usual fashion, make your usual landing at Highport, and let us off. The Merseians will never know, I swear."

"I—but I—"

Flandry snatched an idea from the air. "As for your owners," he said, "you can do them a good turn as well. Our boat had better be jettisoned out here. The enemy has her description. But if we take careful note of the spot, and leave her powerplant going for neutrino tracing, you pick her up on your way home and sell her there. She's worth as much as this entire ship, I'll bet." He winked. "Of course, you'll inform your owners."

Brummelmann's eyes gleamed. "Well. So. Of course." He tossed off the rest of his drink. "By God, yes! Shake!"

He insisted on shaking hands with Persis also. "Ugh," she said to Flandry when they were alone, in an emptied locker where a mattress had been laid. She had refused the captain's offer of his quarters. "How long to Starkad?"

"Couple days." Flandry busied himself checking the spacesuits he had removed from the boat before she was cast adrift.

"I don't know if I can stand it."

"Sorry, but we've burned our britches. Myself, I stick by my claims that we lucked out."

"You have the strangest idea of luck," she sighed. "Oh, well, matters can't get any worse."

They could.

Fifteen hours later, Flandry and Persis were in the saloon. Coveralled against the chill but nonetheless shivering, mucous membranes aching from the dryness, they tried to pass time with a game of rummy. They weren't succeeding very well.

Brummelmann's voice boomed hoarse from the intercom: "You! Ensign Flandry! To the bridge!"

"Huh?" He sprang up. Persis followed his dash, down halls and through a companionway. Stars glared from the viewports. Because the optical compensator was out of adjustment, they had strange colors and were packed fore and aft, as if the ship moved through another reality.

Brummelmann held a wrench. Beside him, his first mate aimed a laser torch, a crude substitute for a gun but lethal at short range. "Hands high!" the captain shrilled.

Flandry's arms lifted. Sickness caught at his gullet. "What is this?"

"Read." Brummelman thrust a printout at him. "You liar, you traitor, thought you could fool me? Look what came."

It was a standard form, transcribed from a hypercast that must have originated in one of several automatic transmitters around Saxo. *Office of Vice Admiral Juan Enriques, commanding Imperial Terrestrial Naval forces in a region—*Flandry's glance flew to the text.

General directive issued under martial law: By statement of his Excellency Lord Markus Hauksberg, Viscount of Ny Kalmar on Terra, special Imperial delegate to the Roidhunate of Merseia . . . Ensign Dominic Flandry, an officer of his Majesty's Navy attached to the delegation . . . mutinied and stole a spaceboat belonging to the realm of Ny Kalmar; description as follows . . . charged with high treason. . . . Pursuant to interstellar law and Imperial policy, Ensign Flandry is to be apprehended and returned to his superiors on Merseia. . . . All ships, including Terran, will be boarded by Merseian inspectors before proceeding to Starkad. . . . Terrans who may apprehend this criminal are to deliver him promptly, in their own persons, to the nearest Merseian authority . . . secrets of state—

Persis closed her eyes and strained fingers together. The blood had left her face.

"Well?" Brummelmann growled. "Well, what have you to say for yourself?"

Flandry leaned against the bulkhead. He didn't know if his legs would upbear him. "I . . . can say . . . that bastard Brechdan thinks of everything."

"You expected you could fool me? You thought I would do your traitor's work? No, no!"

Flandry looked from him, to the mate, to Persis. Weakness vanished in rage. But his brains stayed machine precise. He lowered the hand which held the flimsy paper. "I'd better tell you the whole truth," he husked.

"No, I don't want to hear, I want no secrets."

Flandry let his knees go. As he fell, he yanked

out his blaster. The torch flame boomed blue
where he had been. His own snap shot flared off
that tool. The mate yowled and dropped the red-
hot thing. Flandry regained his feet. "Get rid of
your wrench," he said.

It clattered on the deck. Brummelmann
backed off, past his mate who crouched and
keened in pain. "You cannot get away," he
croaked. "We are detected by now. Surely we are.
You make us turn around, a warship comes after."

"I know," Flandry said. His mind leaped as if
across ice floes. "Listen. This is a misunderstanding. Lord Hauksberg's been fooled. I do have
information, and it does have to reach Admiral
Enriques. I want nothing from you but transportation to Highport. I'll surrender to the Terrans.
Not to the Merseians. The Terrans. What's
wrong with that? They'll do what the Emperor
really wants. If need be, they can turn me over to
the enemy. But not before they've heard what I
have to tell. Are you a man, Captain? Then behave like one!"

"But we will be boarded," Brummelmann
wailed.

"You can hide me. A thousand possible places
on a ship. If they have no reason to suspect you,
the Merseians won't search everywhere. That
could take days. Your crew won't blab. They're
as alien to the Merseians as they are to us. No
common language, gestures, interests, anything.
Let the greenskins come aboard. I'll be down in
the cargo or somewhere. You act natural.
Doesn't matter if you show a bit of strain. I'm

certain everybody they've checked has done so.
Pass me on to the Terrans. A year from now you
could have a knighthood."

Brummelmann's eyes darted back and forth.
The breath rasped sour from his mouth.

"The alternative," Flandry said, "is that I
lock you up and assume command."

"I . . . no—" Tears started forth, down into
the dirty beard. "Please. Too much risk—"
Abruptly, slyly, after a breath: "Why, yes. I will.
I can find a good hiding spot for you."

And tell them when they arrive, Flandry thought.
*I've got the upper hand and it's worthless. What am I
to do?*

Persis stirred. She approached Brummelmann
and took his hands in hers. "Oh, thank you,"
she caroled.

"Eh? Ho?" He gawped at her.

"I knew you were a real man. Like the old
heroes of the League, come back to life."

"But you—lady—"

"The message doesn't include a word about
me," she purred. "I don't feel like sitting in some
dark hole."

"You . . . you aren't registered aboard. They
will read the list. Won't they?"

"What if they do? Would I be registered?"

Hope rushed across Flandry. He felt giddy
with it. "There are some immediate rewards,
you see," he cackled.

"I—why, I—" Brummelmann straightened.
He caught Persis to him. "So there are. Oh, ho,
ho! So there are!"

She threw Flandry a look he wished he could
forget.

He crept from the packing case. The hold was
gut-black. The helmet light of his spacesuit cast
a single beam to guide him. Slowly, awkward in
armor, he wormed among crates to the hatch.

The ship was quiet. Nothing spoke but powerplant, throttled low, and ventilators. Shadows
bobbed grotesque where his beam cut a path.
Orbit around Starkad, awaiting clearance to descend—must be. He had survived. The
Merseians had passed within meters of him, he
heard them talk and curled his finger around the
trigger; but they had gone again and the
Rieskessel resumed acceleration. So Persis had
kept Brummelmann under control; he didn't like
to think how.

The obvious course was to carry on as he had
outlined, let himself be taken planetside and
turn himself in. Thus he would certainly get his
message through, the word which he alone bore.
(He had wondered whether to give Persis those
numbers, but decided against it. A list for her
made another chance of getting caught; and her
untrained mind might not retain the figures exactly, even in the subconscious for narcosyn-
thesis to bring forth.) But he didn't know how
Enriques would react. The admiral was no robot; he would pass the information on to Terra,
one way or another. But he might yield up Flandry. He would most likely not send an armed
scout to check and confirm, without author-
ization from headquarters. Not in the face of

Hauksberg's message, or the command laid on him that he must take no escalating action save in response to a Merseian initiative.

So at best, the obvious course entailed delay, which the enemy might put to good use. It entailed a high probability of Brechdan Ironrede learning how matters stood. Max Abrams (*Are you alive yet, my father?*) had said, "What helps the other fellow most is knowing what you know." And, finally, Dominic Flandry wasn't about to become a God damned pawn again!

He opened the hatch. The corridor stretched empty. Unhuman music squealed from the forecastle. Captain Brummelmann was in no hurry to make planetfall, and his crew was taking the chance to relax.

Flandry sought the nearest lifeboat. If anyone noticed, well, all right, he'd go to Highport. But otherwise, borrowing a boat would be the smallest crime on his docket. He entered the turret, dogged the inner valve, closed his faceplate, and worked the manual controls. Pumps roared, exhausting air. He climbed into the boat and secured her own airlock. The turret's outer valve opened automatically.

Space blazed at him. He nudged through on the last possible impetus. Starkad was a huge wheel of darkness, rimmed with red, day blue on one edge. A crescent moon glimmered among the stars. Weightlessness caught Flandry in an endless falling.

It vanished as he turned on interior gravity and applied a thrust vector. He spiraled down-

ward. The planetary map was clear in his recollection. He could reach Ujanka without trouble
—Ujanka, the city he had saved.

Chapter Sixteen

Dragoika flowed to a couch, reclined on one elbow, and gestured at Flandry. "Don't pace in that caged way, Dommaneek," she urged. "Take ease by my side. We have scant time alone together, we two friends."

Behind her throaty voice, up through the window, came the sounds of feet shuffling about, weapons rattling, a surflike growl. Flandry stared out. Shiv Alley was packed with armed Kursovikians. They spilled past sight, among gray walls, steep red roofs, carved beams: on into the Street Where They Fought, a cordon around this house. Spearheads and axes, helmets and byrnies flashed in the harsh light of Saxo; banners snapped to the wind, shields bore monsters and thunderbolts luridly colored. It was no mob. It was the fighting force of Ujanka, summoned by the Sisterhood. Warriors guarded the parapets on Seatraders' Castle and the ships lay ready in Golden Bay.

Lucifer! Flandry thought, half dismayed. *Did I start this?*

He looked back at Dragoika. Against the gloom of the chamber, the barbaric relics which crowded it, her ruby eyes and the striped

orange-and-white fur seemed to glow, so that the
curves of her body grew disturbingly rich. She
tossed back her blonde mane, and the half-hu-
man face broke into a smile whose warmth was
not lessened by the fangs. "We were too busy
since you came," she said. "Now, while we wait,
we can talk. Come."

He crossed the floor, strewn with aromatic
leaves in his honor, and took the couch by hers.
A small table in the shape of a flower stood be-
tween, bearing a ship model and a flagon.
Dragoika sipped. "Will you not share my cup,
Dommaneek?"

"Well . . . thanks." He couldn't refuse, though
Starkadian wine tasted grim on his palate.
Besides, he'd better get used to native viands; he
might be living off them for a long while. He
fitted a tube to his chowlock and sucked up a bit.

It was good to wear a regular sea-level outfit
again, air helmet, coverall, boots, after being
penned in a spacesuit. The messenger Dragoika
sent for him, to the Terran station in the High
Housing, had insisted on taking back such a rig.

"How have you been?" Flandry asked lamely.

"As always. We missed you, I and Ferok and
your other old comrades. How glad I am the
Archer was in port."

"Lucky for me!"

"No, no, anyone would have helped you.
The folk down there, plain sailors, artisans,
merchants, ranchers, they are as furious as I
am." Dragoika erected her tendrils. Her tail
twitched, the winglike ears spread wide. "That
those vaz-giradek would dare bite you!"

"Hoy," Flandry said. "You have the wrong idea. I haven't disowned Terra. My people are simply the victims of a lie and our task is to set matters right."

"They outlawed you, did they not?"

"I don't know what the situation is. I dare not communicate by radio. The vaz-Merseian could overhear. So I had your messenger give our men a note which they were asked to fly to Admiral Enriques. The note begged him to send a trustworthy man here."

"You told me that already. I told you I would make quite plain to the vaz-Terran, they will not capture my Dommaneek. Not unless they want war."

"But—"

"They don't. They need us worse than we need them, the more so when they failed to reach an accord with the vaz-Siravo of the Zletovar."

"They did?" Flandry's spirit drooped.

"Yes, as I always said would happen. Oh, there have been no new Merseian submarines. A Terran force blasted the Siravo base when we vaz-Kursovikian were unable to. The vaz-Merseian fought them in the air. Heaven burned that night. Since then, our ships often meet gunfire from swimmers, but most of them get through. They tell me combat between Terran and Merseian has become frequent—elsewhere in the world, however."

Another step up the ladder, Flandry thought. *More men killed, Tigeries, seafolk. By now, I suppose, daily. And in a doomed cause.*

"But you have given small word about your

deeds," Dragoika continued. "Only that you bear a great secret. What?"

"I'm sorry." On an impulse, Flandry reached out and stroked her mane. She rubbed her head against his palm. "I may not tell even you."

She sighed. "As you wish." She picked up the model galley. Her fingers traced spars and rigging. "Let me fare with you a ways. Tell me of your journey."

He tried. She struggled for comprehension. "Strange, that yonder," she said. "The little stars become suns, this world of ours shrunk to a dustmote; the weirdness of other races, the terrible huge machines—" She clutched the model tight. "I did not know a story could frighten me."

"You will learn to live with a whole heart in the universe." *You must.*

"Speak on, Dommaneek."

He did, censoring a trifle. Not that Dragoika would mind his having traveled with Persis; but she might think he preferred the woman to her as a friend, and be hurt.

"—trees on Merseia grow taller than here, bearing a different kind of leaf—"

His wristcom buzzed. He stabbed the transmitter button. "Ensign Flandry." His voice sounded high in his ears. "Standing by."

"Admiral Enriques," from the speaker. "I am approaching in a Boudreau X-7 with two men. Where shall I land?"

Enriques in person? My God, have I gotten myself caught in the gears! "A-a-aye aye, sir."

"I asked where to set down, Flandry."

The ensign stammered out directions. A flitter, as his letter had suggested, could settle on the tower of Dragoika's house. "You see, sir, the people here, they're—well, sort of up in arms. Best avoid possible trouble, sir."

"Your doing?"

"No, sir. I mean, not really. But, well, you'll see everyone gathered. In combat order. They don't want to surrender me to . . . uh . . . to anyone they think is hostile to me. They threaten, uh, attack on our station if—Honest, sir, I haven't alienated an ally. I can explain."

"You'd better," Enriques said. "Very well, you are under arrest but we won't take you into custody as yet. We'll be there in about three minutes. Out."

"What did he say?" Dragoika hissed. Her fur stood on end.

Flandry translated. She glided from her couch and took a sword off the wall. "I'll call a few warriors to make sure he keeps his promise."

"He will. I'm certain he will. Uh . . . the sight of his vehicle might cause excitement. Can we tell the city not to start fighting?"

"We can." Dragoika operated a communicator she had lately acquired and spoke with the Sisterhood centrum across the river. Bells pealed forth, the Song of Truce. An uneasy mutter ran through the Tigeries, but they stayed where they were.

Flandry headed for the door. "I'll meet them on the tower," he said.

"You will not," Dragoika answered. "They are coming to see you by your gracious permission. Lirjoz is there, he'll escort them down."

Flandry seated himself, shaking his head in a stunned fashion.

He rocketed up to salute when Enriques entered. The admiral was alone, must have left his men in the flitter. At a signal from Dragoika, Lirjoz returned to watch them. Slowly, she laid her sword on the table.

"At ease," Enriques clipped. He was gray, bladenosed, scarecrow gaunt. His uniform hung flat as armor. "Kindly present me to my hostess."

"Uh. . .Dragoika, captain-director of the Janjevar va-Radovik. . .Vice Admiral Juan Enriques of the Imperial Terrestrial Navy."

The newcomer clicked his heels, but his bow could have been made to the Empress. Dragoika studied him a moment, then touched brow and breasts, the salute of honor.

"I feel more hope," she said to Flandry.

"Translate," Enriques ordered. That narrow skull held too much to leave room for many languages.

"She . . . uh . . . likes you, sir," Flandry said.

Behind the helmet, a smile ghosted at one corner of Enriques' mouth. "I suspect she is merely prepared to trust me to a clearly defined extent."

"Won't the Admiral be seated?"

Enriques glanced at Dragoika. She eased to her couch. He took the other one, sitting straight. Flandry remained on his feet. Sweat prickled him.

"Sir," he blurted, "please, is Donna d'Io all right?"

"Yes, except for being in a bad nervous state. She landed soon after your message arrived. The *Riekessel's* captain had been making one excuse after another to stay in orbit. When we learned from you that Donna d'Io was aboard, we said we would loft a gig for her. He came down at once. What went on there?"

"Well, sir—I mean, I can't say. I wasn't around, sir. She told you about our escape from Merseia?"

"We had a private interview at her request. Her account was sketchy. But it does tend to bear out your claims."

"Sir, I know what the Merseians are planning, and it's monstrous. I can prove—"

"You will need considerable proof, Ensign," Enriques said bleakly. "Lord Hauksberg's communication laid capital charges against you."

Flandry felt nervousness slide from him. He doubled his fists and cried, with tears of rage stinging his eyes: "Sir, I'm entitled to a court-martial. By my own people. And you'd have let the Merseians have me!"

The lean visage beneath his hardly stirred. The voice was flat. "Regulations provide that personnel under charges are to be handed over to their assigned superiors if this is demanded. The Empire is too big for any other rule to work. By virtue of being a nobleman, Lord Hauksberg holds a reserve commission, equivalent rank of captain, which was automatically activated when Commander Abrams was posted to him. Until you are detached from your assignment, he is your senior commanding officer. He declared

in proper form that state secrets and his mission
on behalf of the Imperium have been endangered
by you. The Merseians will return you to him for
examination. It is true that courts-martial must
be held on an Imperial ship or planet, but the
time for this may be set by him within a one-year
limit."

"Will be never! Sir, they'll scrub my brain
and kill me!"

"Restrain yourself, Ensign."

Flandry gulped. Dragoika bared teeth but
stayed put. "May I hear the exact charges
against me, sir?" Flandry asked.

"High treason," Enriques told him. "Mutiny.
Desertion. Kidnapping. Threat and menace. Assault and battery. Theft. Insubordination. Shall
I recite the entire bill? I thought not. You have
subsequently added several items. Knowing that
you were wanted, you did not surrender yourself. You created dissension between the Empire
and an associated country. This, among other
things, imperils his Majesty's forces on Starkad.
At the moment, you are resisting arrest. Ensign,
you have a great deal to answer for."

"I'll answer to you, sir, not to . . . to those
damned gatortails. Nor to a Terran who's so
busy toadying to them he doesn't care what happens to his fellow human beings. My God, sir,
you let Merseians search Imperial ships!"

"I had my orders," Enriques replied.

"But Hauksberg, you rank him!"

"Formally and in certain procedural matters.
He holds a direct Imperial mandate, though. It
empowers him to negotiate temporary agree-

ments with Merseia, which then become policy determinants."

Flandry heard the least waver in those tones. He pounced. "You protested your orders, sir. Didn't you?"

"I sent a report on my opinion to frontier HQ. No reply has yet been received. In any event, there are only six Merseian men-of-war here, none above Planet class, plus some unarmed cargo carriers told off to help them." Enriques smacked hand on knee. "Why am I arguing with you? At the very least, if you wanted to see me, you could have stayed aboard the *Rieskessel*."

"And afterward been given to the Merseians, sir?"

"Perhaps. The possibility should not have influenced you. Remember your oath."

Flandry made a circle around the room. His hands writhed behind his back. Dragoika laid fingers on sword hilt. "No," he said to her in Kursovikian. "No matter what happens."

He spun on his heel and looked straight at Enriques. "Sir, I had another reason. What I brought from Merseia is a list of numbers. You'd undoubtedly have passed them on. But they do need a direct check, to make sure I'm right about what they mean. And if I am right, whoever goes to look may run into a fight. A space battle. Escalation, which you're forbidden to practice. You couldn't order such a mission the way things have been set up to bind you. You'd have to ask for the authority. And on what basis? On my say-so, me, a baby ex-cadet, a mutineer, a traitor. You can imagine how they'd buckpass.

At best, a favorable decision wouldn't come for weeks. Months, more likely. Meanwhile the war would drag on. Men would get killed. Men like my buddy, Jan van Zuyl, with his life hardly begun. With forty or fifty years of Imperial service in him."

Enriques spoke so softly that one heard the wind whittering off the sea, through the ancient streets outside. "Ensign van Zuyl was killed in action four days ago."

"Oh, no." Flandry closed his eyes.

"Conflict has gotten to the point where—we and the Merseians respect each other's base areas, but roving aircraft fight anyplace else they happen to meet."

"And *still* you let them search us." Flandry paused. "I'm sorry, sir. I know you hadn't any choice. Please let me finish. It's even possible my information would be discredited, never acted on. Hard to imagine, but . . . well, we have so many bureaucrats, so many people in high places like Lord Hauksberg who insists the enemy doesn't really mean harm . . . and Brechdan Ironrede, God, but he's clever. . . . I couldn't risk it. I had to work things so you, sir, would have a free choice."

"You?" Enriques raised his brows. "Ensign Dominic Flandry, all by himself?"

"Yes, sir. You have discretionary power, don't you? I mean, when extraordinary situations arise, you can take what measures are indicated, without asking HQ first. Can't you?"

"Of course. As witness these atmospheric combats." Enriques leaned forward, forgetting to stay sarcastic.

"Well, sir, this is an extraordinary situation. You're supposed to stay friends with the Kursovikians. But you can see I'm the Terran they care about. Their minds work that way. They're barbaric, used to personal leadership; to them, a distant government is no government; they feel a blood obligation to me—that sort of thing. So to preserve the alliance, you must deal with me. I'm a renegade, but you must."

"And so?"

"So if you don't dispatch a scout into space, I'll tell the Sisterhood to dissolve the alliance."

"What?" Enriques started. Dragoika bristled.

"I'll sabotage the whole Terran effort," Flandry said. "Terra has no business on Starkad. We've been trapped, conned, blued and tattooed. When you present physical evidence, photographs, measurements, we'll all go home. Hell, I'll give you eight to one the Merseians go home as soon as you tell old Runei what you've done. Get your courier off first, of course, to make sure he doesn't use those warships to blast us into silence. But then call him and tell him."

"There are no Terran space combat units in this system."

Flandry grinned. The blood was running high in him. "Sir, I don't believe the Imperium is that stupid. There has to be some provision against the Merseians suddenly marshaling strength. If nothing else, a few warcraft orbiting 'way outside. We can flit men to them. A round-about course, so the enemy'll think it's only another homebound ship. Right?"

"Well—" Enriques got up. Dragoika stayed where she was, but closed hand on hilt. "You haven't yet revealed your vast secret," the admiral declared.

Flandry recited the figures.

Enriques stood totem-post erect. "Is that everything?"

"Yes, sir. Everything that was needed."

"How do you interpret it?"

Flandry told him.

Enriques was still for a long moment. The Tigeries growled in Shiv Alley. He turned, went to the window, stared down and then out at the sky.

"Do you believe this?" he asked most quietly.

"Yes, sir," Flandry said. "I can't think of anything else that fits, and I had plenty of time to try. I'd bet my life on it."

Enriques faced him again. "Would you?"

"I'm doing it, sir."

"Maybe. Suppose I order a reconnaissance. As you say, it's not unlikely to run into Merseian pickets. Will you come along?"

A roar went through Flandry's head. "Yes, sir!" he yelled.

"Hm. You trust me that much, eh? And it would be advisable for you to go: a hostage for your claims, with special experience which might prove useful. Although if you didn't return here, we could look for trouble."

"You wouldn't need Kursoviki any longer," Flandry said. He was beginning to tremble.

"If you are truthful and correct in your assertion." Enriques was motionless a while more. The silence grew and grew.

All at once the admiral said, "Very good,

Ensign Flandry. The charges against you are held in abeyance and you are hereby re-attached temporarily to my command. You will return to Highport with me and await further orders."

Flandry saluted. Joy sang in him. "Aye, aye, sir!"

Dragoika rose. "What were you saying, Dommaneek?" she asked anxiously.

"Excuse me, sir, I have to tell her." In Kursovikian: "The misunderstanding has been dissolved, for the time being anyhow. I'm leaving with my skipper."

"Hr-r-r." She looked down. "And then what?"

"Well uh, then we'll go on a flying ship, to a battle which may end this whole war."

"You have only his word," she objected.

"Did you not judge him honorable?"

"Yes. I could be wrong. Surely there are those in the Sisterhood who will suspect a ruse, not to speak of the commons. Blood binds us to you. I think it would look best if I went along. Thus there is a living pledge."

"But—but—"

"Also," Dragoika said, "this is our war too. Shall none of us take part?" Her eyes went back to him. "On behalf of the Sisterhood and myself, I claim a right. You shall not leave without me."

"Problems?" Enriques barked.

Helplessly, Flandry tried to explain.

Chapter Seventeen

The Imperial squadron deployed and accelerated. It was no big force to cast out in so much blackness. True, at the core was the *Sabik,* a Star-class, what some called a pocket battleship; but she was old and worn, obsolete in several respects, shunted off to Saxo as the last step before the scrap orbit. No one had really expected her to see action again. Flanking her went the light cruiser *Umbriel,* equally tired, and the destroyers *Antarctica, New Brazil,* and *Murdoch's Land.* Two scoutships, *Encke* and *Ikeya-Seki,* did not count as fighting units; they carried one energy gun apiece, possibly useful against aircraft, and their sole real value lay in speed and maneuverability. Yet theirs was the ultimate mission, the rest merely their helpers. Aboard each of them reposed a document signed by Admiral Enriques.

At first the squadron moved on gravitics. It would not continue thus. The distance to be traversed was a few light-days, negligible under hyperdrive, appalling under true velocity. However, a sudden burst of wakes, outbound from a large orbit, would be detected by the Merseians. Their suspicions would be excited. And their strength in the Saxonian System, let alone what else they might have up ahead, was fully comparable to Captain Einarsen's command. He wanted to enter this water carefully. It was deep.

But when twenty-four hours had passed without incident, he ordered the *New Brazil* to proceed at superlight toward the destination. At the first sign of an enemy waiting there, she was to come back.

Flandry and Dragoika sat in a wardroom of the *Sabik* with Lieutenant (j.g.) Sergei Karamzin, who happened to be off watch. He was as frantic to see new faces and hear something new from the universe as everyone else aboard. "Almost a year on station," he said. "A year out of my life, bang, like that. Only it wasn't sudden, you understand. Felt more like a decade."

Flandry's glance traveled around the cabin. An attempt had been made to brighten it with pictures and home-sewn draperies. The attempt had not been very successful. Today the place had come alive with the thrum of power, low and bone-deep. A clean tang of oil touched air which circulated briskly again. But he hated to think what this environment had felt like after a year of absolutely eventless orbit. Dragoika saw matters otherwise, of course; the ship dazzled, puzzled, frightened, delighted, enthralled her, never had she known such wonder! She poised in her chair with fur standing straight and eyes bouncing around.

"You had your surrogates, didn't you?" Flandry asked. "Pseudosensory inputs and the rest."

"Sure," Karamzin said. "The galley's good, too. But those things are just medicine, to keep you from spinning off altogether." His young features hardened. "I hope we meet some opposition. I really do."

"Myself," Flandry said, "I've met enough opposition to last me for quite a while."

His lighter kindled a cigarette. He felt odd, back in horizon blue; jetflares on his shoulders and no blaster at his waist: back in a ship, in discipline, in tradition. He wasn't sure he liked it.

At least his position was refreshingly anomalous. Captain Einarsen had been aghast when Dragoika boarded—an Iron Age xeno on *his* vessel? But the orders from Enriques were clear. This was a vip who insisted on riding along and could cause trouble if she wasn't humored. Thus Ensign Flandry was appointed "liaison officer," the clause being added in private that he'd keep his pet savage out of the way or be busted to midshipman. (Nothing was said on either side about his being technically a prisoner. Einarsen had received the broadcast, but judged it would be dangerous to let his men know that Merseians were stopping Terran craft. And Enriques' message had clarified his understanding.) At the age of nineteen, how could Flandry resist conveying the impression that the vip really had some grasp of astronautics and must be kept posted on developments? So he was granted communication with the bridge.

Under all cheer and excitement, a knot of ten-

sion was in him. He figured that word from the
New Brazil would arrive at any minute.

"Your pardon," Dragoika interrupted. "I
must go to the—what you say—the head." She
thought that installation the most amusing thing
aboard.

Karamzin watched her leave. Her supple gait
was not impeded by the air helmet she required
in a Terran atmosphere. The chief problem had
been coiling her mane to fit inside. Otherwise
her garments consisted of a sword and a knife.

"Way-hay," Karamzin murmured. "What a
shape! How is she?"

"Be so good as not to talk about her like that,"
Flandry rapped.

"What? I didn't mean any harm. She's only a
xeno."

"She's my friend. She's worth a hundred Imperial sheep. And what she's got to face and survive, the rest of her life—"

Karamzin leaned across the table. "How's
that? What sort of cruise are we on, anyway?
Supposed to check on something the gatortails
might have out in space; they didn't tell us
more."

"I can't, either."

"I wasn't ordered to stop thinking. And you
know, I think this Starkad affair is a blind.
They'll develop the war here, get our whole attention on this sinkhole, then bang, they'll hit
someplace else."

Flandry blew a smoke ring. "Maybe." *I wish I
could tell you. You have no military right to know, but
haven't you a human right?*

"What's Starkad like, anyway? Our briefing didn't say much."

"Well—" Flandry hunted for words. They were bloodless things at best. You could describe, but you could not make real: dawn white over a running sea, slow heavy winds that roared on wooded mountainsides, an old and proud city, loveliness on a shadowy ocean floor, two brave races, billions of years since first the planet coalesced, the great globe itself. . . . He was still trying when Dragoika returned. She sat down quietly and watched him.

"—and, uh, a very interesting paleolithic culture on an island they call Rayadan—"

Alarms hooted.

Karamzin was through the door first. Feet clattered, metal clanged, voices shouted, under the shrill *woop-woop-woop* that echoed from end to end of the long hull. Dragoika snatched the sword off her shoulder. "What's happening?" she yelled.

"Battle stations." Flandry realized he had spoken in Anglic. "An enemy has been . . . sighted."

"Where is he?"

"Out there, put away that steel. Strength and courage won't help you now. Come." Flandry led her into the corridor.

They wove among men who themselves pelted toward their posts. Near the navigation bridge was a planetary chartroom equipped for full audiovisual intercom. The exec had decided this would serve the vip and her keeper. Two spacesuits hung ready. One was modified for Starka-

dian use. Dragoika had gotten some drill with it
en route to the squadron, but Flandry thought
he'd better help her before armoring himself.
"Here; this fastens so. Now hold your breath till
we change helmets on you. . . . Why did you
come?"

"I would not let you fare alone on my behalf,"
Dragoika said after her faceplate was closed.

Flandry left his own open, but heard her in his
radio earplugs. The alarm penetrated them;
and, presently, a voice:

"Now hear this. Now hear this. Captain to all
officers and men. The *New Brazil* reports two hyperdrives activated as she approached destination. She is returning to us and the bogies are in
pursuit. We shall proceed. Stand by for hyperdrive. Stand by for combat. Glory to the Emperor."

Flandry worked the com dials. Turning in on
a bridge viewscreen, he saw space on his own
panel, black and star-strewn. Briefly, as the
quantum field built up, the cosmos twisted.
Compensators clicked in and the scene grew
steady; but now *Sabik* outran light and kilometers reeled aft more swiftly than imagination
could follow. The power throb was a leonine
growl through every cell of his body.

"What does this mean?" Dragoika pressed
close to him, seeking comfort.

Flandry switched to a view of the operations
tank. Seven green dots of varying size moved
against a stellar background. "See, those are our
ships. The big one, that's this." Two red dots
appeared. "Those are the enemy, as near as we

can tell his positions. Um-m-m, look at their
size. That's because we detect very powerful engines. I'd say one is roughly equal to ours,
though probably newer and better armed. The
other seems to be a heavy destroyer."

Her gauntlets clapped together. "But this is
like magic!" she cried with glee.

"Not much use, actually, except to give a
quick overall picture. What the captain uses is
figures and calculations from our machines."

Dragoika's enthusiasm died. "Always machines," she said in a troubled voice. "Glad I am
not to live in your world, Dommaneek."

You'll have to, I'm afraid, he thought. *For a while,
anyway. If we live.*

He scanned the communications office. Men
sat before banks of meters, as if hypnotized. Occasionally someone touched a control or spoke a
few words to his neighbor. Electro-magnetic radio was mute beyond the hull. But with hyperdrive going, a slight modulation could be im-
posed on the wake to carry messages. *Sabik* could
transmit instantaneously, as well as receive.

As Flandry watched, a man stiffened in his
seat. His hands shook a little when he ripped off
a printout and gave it to his pacing superior.
That officer strode to an intercom and called the
command bridge. Flandry listened and nodded.

"Tell me," Dragoika begged. "I feel so alone
here."

"Shhh!"

Announcement: "Now hear this. Now hear
this. Captain to all officers and men. It is known
that there are six Merseian warships in Saxo or-

bit. They have gone hyper and are seeking junction with the two bogies in pursuit of *New Brazil*. We detect scrambled communication between these various units. It is expected they will attack us. First contact is estimated in ten minutes. Stand by to open fire upon command. The composition of the hostiles is—"

Flandry showed Dragoika the tank. Half a dozen sparks drove outward from the luminous globelet which represented her sun. "They are one light cruiser, about like our *Umbriel,* and five destroyers. Then ahead, remember, we have a battleship and a quite heavy destroyer."

"Eight against five of us." Tendrils rose behind the faceplace, fur crackled, the lost child dropped out of her and she said low and resonant: "But we will catch those first two by themselves."

"Right. I wonder. . . ." Flandry tried a different setting. It should have been blocked off, but someone had forgotten and he looked over Captain Einarsen's shoulder.

Yes, a Merseian in the outercom screen! And a high-ranking one, too.

"—interdicted region," he said in thickly accented Anglic. "Turn back at once."

"His Majesty's government does not recognize interdictions in unclaimed space," Einarsen said. "You will interfere with us at your peril."

"Where are you bound? What is your purpose?"

"That is of no concern to you, Fodaich. My command is bound on its lawful occasions. Do we pass peacefully or must we fight?"

Flandry translated for Dragoika as he listened. The Merseian paused, and she whispered: "He will say we can go on, surely. Thus he can join the others."

Flandry wiped his brow. The room felt hot, and he stank with perspiration in his suit. "I wish you'd been born in our civilization," he said. "You have a Navy mind."

"Pass, then," the Merseian said slowly. "Under protest, I let you by."

Flandry leaned forward, gripping a table edge, struggling not to shout what Einarsen must do.

The Terran commander said, "Very good. But in view of the fact that other units are moving to link with yours, I am forced to require guarantees of good faith. You will immediately head due galactic north at full speed, without halt until I return to Saxo."

"Outrageous! You have no right—"

"I have the right of my responsibility for this squadron. If your government wishes to protest to mine, let it do so. Unless you withdraw as requested, I shall consider your intentions hostile and take appropriate measures. My compliments to you sir. Good day." The screen was blanked.

Flandry switched away from Einarsen's expressionless countenance and stood shaking. There trickled through the turmoil in him, *I guess an old-line officer does have as much sense as a fresh-caught ensign*.

When he brought Dragoika up to date, she said coolly, "Let us see that tank again."

The Merseians ahead were not heeding the Terran order. They were, though, sheering off, one in either direction, obviously hoping to delay matters until help arrived. Einarsen didn't cooperate. Like a wolf brought to bay, *New Brazil* turned on her lesser pursuer. *Murdoch's Land* hurried to her aid. On the other side, *Umbriel* and *Sabik* herself accelerated toward the Merseian battlewagon. *Antarctica* continued as before, convoying the scoutboats.

"Here we go," Flandry said between clenched jaws. His first space battle, as terrifying, bewildering, and exalting as his first woman. He lusted to be in a gun turret. After dogging his faceplate, he sought an exterior view.

For a minute, nothing was visible but stars. Then the ship boomed and shuddered. She had fired a missile salvo: the monster missiles which nothing smaller than a battleship could carry, which had their own hyperdrives and phase-in computers. He could not see them arrive. The distance was as yet too great. But close at hand, explosions burst in space, one immense fireball after another, swelling, raging, and vanishing. Had the screen carried their real intensity, his eyeballs would have melted. Even through airlessness, he felt the buffet of expanding gases; the deck rocked and the hull belled.

"What was that?" Dragoika cried.

"The enemy shot at us. We managed to intercept and destroy his missiles with smaller ones. Look there." A lean metal thing prowled across the screen. "It seeks its own target. We have a cloud of them out."

Again and again energies ran wild. One blast almost knocked Flandry off his feet. His ears buzzed from it. He tuned in on damage control. The strike had been so near that the hull was bashed open. Bulkheads sealed off that section. A gun turret was wrecked, its crew blown to fragments. But another nearby reported itself still functional. Behind heavy material and electromagnetic shielding, its men had not gotten a lethal dose of radiation: not if they received medical help within a day. They stayed at their post.

Flandry checked the tank once more. Faster than either battleship, *Umbriel* had overhauled her giant foe. When drive fields touched, she went out of phase, just sufficient to be unhittable, not enough that her added mass did not serve as a drag. The Merseian must be trying to get in phase and wipe her out before—No, here *Sabik* came!

Generators that powerful extended their fields for a long radius. When she first intermeshed, the enemy seemed a toy, lost among so many stars. But she grew in the screen, a shark, a whale, Leviathan in steel, bristling with weapons, livid with lightnings.

The combat was not waged by living creatures. Not really. They did nothing but serve guns, tend machines, and die. When such speeds, masses, intensities met, robots took over. Missile raced at missile; computer matched wits with computer in the weird dance of phasing. Human and Merseian hands did operate blaster cannon, probing, searing, slicing through metal like a knife through flesh. But their chance of doing important harm, in the short time they had, was small.

Fire sheeted across space. Thunder brawled in hulls. Decks twisted, girders buckled, plates melted. An explosion pitched Flandry and Dragoika down. They lay in each other's arms, bruised, bleeding, deafened, while the storm prevailed.

And passed.

Slowly, incredulously, they climbed to their feet. Shouts from outside told them their eardrums were not ruptured. The door sagged and smoke curled through. Chemical extinguishers rumbled. Someone called for a medic. The voice was raw with pain.

The screen still worked. Flandry glimpsed *Umbriel* before relative speed made her unseeable. Her bows gaped open, a gun barrel was bent in a quarter circle, plates resembled seafoam where they had liquefied and congealed. But she ran yet. And so did *Sabik*.

He looked and listened awhile before he could reconstruct the picture for Dragoika. "We got them. Our two destroyers took care of the enemy's without suffering much damage. We're hulled in several places ourselves, three turrets and a missile launcher are knocked out, some lines leading from the main computer bank are cut, we're using auxiliary generators till the engineers can fix the primary one, and the casualties are pretty bad. We're operational, though, sort of."

"What became of the battleship we fought?"

"We sank a warhead in her midriff. One

megaton, I believe . . . no, you don't know about
that, do you? She's dust and gas."

The squadron reunited and moved onward.
Two tiny green flecks in the tank detached themselves and hastened ahead. "See those? Our
scoutboats. We have to screen them while they
perform their task. This means we have to fight
those Merseians from Saxo."

"Six of them to five of us," Dragoika counted.
"Well, the odds are improving. And then, we
have a bigger ship, this one, than remains to
them."

Flandry watched the green lights deploy. The
objective was to prevent even one of the red
sparks from getting through and attacking the
scouts. This invited annihilation in detail, but—
Yes, evidently the Merseian commander had
told off one of his destroyers to each of
Einarsen's. That left him with his cruiser and
two destroyers against *Sabik* and *Umbriel,* which
would have been fine were the latter pair not half
crippled. "I'd call the odds even, myself," Flandry said. "But that may be good enough. If we
stand off the enemy for . . . a couple of hours, I'd
guess . . we've done what we were supposed."

"But what is that, Dommaneek? You spoke
only of some menace out here." Dragoika took
him by the shoulders and regarded him levelly.
"Can you not tell me?"

He could, without violating any secrecy that
mattered any longer. But he didn't want to. He
tried to stall, and hoped the next stage of combat
would begin before she realized what he was
doing. "Well," he said, "we have news about,

uh, an object. What the scouts must do is go to it, find out what it is like, and plot its path. They'll do that in an interesting way. They'll retreat from it, faster than light, so they can take pictures of it not where it is at this moment but where it was at different times in the past. Since they know where to look, their instruments can pinpoint it at more than a light year. That is, across more than a year of time. On such basis, they can easily calculate how it will move for the next several years to come."

Again dread stirred behind her eyes. "They can reach over time itself?" she whispered. "To the past and its ghosts? You dare too much, you vaz-Terran. One night the hidden powers will set free their anger on you."

He bit his lip—and winced, for it was swollen where his face had been thrown against a mouth-control radio switch. "I often wonder if that may not be so, Dragoika. But what can we do? Our course was set for us ages agone, before ever we left our home world, and there is no turning back."

"Then . . . you fare bravely." She straightened in her armor. "I may do no less. Tell me what the thing is that you hunt through time."

"It—" The ship recoiled. A drumroll ran. "Missiles fired off! We're engaging!"

Another salvo and another. Einarsen must be shooting off every last hyperdrive weapon in his magazines. If one or two connected, they might decide the outcome. If not, then none of his present foes could reply in kind.

Flandry saw, in the tank, how the Merseian

destroyers scattered. They could do little but try
to outdodge those killers, or outphase them if
field contact was made. As formation broke up,
Murdoch's Land and *Antarctica* closed in together
on a single enemy of their class. That would be
slugfest, minor missiles and energy cannon and
artillery, more slow and perhaps more brutal
than the nearly abstract encounter between two
capital ships, but also somehow more human.

The volleys ended. Dragoika howled. "Look,
Dommaneek! A red light went out! There! First
blood for us!"

"Yes . . . yes, we did get a destroyer.
Whoopee!" The exec announced it on the intercom, and cheers sounded faintly from those
who still had their faceplates open. The other
missiles must have been avoided or parried, and
by now were destroying themselves lest they become threats to navigation. Max Abrams would
have called that rule a hopeful sign.

Another Merseian ship sped to assist the one
on which the two Terrans were converging,
while *New Brazil* and a third enemy stalked each
other. *Umbriel* limped on an intercept course for
the heavy cruiser and her attendant. Those
drove straight for *Sabik,* which lay in wait licking
her wounds.

The lights flickered and died. They came
back, but feebly. So there was trouble with the
spare powerplant, too. And damn, damn, damn,
Flandry couldn't do a thing except watch that
tank!

The cruiser's escort detached herself and ran
toward *Umbriel* to harry and hinder. Flandry

clenched his teeth till his jaws ached. "The greenskins can see we have problems here," he said. "They figure a cruiser can take us. And they may be right."

Red crept up on green. "Stand by for straight-phase engagement," said the intercom.

"What did that mean?" Dragoika asked.

"We can't dodge till a certain machine has been fixed." It was as near as Flandry could come to saying in Kursovikian that phase change was impossible. "We shall have to sit and shoot."

Sabik wasn't quite a wingless duck. She could revert to sublight, though that was a desperation maneuver. At superlight, the enemy must be in phase with her to inflict damage, and therefore equally vulnerable. But the cruiser did, now, possess an extra capability of eluding her opponent's fire. *Sabik* had no shield except her antimissiles. To be sure, she was better supplied with those.

It looked as if a toe-to-toe match was coming.

"Hyperfield contact made," said the intercom. "All units fire at will."

Flandry switched to exterior view. The Merseian zigzagged among the stars. Sometimes she vanished, always she reappeared. She was a strictly spacegoing vessel, bulged at the waist like a double-ended pear. Starlight and shadow picked out her armament. Dragoika hissed in a breath. Again fire erupted.

A titan's fist smote. A noise so enormous that it transcended noise bellowed through the hull. Bulkheads split asunder. The deck crashed against Flandry. He whirled into night.

Moments later he regained consciousness. He was falling, falling, forever, and blind . . . no, he thought through the ringing in his head, the lights were out, the gravs were out, he floated free amidst the moan of escaping air. Blood from his nose formed globules which, weightless, threatened to strangle him. He sucked to draw them down his throat. "Dragoika!" he rasped. "Dragoika!"

Her helmet beam sprang forth. She was a shadow behind it, but the voice came clear and taut: "Dommaneek, are you hale? What happened? Here, here is my hand."

"We took a direct hit." He shook himself, limb by limb, felt pain boil in his body but marveled that nothing appeared seriously injured. Well, space armor was designed to take shocks. "Nothing in here is working, so I don't know what the ship's condition is. Let's try to find out. Yes, hang onto me. Push against things, not too hard. It's like swimming. Do you feel sick?"

"No. I feel as in a dream, nothing else." She got the basic technique of null-gee motion fast.

They entered the corridor. Undiffused, their lamplight made dull puddles amidst a crowding murk. Ribs thrust out past twisted, buckled plates. Half of a space-suited man drifted in a blood-cloud which Flandry must wipe off his helmet. No radio spoke. The silence was of a tomb.

The nuclear warhead that got through could not have been very large. But where it struck, ruin was total. Elsewhere, though, forcefields, bulkheads, baffles, breakaway lines had given what protection they could. Thus Flandry and Dragoika survived. Did anyone else? He called and called, but got no answer.

A hole filled with stars yawned before him. He told her to stay put and flitted forth on impellers. Saxo, nearly the brightest of the diamond points around him, transited the specter arch of the Milky Way. It cast enough light for him to see. The fragment of ship from which he had emerged spun slowly—luck, that, or Coriolis force would have sickened him and perhaps her. An energy cannon turret looked intact. Further off tumbled larger pieces, ugly against cold serene heaven.

He tried his radio again, now when he was outside screening metal. With her secondary engines gone, the remnants of *Sabik* had reverted to normal state. "Ensign Flandry from Section Four. Come in, anyone. Come in!"

A voice trickled through. Cosmic interference seethed behind it. "Commander Ranjit Singh in Section Two. I am assuming command unless a superior officer turns out to be alive. Report your condition."

Flandry did. "Shall we join you, sir?" he finished.

"No. Check that gun. Report whether it's in working order. If so, man it."

"But sir, we're disabled. The cruiser's gone on to fight elsewhere. Nobody'll bother with us."

"That remains to be seen, Ensign. If the battle pattern should release a bogie, he may decide he'll make sure of us. Go to your gun."

"Aye, aye, sir."

Dead bodies floated in the turret. They were not mutilated; but two or three roentgens must have sleeted through all shielding. Flandry and Dragoika hauled them out and cast them adrift. As they dwindled among the stars, she sang to them the Song of Mourning. *I wouldn't mind such a sendoff,* he thought.

The gun was useable. Flandry rehearsed Dragoika in emergency manual control. They'd alternate at the hydraulic aiming system and the handwheel which recharged the batteries that drove it. She was as strong as he.

Thereafter they waited. "I never thought to die in a place like this," she said. "But my end will be in battle, and with the finest of comrades. How we shall yarn, in the Land of Trees Beyond!"

"We might survive yet," he said. Starlight flashed off the teeth in his bruised and blood-smeared face.

"Don't fool yourself. Unworthy of you."

"Unworthy my left one! I plain don't intend to quit till I'm dead."

"I see. Maybe that is what has made you vaz-Terran great."

The Merseian came.

She was a destroyer. *Umbriel,* locked in combat with the badly hurt enemy cruiser, had inflicted grave harm on her, too. *Murdoch's Land* was shattered, *Antarctica* out of action until repairs could be made, but they had accounted for two of her fellows. *New Brazil* dueled yet with the third.

This fourth one suffered from a damaged hyper-drive alternator. Until her sweating engineers could repair it, which would take an hour or so, her superlight speed was a crawl; any vessel in better shape could wipe her from the universe. Her captain resolved he would go back to where the remnants of *Sabik* orbited and spend the interim cleaning them out. For the general order was that none but Merseians might enter this region and live.

She flashed into reality. Her missiles were spent, but guns licked with fire-tongues and shells. The main part of the battleship's dismembered hulk took their impact, glowed, broke, and returned the attack.

"Yow-w-w!" Dragoika's yell was pure exultation. She spun the handwheel demoniacally fast. Flandry pushed himself into the saddle. His cannon swung about. The bit of hull counter-rotated. He adjusted, got the destroyer's after section in his cross-hairs, and pulled trigger.

Capacitors discharged. Their energy content was limited; that was why the gun must be laid by hand, to conserve every last erg for revenge. Flame spat across kilometers. Steel sublimed. A wound opened. Air gushed forth, white with condensing water vapour.

The destroyer applied backward thrust. Flandry followed, holding his beam to the same spot, driving inward and inward. From four other pieces of *Sabik,* death vomited.

"Man," Flandry chanted, "but you've got a Tigery by the tail!"

Remorselessly, spin took him out of sight. He

waited fuming. When he could again aim, the destroyer was further away, and she had turned one battleship section into gas. But the rest fought on. He joined his beam to theirs. She was retreating under gravitics. Why didn't she go hyper and get the hell out of here? Maybe she couldn't. He himself had been shooting to disable her quantum-field generator. Maybe he'd succeeded.

"Kursoviki!" Dragoika shrieked at the wheel. "Archers all! Janjevar va-Radovik for aye!"

A gun swiveled toward them. He could see it, tiny at its distance, thin and deadly. He shifted aim. His fire melted the muzzle shut.

The destroyer scuttled away. And then, suddenly, there was *New Brazil*. Flandry darted from his seat, caught Dragoika to him, held her faceplate against his breast and closed his own eyes. When they looked again, the Merseian was white-hot meteorites. They hugged each other in their armor.

Umbriel, Antarctica, and *New Brazil:* torn, battered, lame, filled with the horribly wounded, haunted by their dead, but victorious, victorious —neared the planet. The scoutships had long since finished their work and departed Empireward. Yet Ranjit Singh would give his men a look at the prize they had won.

On the cruiser's bridge, Flandry and Dragoika stood with him. The planet filled the foreward viewscreen. It was hardly larger than Luna. Like Terra's moon, it was bereft of air, water, life; such had bled away to space over billions of years. Mountains bared fangs at the stars, above ashen plains. Barren, empty, blind as a skull, the rogue rushed on to its destiny.

"One planet," the acting captain breathed. "One wretched sunless planet."

"It's enough, sir," Flandry said. Exhaustion pulsed through him in huge soft waves. To sleep . . . to sleep, perchance to dream. . . . "On a collision course with Saxo. It'll strike inside of five years. That much mass, simply falling from infinity, carries the energy of three years' stellar radiation. Which will have to be discharged somehow, in a matter of seconds. And Saxo is an F5, short lived, due to start expanding in less than a begayear. The instabilities must already be building up. The impact—Saxo will go nova. Explode."

"And our fleet—"

"Yes, sir. What else? The thing's wildly improbable. Interstellar distances are so big. But the universe is bigger still. No matter how unlikely, anything which is possible must happen sometime. This is one occasion when it does. Merseian explorers chanced on the datum. Brechdan saw what it meant. He could develop the conflict on Starkad, step by step, guiding it, nursing it, keeping it on schedule . . . till our main strength was marshaled there, just before the blowup came. We wouldn't be likely to see the invader. It's coming in 'way off the ecliptic, and has a very low albedo, and toward the end would be lost in Saxo's glare and traveling at more than 700 kilometers per second. Nor would we be looking in that direction. Our attention would be all on Brechdan's forces. They'd be prepared, after the captains opened their sealed orders. They'd know exactly when to dash away on hyperdrive. Ours—well, the initial radiation will move at the speed of light. It would kill the crews before they knew they were dead. An hour or so later, the first wave of gases would vaporize their ships. The Empire would be crippled and the Merseians could move in. That's why there's war on Starkad."

Ranjit Singh tugged his beard. The pain seemed to strengthen him. "Can we do anything? Plant bombs to blow this object apart, maybe?"

"I don't know, sir. Offhand, I doubt it. Too many fragments would stay on essentially the same path, I believe. Of course, we can evacuate Starkad. There are other planets."

"Yes. We can do that."

"Will you tell me now?" Dragoika asked.

Flandry did. He had not known she could weep.

Chapter Eighteen

Highport lay quiet. Men filled the ugly barracks, drifted along the dusty streets, waited for orders and longed for home. Clamor of construction work, grumble of traffic, whine of aircraft bound to battle, were ended. So likewise, after the first tumultuous celebrations, was most merrymaking. The war's conclusion had left people too dazed. First, the curt announcement that Admiral Enriques and Fodaich Runei were agreed on a cease-fire while they communicated with their respective governments. Then, day after day of not knowing. Then the arrival of ships; the proclamation that, Starkad being doomed, Empire and Roidhunate joined in hoping for a termination of the interracial conflict; the quick departure of the Merseians, save for a few observers; the imminent departure of most Imperial Navy personnel; the advent of civilian experts to make preliminary studies for a massive Terran project of another sort. And always the rumors, scuttlebutt, so-and-so knew somebody who knew for a fact that—How could you carry on as if this were ordinary? Nothing would ever again be quite ordinary. At night, you saw the stars and shivered.

Dominic Flandry walked in silence. His boots made a soft, rhythmic thud. The air was cool around him. Saxo spilled radiance from an enormous blue sky. The peaks beyond Mount Narpa thrust snowfields toward the ghost of a moon. Never had the planet looked so fair.

The door was ajar to the xenological office. He entered. Desks stood vacant. John Ridenour's staff was in the field. Their chief stayed behind, replacing sleep with stimulants as he tried to co-ordinate their efforts around an entire world. He was in conversation with a visitor. Flandry's heart climbed into his throat. Lord Hauksberg!

Everyone knew *Dronning Margrete* had arrived yesterday, in order that his Majesty's delegate might make a final inspection tour. Flandry had planned on keeping far out of sight. He snapped to a salute.

"Well, well." The viscount did not rise from his chair. Only the blond sharp face turned. The elegantly clad body stayed relaxed, the voice was amused. "What have we here?"

"Ensign Flandry, sir. I—I beg pardon. Didn't mean to interrupt. I'll go."

"No. Sit. Been meanin' to get hold of you. I do remember your name, strange as that may seem." Hauksberg nodded at Ridenour. "Go ahead. Just what is this difficulty you mention?"

The xenologist scarcely noticed the new-comer, miserable on a chair. Weariness harshened his tone. "Perhaps I can best il-lustrate with a typical scene, my lord, taken last week. Here's the Sisterhood HQ in Ujanka."

A screen showed a room whose murals related

ancient glories. A Terran and several Tigery
females in the plumes and striped cloaks of authority sat in front of a vidiphone. Flandry recognized some. He cursed the accident which
brought him here at this minute. His farewells in
the city had hurt so much.

Ostrova, the mistress, glared at the piscine
face projected before her. "Never," she snapped.
"Our rights and needs remain with us. Better
death than surrender what our mothers died to
gain."

The view shifted, went underwater, where also
a human team observed and recorded. Again
Flandry saw the Temple of Sky, from within.
Light pervaded the water, turned it into one emerald where the lords of the Seafolk floated free.
They had summoned Isinglass and Evenfall for
expert knowledge. *Those I never did get a chance to
say good-bye to,* Flandry thought, *and now I never
will.* Through the colonnade he looked down on
elfin Shell-gleam.

"You would steal everything, then, through
the whole cycle, as always you have done," said
he who spoke for them. "It shall not be. We must
have those resources, when great toil is coming
upon us. Do not forget, we keep our guns."

The record included the back-and-forth in-
terpretation of Ridenour's men at either end, so
Flandry followed the bitter argument in
Kursovikian. Hauksberg could not, and grew
restless. After a few minutes, he said, "Most
int'restin', but s'pose you tell me what's goin'
on."

"A summary was prepared by our station in

the Chain," Ridenour said. He flicked a switch. In the screen appeared a lagoon where sunlight glittered on wavelets and trees rustled behind a wide white beach: heartbreakingly beautiful. It was seen from the cabin of a waterboat, where a man with dark-rimmed eyes sat. He gave date and topic, and stated:

"Both factions continue to assert exclusive rights to the archipelago fishing grounds. Largely by shading their translations, our teams have managed to prevent irrevocable loss of temper, but no compromise is yet in sight. We shall continue to press for an equitable arrangement. Success is anticipated, though not for a considerable time."

Ridenour switched off. "You see, my lord?" he said. "We can't simply load these people aboard spaceships. We have to determine which of several possible planets are most suitable for them; and we have to prepare them, both in organization and education. Under ideal conditions, the psychic and cultural shock will still be terrible. Groundlaying will take years. Meanwhile, both races have to maintain themselves."

"Squabblin' over somethin' that'll be a whiff of gas in half a decade? Are such idiots worth savin'?"

"They're not idiots, my lord. But our news, that their world is under a death sentence, has been shattering. Most of them will need a long while to adapt, to heal the wound, before they can think about it rationally. Many never will. And .. my lord, no matter how logical one believes he is, no matter how sophisticated he claims to be, he stays an animal. His forebrain is nothing but the hand-maiden of instinct. Let's not look down on these Starkadians. If we and the Merseians, we big flashy space-conquering races, had any better sense, there'd be no war between us."

"There isn't," Hauksberg said.

"That remains to be seen, my lord."

Hauksberg flushed. "Thank you for your show," he said coldly. "I'll mention it in my report."

Ridenour pleaded. "If your Lordship would stress the need for more trained personnel here. . . . You've seen a little bit of what needs doing in this little bit of the planet. Ahead of us is the whole sphere, millions of individuals, thousands of societies. Many aren't even known to us, not so much as names, only blank spots on the map. But those blank spots are filled with living, thinking, feeling beings. We have to reach them, save them. We won't get them all, we can't, but each that we do rescue is one more justification for mankind's existence. Which God knows, my lord, needs every justification it can find."

"Eloquent," Hauksberg said. "His Majesty's government'll have to decide how big a bureaucratic empire it wants to create for the benefit of some primitives. Out o' my department." He got up. Ridenour did too. "Good day."

"Good day, my lord," the xenologist said. "Thank you for calling. Oh. Ensign Flandry. What'd you want?"

"I came to say good-bye, sir." Flandry stood

at attention. "My transport leaves in a few hours."

"Well, good-bye, then. Good luck." Ridenour went so far as to come shake hands. But even before Hauksberg, with Flandry behind, was out of the door, Ridenour was back at his desk.

"Let's take a stroll beyond town," Hauksberg said. "Want to stretch my legs. No, beside me. We've things to discuss, boy."

"Yes, sir."

Nothing further was said until they halted in a meadow of long silvery quasigrass. A breeze slid from the glaciers where mountains dreamed. A pair of wings cruised overhead. Were every last sentient Starkadian rescued, Flandry thought, they would be no more than the tiniest fraction of the life which joyed on this world.

Hauksberg's cloak flapped. He drew it about him. "Well," he said, looking steadily at the other. "We meet again, eh?"

Flandry made himself give stare for stare. "Yes, sir. I trust the remainder of my lord's stay on Merseia was pleasant."

Hauksberg uttered a laugh. "You are shameless! Will go far indeed, if no one shoots you first. Yes, I may say Councillor Brechdan and I had some rather int'restin' talks after the word came from here."

"I . . . I understand you agreed to, uh, say the space battle was only due to both commanders mistaking their orders."

"Right. Merseia was astonished as us to learn about the rogue after our forces found it by accident." Hauksberg's geniality vanished. He seized Flandry's arm with unexpected force and said sternly: "Any information to the contrary is a secret of state. Revealin' it to anyone, even so much as hintin' at it, will be high treason. Is that clear?"

"Yes, my lord. I've been briefed."

"And's to your benefit, too." Hauksberg said in a milder voice. "Keepin' the secret necessarily involves quashin' the charges against you. The very fact that they were ever brought, that anything very special happened after we reached Merseia, goes in the ultrasecret file also. You're safe, my boy."

Flandry put his hands behind his back, to hide how they doubled into fists. He'd have given ten years, off this end of his life, to smash that smiling face. Instead he must say, "Is my lord so kind as to add his personal pardon?"

"Oh, my, yes!" Hauksberg beamed and clapped his shoulder. "You did absolutely right. For absolutely the wrong reasons, to be sure, but by pure luck you accomplished my purpose for me, peace with Merseia. Why should I carry a grudge?" He winked. "Regardin' a certain lady, nothin' between friends, eh? Forgotten."

Flandry could not play along. "But we have no peace!" he exploded.

"Hey? Now, now, realize you've been under strain and so forth, but—"

"My lord, they were planning to destroy us. How can we let them go without even a scolding?"

"Ease down. I'm sure they'd no such intention. It was a weapon to use against us if we forced 'em to. Nothin' else. If we'd shown a genuine desire to cooperate, they'd've warned us in ample time."

"How can you say that?" Flandry choked. "Haven't you read any history? Haven't you listened to Merseian speeches, looked at Merseian books, seen our dead and wounded come back from meeting Merseians in space? They want us out of the universe!"

Hauksberg's nostrils dilated. "That will do, Ensign. Don't get above yourself. And spare me the spewed-back propaganda. The full story of this incident is bein' suppressed precisely because it'd be subject to your kind of misinterpretation and so embarrass future relations between the governments. Brechdan's already shown his desire for peace, by withdrawin' his forces in toto from Starkad."

"Throwing the whole expensive job of rescue onto us. Sure."

"I told you to control yourself, Ensign. You're not quite old enough to set Imperial policy."

Flandry swallowed a foul taste. "Apologies, my lord."

Hauksberg regarded him for a minute. Abruptly the viscount smiled. "No. Now I was gloatin'. Apologies to you. Really, I'm not a bad sort. And you mean well too. One day you'll be wiser. Let's shake on that."

Flandry saw no choice. Hauksberg winked again. "B'lieve I'll continue my stroll alone. If you'd like to say good-bye to Donna d'Io, she's in the guest suite."

Flandry departed with long strides.

By the time he had reached HQ and gone through the rigamarole of gaining admittance, fury had faded. In its place lay emptiness. He walked into the living room and stopped. Why go further? Why do anything?

Persis ran to him. She wore a golden gown and diamonds in her hair. "Oh, Nicky, Nicky!" She laid her head on his breast and sobbed.

He consoled her in a mechanical fashion. They hadn't had many times together since he came back from the rogue. There had been too much work for him, in Ujanka on Ridenour's behalf. And that had occupied him so greatly that he almost resented the occasions when he must return to Highport. She was brave and intelligent and fun, and twice she had stepped between him and catastrophe, but she did not face the end of her world. Nor was her own world the same as his: could never be.

They sat down on a divan. He had an arm around her waist, a cigarette in his free hand. She looked at the floor. "Will I see you on Terra?" she asked dully.

"I don't know," he said. "Not for some time anyway, I'm afraid. My orders have come through officially, I'm posted to the Intelligence academy for training, and Commander Abrams warns me they work the candidates hard."

"You couldn't transfer out again? I'm sure I could arrange an assignment—"

"A nice, cushy office job with regular hours? No, thanks, I'm not about to become anyone's kept man."

She stiffened as if he had struck her. "I'm

sorry," he floundered. "Didn't mean that. It's only, well, here's a job I am fitted for, that serves a purpose. If I don't take it, what meaning has life got?"

"I could answer that," she said low, "but I guess you wouldn't understand."

He wondered what the devil to say.

Her lips brushed his cheek. "Go ahead, then," she said. "Fly."

"Uh . . . you're not in trouble, Persis?"

"No, no. Mark's a most civilized man. We might even stay together a while longer, on Terra. Not that that makes any big difference. No matter how censored, some account of my adventures is bound to circulate. I'll be quite a novelty, quite in demand. Don't worry about me. Dancers know how to land on their feet."

A slight gladness stirred in him, largely because he was relieved of any obligation to fret about her. He kissed her farewell with a good imitation of warmth.

It was so good, in fact, that his loneliness returned redoubled once he was in the street again. He fled to Max Abrams.

The commander was in his office, straightening out details before leaving on the same transport that would bear Flandry home. From Terra, though, he would go on furlough to Dayan. His stocky frame leaned back as Flandry burst through the doorway. "Well, hello, hero," he said. "What ails you?"

The ensign flung himself into a chair. "Why do we keep trying?" he cried. "What's the use?"

"Hey-hey. You need a drink." Abrams took a

bottle from a drawer and poured into two glasses. "Wouldn't mind one myself. Hardly set foot on Starkad before they tell me I'm shipping out again." He lifted his tumbler. *"Shalom."*

Flandry's hand shook. He drained his whisky at a gulp. It burned on the way down.

Abrams made a production of lighting a cigar. "All right, son," he said. "Talk."

"I've seen Hauksberg," jerked from Flandry.

"Nu? Is he that hideous?"

"He . . . he . . . the bastard gets home free. Not a stain on his bloody damned escutcheon. He'll probably pull a medal. And still he quacks about peace!"

"Whoa. He's no villain. He merely suffers from a strong will to believe. Of course, his political career is bound up with the position he's taken. He can't afford to admit he was wrong. Not even to himself, I imagine. Wouldn't be fair to destroy him, supposing we could. Not expedient. Our side needs him."

"Sir?"

"Think. Never mind what the public hears. Consider what they'll hear on the Board. How they'll regard him. How neatly he can be pressured if he should get a seat on it, which I hope he does. No blackmail, nothing so crude, especially when the truth can't be told. But an eyebrow lifted at a strategic moment. A recollection, each time he opens his mouth, of what he nearly got us into last time around. Sure, he'll be popular with the masses. He'll have influence. So, fine. Better him than somebody else, with the same views, that hasn't yet bungled. If you had any charity in you, young man—which no one does at your age—you'd feel sorry for Lord Hauksberg."

"But . . . I . . . well—"

Abrams frowned into a cloud of smoke. "Also," he said, "in the longer view, we need the pacifists as a counterweight to the armchair missileers. We can't make peace, but we can't make real war either. All we can do is hold the line. And man is not an especially patient animal by nature."

"So the entire thing is for zero?" Flandry nigh screamed. "Only to keep what little we have?"

The grizzled head bent. "If the Lord God grants us that much," Abrams said. "He is more merciful than He is just."

"Starkad, though—Death, pain, ruin, and at last, the rotten status quo! What were we doing here?"

Abrams caught Flandry's gaze and would not let go. "I'll tell you," he said. "We had to come. The fact that we did, however futile it looked, however distant and alien and no-business-of-ours these poor people seemed, gives me a little hope for my grandchildren. We were resisting the enemy, refusing to let any aggression whatsoever go unpunished, taking the chance he presented us to wear him down. And we were proving once more to him, to ourselves, to the universe, that we will not give up to him even the least of these. Oh, yes, we belonged here."

Flandry swallowed and had no words.

"In this particular case," Abrams went on, "because we came, we can save two whole thinking races and everything they might mean to the future. We'd no way of knowing that beforehand; but there we were when the time arrived. Suppose we hadn't been? Suppose we'd said it didn't matter what the enemy did in these marches. Would he have rescued the natives? I doubt it. Not unless there happened to be a political profit in it. He's that kind of people."

Abrams puffed harder. "You know," he said, "ever since Akhnaton ruled in Egypt, probably since before then, a school of thought has held we ought to lay down our weapons and rely on love. That, if love doesn't work, at least we'll die guiltless. Usually even its opponents have said this is a noble idea. I say it stinks. I say it's not just unrealistic, not just infantile, it's evil. It denies we have any duty to *act* in this life. Because how can we, if we let go of our capability?

"No, son, we're mortal—which is to say, we're ignorant, stupid and sinful—but those are only handicaps. Our pride is that nevertheless, now and then, we do our best. A few times we succeed. What more dare we ask for?"

Flandry remained silent.

Abrams chuckled and poured two fresh drinks. "End of lecture," he said. "Let's examine what's waiting for you. I wouldn't ordinarily say this to a fellow at your arrogant age, but since you need cheering up . . . well, I will say, once you hit your stride, Lord help the opposition!"

He talked for an hour longer. And Flandry left the office whistling.

POUL ANDERSON
Masterpieces of Science Fiction